R 164

Russian Language Ministries
P. O. Box 212667
Columbia, SC 29221-2667
(803) 333-9119 Fax (803) 333-9117

ZIP *and Other Stories*
CHILDHOOD
N E W   R U S S I A N   W R I T I N G   glas

Editors:
NATASHA PEROVA & ARCH TAIT

Cover design: Andrei Bondarenko
Camera-ready copy: Tatiana Shaposhnikova
Contributing editor: Joanne Turnbull
Front cover: detail from Alexander Rodchenko's photograph "Young Pioneer"

GLAS Publishers (Russia)
Moscow 119517, P.O.Box 47, Russia
Tel./Fax: +7(095)441 9157; E-mail: perova@glas.msk.su

GLAS Publishers (UK)
Dept. of Russian Literature, University of Birmingham, Birmingham, B15 2TT, UK
Tel/Fax: +44(0)121-414 6047; E-mail: a.l.tait@bham.ac.uk

world wide web: http://www.bham.ac.uk/russian/glascover.html

European Distribution:
Password Books,
Sunhouse, 2 Little Peter Street, Knott Mill, Manchester M15 4PS, UK
Tel: +44 161 834 8767; Fax: +44 161 834 8656
E-mail: password@dircon.co.uk

USA and Canada:
Ivan R. Dee Inc:
1332 North Halsted St., Chicago, Illinois 60622-2637, USA
Tel: 1-312-787 6262; Fax: 1-312-787 6269; Toll-free: 1-800-634-0226
E-mail: elephant@enteract.com

Back issues of Glas are available:
REVOLUTION • SOVIET GROTESQUE • WOMEN'S VIEW
LOVE & FEAR • BULGAKOV & MANDELSTAM
JEWS & STRANGERS • BOOKER WINNERS & OTHERS
LOVE RUSSIAN STYLE • THE SCARED GENERATION
BOOKER WINNERS & OTHERS — II • CAPTIVES
BEYOND THE LOOKING-GLAS • A WILL & A WAY
Peter Aleshkovsky, SKUNK: A LIFE

GLAS gratefully acknowledges the financial and moral support of
the Arts Council of England and the Fund for Central and
East European Book Projects, Amsterdam.

ISBN 1-56663-198-X
© Glas New Russian Writing 1998
Copyright reverts to authors and translators upon publication

CONTENTS

Andrei BITOV
Zip
8
Friday, Evening
14

Andrei PLATONOV
Nikita
23

Ludmilla ULITSKAYA
The Foundling
35

Zufar GAREEV
The Holidays
67

Leonid LATYNIN
The Bear Fight
81

Alan CHERCHESOV
Requiem for the Living
107

Anatoly PRISTAVKIN
Kukushkin Kids or the Cuckoos
133

Misha NIKOLAYEV
Orphanage
165

Julia NEMIROVSKAYA
The Garage
182
Insight
189

Andrei SERGEEV
Stamp Album
194

Sergei GANDLEVSKY
Opening the Skull
207
Poems
220

The Child Is Father to the Man

These days Russian readers tend to prefer reminiscences and documentaries to pure fiction, which has been demoted to the domain of mass culture. This is because they feel now that their greatest need is to have all the facts at their disposal so that they can re-appraise the past and draw lessons for the future. Most popular are memoir-like works and novels which show the hidden springs behind surface reality, show familiar things in a new light, and question received wisdom.

Take for example the shortlist for the 1996 Booker Russian Novel Prize: the "novels" of Andrei Sergeev, winner of the main prize, and of Sergei Gandlevsky, who won the Little Booker Prize, are in fact well-written reminiscences. These two works have been widely read and discussed in Russia. This issue includes fairly long excerpts from both as examples of the kind of reading currently most in vogue among serious Russian readers.

The Grotesque has ceased to be the dominant trend, although it remains highly popular with younger readers. Everyone is looking for new rules for living now that the old guidelines have disappeared in the process of massive social change. This perhaps explains why de-mythologization and confession are currently of greater interest than the playful literature of the Absurd. The opponents of the latter trend say that Absurdity is already so much a part of everyday reality in Russia that they do not need to read about it in literature: what new absurdity can writers invent that has not already befallen real life?

There is a clear tendency to debunk former heroes, digging up dirt and leaving no stone unturned. Traditionally minded critics insist that the revision of ideas can only be successful after a new hierarchy of moral and social values has evolved. They don't care at all for the ideological about-turn evident in Russia today where whatever was considered good in Soviet times is automatically rejected today and vice versa, and any attempt to defend old values results in major unpopularity.

Despite the atmosphere of general disillusionment with literature, compelling new works continue to appear, probing ever new areas of life and thought.

In the current collection, centred on the theme of Childhood we offer two early stories by Andrei Bitov which reflect the growing awareness in children of life's mystery and beauty; a story by Andrei Platonov, bearing the stamp of his inimitable style, more fully developed in *The Foundation Pit* and *Chevengur*, Ludmilla Ulitskaya's perspicacious story of the complex relationship between twin sisters; an impressionistic story by Zufar Gareev about the torments of adolescence; Leonid Latynin's epic, set in pre-Christian Russia and giving us a glimpse of the dawn of Russian civilisation; Alan Cherchesov's account of an unusually bright Chechen boy living alone in a highland village in the Caucasus; stories by Anatoly Pristavkin and Misha Nikolayev about life in the special orphanages for children of "enemies of the people"; and Julia Nemirovskaya about her childhood under the Soviets.

Finally, quite a few of our readers and some of our reviewers have suggested that they would prefer complete works rather than excerpts from novels that we publish occasionally. Accordingly, your listening editors are moving over to publication of single-author volumes, mostly novels. The first of these has already appeared: Peter Aleshkovsky's *Skunk: A Life*. *Glas* does, however, aim to provide the broadest possible overview of contemporary Russian literature, so we will continue to bring out at least one anthology a year to help those of you with a professional interest in contemporary Russian literature to stay up to date. We hope, too, that this will encourage other publishers to translate more new Russian writers.

The editors

Russian Language Ministries
P. O. Box 212667
Columbia, SC 29221-2667
(803) 333-9119 Fax (803) 333-9117

Andrei
BITOV

Zip
Friday, Evening

Translated by Susan Brownsberger

Zip

He inspected the pencil – it had come out very well! – and took up the next one. Slowly, carefully, he began to sharpen it.

Slowly, evenly, the shavings fell away, curled into a crescent.

If you chew on a shaving, there's such a fresh taste...

"While I'm at it, I'll do the colored ones, too..."

The green one. And the red. And the blue. Neatly he gathered the shavings in his cupped hand and went to Mama's room.

"Alyosha, what are you doing?" asked Mama.

"Studying," said Alyosha.

"What's that?" She pointed at Alyosha's fist.

"But I can't draw with stubs!"

"You sharpened your pencils yesterday, too."

Alyosha scattered the shavings in the ashtray. He thought a moment and picked up the ashtray.

"What do you want with the ashtray?"

"I'm going to empty it."

"What's the matter, don't you have anything better to do?"

"I got it dirty – I have to clean it," Alyosha said firmly.

He went out to the front hall. In the front hall there was a table with newspapers lying on it.

He turned the pages for a while.

He started walking down the corridor, walking down the corridor. Coats hung there. A telephone hung there. Alyosha set the ashtray on the telephone table and fished in a pocket. A second pocket, a third. A button, a coin, a streetcar ticket... A letter. This was Lucy's coat...

"Darling Lucy," he read, "I'm sorry I..."

"O-ho, just wait, 'darling Lucy'!" Alyosha sang out. "Today it's my turn!"

Zip

When the corridor ended, the kitchen began. No one was there. The cat scooted away from Alyosha.

"Idiot," Alyosha said, "maybe I wanted to pet you."

He tried to sneak up from the rear – the cat sprang lightly to the windowsill, from the windowsill to the refrigerator, from the refrigerator to the sideboard. Alyosha unhurriedly took a wet rag and unhurriedly climbed up on a chair. The cat flattened itself against the wall with its tail curled under and started to hiss.

"Hissing?" Alyosha said. "But maybe I wanted to dust..."

He took aim, swung... He missed the cat, but one of the finial knobs snapped off the sideboard. The cat described an arc and went scuttling around the kitchen. Alyosha unhurriedly climbed down from the chair, inwardly seething: not that knob again! "A high-strung child," Mama often said...

The cat had taken refuge under the sideboard. A loud rumble could be heard down there. Such a worthless beast – and such a growl, thought Alyosha. He rapped on the sideboard, and the rumble grew even louder.

"Now, there's a nasty animal," Alyosha said. The sideboard droned steadily. "Just you growl at me some more! Just you growl!"

Alyosha sighed and carried the ashtray to the garbage chute. He opened the chute, laid his ear to it: a steady droning there, too.

"Knowledge is light, ignorance darkness," he complained into the chute.

The chute roared something in reply. It smelled of wet ashes. Alyosha thrust his arm into the chute and emptied the shavings: they swished. He very much wanted to drop the ashtray down too. He picked up the knob, and it clattered in the chute.

"I should drop the cat down," Alyosha thought absently. "Now, that would be a symphony!" He sighed.

"How about some water?"

He filled a glass at the faucet. Took a sip. Another sip. Dumped it in the sink.

9

On the way back he walked quickly, without looking at the droning sideboard, the chute, the coat rack.

"Where have you been?!" said Mama.

Alyosha went to his room. He sat down. A white sheet of paper lay in front of him. The pencils stuck up from the tumbler with sharp points, and he had no other pencils. His glance fell on the razor blade. Alyosha jabbed it into the edge of the desk.

He drew it out – zing! sang the blade. He jabbed it in deeper – zeng! it sang. "Re," Alyosha thought. He emptied out all his blades. After lengthy exertions – zong! zeng! zing! zang! sang the blades, "do, re, mi, fa," they sang. He couldn't seem to get sol.

Mama said, "Have you played the piano today?"

"I have a whole lot of homework, Mama," Alyosha said, and cut his finger.

He sucked his finger and stared at the sheet of paper.

"Alyosha," he heard from Mama's room, "I'm going out now for a little while, but you stay and study. It's simply a disgrace the way I have to blush for you at PTA meetings. And it's Skorpyshev's grandson!" she added with sorrow. "Play the piano. Have your lunch – I've left it in the kitchen. I'm off."

Alyosha stood at the big mirror in Mama's room, holding a large wine-glass full of milk. He held the hand with the wine-glass out to one side, and watched himself holding the hand with the wine-glass out to one side. Then he took a small sip and smacked his lips and shook his head, and watched himself taking a sip, smacking his lips, and shaking his head. Then he made several mutual bows, held the hand with the wine-glass out even farther, looked to see the effect of all this, and cleared his throat. Said nothing for a moment. Cleared his throat.

"No," he said, "too white."

He set the glass on a small table. And began to walk with his hands folded behind his back, the way Grandfather used to. "Don't bother Grandfather – he's thinking," Mama used to say

Zip

then. Alyosha walked back and forth past the mirror – and as he passed kept turning his head to the left, to the right.

"What should I think about?" Alyosha thought.

Only Mama, teachers, and homework came to mind.

"What should I think about...," Alyosha said aloud.

The door slammed. In two bounds he was at the white sheet of paper, and the wine-glass stood under the desk.

"Why haven't you had your lunch?" Mama said.

"I was studying."

Alyosha sat in the kitchen and listlessly munched cheese pancakes. They didn't taste good, but he was making them last.

The door slammed. Footsteps sounded – not steps but stomps – and a deep voice sang out, "Underneath the lamplight, by the barrack gate, Tell that noisy nightingale it's keeping us awake..." And the same voice burst out laughing.

"Uncle!" Alyosha said happily.

"The writer!" Mama muttered with irritation.

Uncle glanced into the kitchen, sniffed, and said, "Something stinks here."

Mama said, "You're forever making nasty remarks in front of the child!"

"You're a beautiful woman, but an idiot!" Uncle said, and his footsteps moved off down the corridor.

Mama grumbled by the sideboard.

Uncle was a writer, and he was writing a book about Grandfather. He said Grandfather had left no other legacy.

Alyosha hastily swallowed his cheese pancake and slipped out into the corridor.

"Ah, it's you, Zip!" Uncle said in his bass voice. He was standing there poking a finger into the typewriter. "Why don't you say something?" Uncle pulled at his suspenders and snapped them against his own fleshy belly. "You mean you're not Zip?"

"No, I'm not," Alyosha said.

"Yes, you are Zip." Uncle emitted a cloud of cognac breath. "What else would you be?"

11

"I'm a human being," Alyosha said. Talking with Uncle was fun.

"Ah, yes! Sorry, sorry... Then again, that still doesn't mean you aren't zip." Uncle removed the cigarette stub from his lip and pasted it to the edge of the desk. There was already a handsome border there.

"But don't you think the place stinks of something?"

"No."

"Odd, very odd...," Uncle said. "Well, why have you honored me with a visit? Too lazy to study? Tch, tch! For shame, for shame... I won't tell you about how I was first in my class, though... Really and truly, I won't! I won't give you any cognac, either."

"Then give me something to read."

"But what can I give you to read? You've already read all about boats."

"Come on. Even just something of your own."

"See here, Alyosha – I respect you, but you're zip! Let's settle this, once and for all: you will not make any more nasty remarks to me."

"All right," Alyosha agreed. "Then give me the *Decameron*."

"The *Decameron*," Uncle said dreamily. "First stirrings of the flesh. Distant youth... I won't."

"Why not?" Alyosha whined.

"I won't – and don't beg."

"Many in my class have already read it," Alyosha informed him.

"Oh? That's different, I suppose. You mustn't fall behind... I won't."

"Come on, Uncle..."

"Did she give you permission?"

"Oh, Uncle! That's a laugh!"

"The place does stink." Uncle sniffed. "So she didn't give you permission?"

"No! She'd never let me," Alyosha said with conviction.

"So she'd never let you... But did you ask her?"

Zip

"Oh, Uncle! You know her as well as I do."

"Hm-m, as well as you do... I wouldn't put it just like that. Well, so, she'd never let you."

"No," Alyosha snapped categorically.

"Go ahead, then, take it. Take it, carrot-haired zip, and run along. I still have to write the hardest chapter about your Grandpa – how he welcomed the revolution... The hardest chapter. And any minute she'll come flying in to get you."

Alyosha sat in front of the blank sheet of paper, and the *Decameron* lay in the pulled-out drawer. A boring book, he thought. The only entertaining part was that he had to watch out Mama didn't catch him. Several times already he had imagined Mama was heading his way, and he had banged the drawer shut and begun twirling his pencil in concentration. His heart had thumped. Mama had not come. When he slammed the drawer yet again –

"What's all the racket in there?" Mama said from the next room.

"I dropped my textbook..."

In the end, Mama came in so soundlessly, somehow, that Alyosha failed not only to slam the drawer but also to wake up. He raised his head and looked around with unseeing eyes. On the open book lay a puddle of sweet, sleepy spittle.

"So that's it!" Mama managed to say. She grabbed the book and rushed off to have a scene with Uncle.

"Oh, no!" Alyosha groaned. "Where can I hide..."

They bumped into each other downstairs in the doorway.

"Zip!" Uncle said in surprise. "Where are you going?"

"Out...," Alyosha said.

"Ah. Out... Well, walk me to the corner, then."

They walked to the corner. Port Avenue began here. They stood for a moment.

"Well, how about it, shall we go look at the boats?" said Uncle.

1959

Friday, Evening

Kostya had worn his new shoes that day for the first time. Now he added a starched white shirt. He felt handsome. He had no place special to go, but the shoes gave him no peace, and he went out to the street. Not walking – carrying himself. Women looked at him.

The day before, new fluorescent lamps had been installed on Nevsky Prospect. Their unaccustomed light, at once strong and soft, made the contours of the buildings less weighty and altered his accustomed sense of scale. The women, too, were strange and attractive in this light. They looked at Kostya. Tiny balls of fluorescent light bounced on the narrow toes of the new shoes. His own stride and the glances of women coming toward him excited Kostya.

He walked like this for a long while, and already it was time to go home.

He stood in line at the bus stop. Buses pulled up, buses other than he needed. They drove up and drove away, showing Kostya all their passengers. The windows past his eyes were like a harmonica across the lips: *tren-n-ng...*

Among the passengers there were women. Many cast glances at Kostya. Some averted their eyes afterwards, because Kostya would begin to stare too hard. There were even beautiful women. They were driven up and driven away on the buses. The beautiful women exchanged glances with Kostya and rode away somewhere. Like on a harmonica... *Tren-n-ng.*

Just one thing: it was evening, the buses were lighted from inside – and you couldn't make out your own reflection in the bus windows. Couldn't see how brave or stern your face was. But Kostya liked himself even without a reflection. He made a face.

Standing at a bus stop – this, too, had its charm.

Friday, Evening

Tren-n-ng... A window. Inside the window is an unknown woman. Kostya sees the stranger. Makes a handsome face and stares. The stranger sees Kostya's silly face. She averts her eyes. Kostya executes a maneuver: he, too, averts his eyes, makes his face indifferent, then suddenly looks at the stranger again. And yes – catches her eye. A smile – a smile. Dust on the window... *Tren-n-ng.* And the bus is gone. The passenger is gone.

Now here was Kostya's bus.

Kostya jostled his way up the steps. Looked around. Right there, on the back seat, was a young woman. Attractive. She had watched Kostya get on. But now, when Kostya purposely stood facing her, she began to look out the window. Curious, the way she could turn her head to both right and left while avoiding Kostya's eyes in the middle. She looked now out the left window, now out the right.

This, too, could be figured out. If Kostya, too, should start to look out the window – she would look at Kostya. And she could be caught at this. He caught her, embarrassed her. She looked out the window again.

At the next stop a lot of people got on. Kostya, unresisting, allowed them to draw him away from the young woman, and at the point where he stopped he was able to study four women at once. The first was really pretty. She never once raised her head, never glanced at Kostya. Beside her was a woman of about thirty, plump and fair. That one was sleeping. Across the aisle was a very young, rather dark girl with a homely, sensual face. She played a game of "catch my eye" with Kostya and then stared out the window more and more stubbornly, embarrassed. The fourth woman, about thirty-five, had sharp separate creases on her bony face; she was heavily rouged. A gray, lifeless lock of permed hair straggled from under a green wool headband with a little bouquet on it. Her red coat was of a style long out of fashion. This woman looked at Kostya only once, at the very beginning. Then she looked nowhere. Kostya, too, avoided looking at her – he was ashamed.

Nothing special on these two seats.

Andrei Bitov

But Kostya did not want to move up front: the bus was too crowded to push his way forward, and his stop would be soon.

Kostya stood holding the grab-handle above his head.

The next stop would be his.

Everyone would be getting off here. The woman in green and red stood up. "Young man, are you getting off?" "Yes," Kostya said, and his face became especially hard and disdainful. Kostya was ashamed that this woman had spoken to him in front of the other women passengers. He imagined, of course, that they were all looking at him "peculiarly." He made a face. The bus swayed. The woman could perfectly well have grabbed a handle, but for some reason she grabbed the crook of Kostya's arm. Kostya's face became even more independent and disdainful, but at the same time he flexed his biceps, on which her hand lay. She sensed his biceps under her hand and gripped much more firmly and gently than was necessary to keep her balance. She threw him a predatory glance, he thought. Kostya did the impossible: made his face even colder. But he still kept his biceps inflated. "Do we get off at the front?" Her voice quavered, and she was pressing Kostya's biceps. She could have grasped the handle long ago. She was about to let go of him. But at the first quite trivial little jolt she tightened her grip on Kostya's arm, and Kostya's biceps flexed again. She could have held the handle! Kostya was afraid to look at the women passengers: what if they thought she was with him? He saw his frozen face in the window. "I won't be able to get off," she quavered. "I'd better follow the young man...." Kostya turned to face the exit, so as to somehow escape the passengers he thought were looking at him. The woman was forced to let go of his arm. But no sooner had Kostya turned his back on her than the woman pressed her whole body against him. "I'll follow you, follow you..." She pressed harder against Kostya's back. The other women could no longer see them, and Kostya felt relieved. But she seemed to keep pressing against him harder and harder. The frozen expression did not leave his face.

The doors opened. People were jumping off the bus – jumping

Friday, Evening

left and right, left and right. In that instant the woman was torn away from Kostya. He got off first. Something stopped him in his intention to go straight home. He waited, and as she got off he gave her his hand. The woman gripped it tightly and stepped down. Her hand was still in Kostya's, but the expression frozen on Kostya's face had not changed. He became aware of this when she said thank-you and for some reason fled from him, her legs flailing absurdly, a small bundle clasped to her bosom. She ran about five steps. After that she walked. On reaching the crosswalk she glanced back and saw Kostya. For some reason she ran again as she crossed the street.

Kostya followed her. He passed pretty girls coming toward him but paid no attention. To them or their glances. The woman looked back again once or twice. Kostya did not succeed in catching her eye. Again she ran across a street. Kostya walked across behind her. She slowed her step and suddenly disappeared. She did not disappear, she went into a bakery.

Kostya watched the bakery door from an alley. "Should I go in or not?" he thought. He decided it wasn't worth it: there were a lot of other people in the bakery. The woman was already taking too long to come out. And already it was more and more absurd — why was he, Kostya, here in an alley, watching the door of a bakery... And then the door flew open. Her!

Kostya thought it was odd that her package had become so large. But it was her.

The woman hurried across the street and started up a dark, narrow lane. Kostya hurried after her. She went in at a front door. Only for an instant did something stop Kostya. Now he, too, went in. Her shoes were tapping, one flight up. Kostya ran up the stairs. A door slammed. So much for that. Kostya stood still a moment, started down. Cursed himself. And felt relieved.

With a grim expression he went back down the lane and crossed the street, heading home. And now, at the bakery, he came face to face with the very same woman. In addition to the bundle, she was clasping a long loaf of bread to her bosom. Kostya was so astonished that he went right past her.

17

Having rushed past, Kostya stopped. And stared after her, undecided. A weight fell on him again. "A delusion... But how could I mistake her?"

Kostya dashed to catch up.

"After all, it was obvious," Kostya thought, striding after her. "Why didn't I say right off, 'Could I help you carry your package?' Now, though, she has the loaf of bread besides... Hell! What does the bread matter!"

And he paced himself so that he neither lagged behind nor gained on her. They walked all the way to the end of the street. A dark street with bright store windows. The street lamps were no longer burning. The merchandise in the windows looked abstract and strange. The mannequins cast ironic glances. They held hats in their hands. Young women were still coming toward him. Without men. They looked at Kostya. He hurried past them. He did not notice himself moving. As if carried by a stream.

"What's wrong with me!" he was on the point of thinking, but the thought was disagreeable, and he dismissed it. "I'm losing my mind," he told himself, and felt calmer.

Having walked to the end of the street, they turned into one that was totally dark. Only the house numbers were dimly lighted. "Exactly like in that lane," Kostya thought.

Of course she knew that Kostya was following her... The street was deserted, after all, and Kostya's new shoes made such a resounding clatter with their metal heel-plates. But she did not look back.

"Offering to carry it now would be pointless. I'll go up to her and ask: Why did you press against me like that on the bus?"

Kostya lengthened his stride to catch up. He glanced back to see if anyone was there. Walking behind him (Kostya even started) was a woman janitor. "They all know each other here," Kostya thought in fright, "they all know..." Kostya stopped. He put his foot on the curb and began to tie his shoe laces. They had come untied long ago and were hampering his stride, the silky laces of the new shoes. The janitor passed Kostya and turned into an alley.

Friday, Evening

Striding swiftly along, Kostya narrowed the gap again and followed. Up ahead something loomed even darker than the dark street – a dead end.

Why did you press against me like that on the bus?

The last apartment building.

The woman turned in at the driveway.

Kostya followed. The driveway was paved with cobblestones. Kostya thought of his new shoes for some reason: he stepped carefully, lest he knock off a heel.

The courtyard, too, was badly lighted: only a few solitary windows had not yet gone dark. Piles of firewood. A great many of them. On the right, a lighted staircase. There, unexpectedly close, Kostya caught sight of the woman. She stopped and recoiled, pressed her back against a woodpile. She had one arm around the bundle, the other around the loaf of bread. Her mouth twisted.

Kostya passed her, somehow hastily, making a stony, independent face again for some reason, and found himself on the staircase. He was aware of her eyes on his back, and felt awful. On the staircase he did not know what to do. Slowly he began to climb up, listening for footsteps below. He went up and up, sometimes stopping, listening, but there was no one on the staircase – only him. Suddenly he was on the top floor. He did not know what to do. He wanted to leave. But suddenly he thought he simply hadn't heard, and the woman was now somewhere one landing below. So he couldn't just go up and come down like that... He pushed a doorbell. He felt agonizingly awkward. Had an urge to go running down the stairs. But did not run. Someone shuffled to the door: "Who's there?" he asked, without opening it. "Is Yura home?" Kostya said. "No Yura here." The footsteps moved away.

After delaying a bit longer, Kostya started down. He went more and more slowly, and his fear that the woman would be downstairs kept growing. But no matter how he delayed, he arrived downstairs. He walked out into the courtyard.

There was no one by the woodpile. The sensation that a

19

weight had fallen from him was so acute and total that Kostya felt he could fly. Lightly and rapidly he went out to the street.

"Here I am, just going home from a friend's house," Kostya imagined. "Nothing happened. Of course nothing happened. It was a dream. Not even a dream... But look what funny numbers on these houses – they're like little houses. They have house-spirits living in them."

That's not it, not it... Something was spinning in his mind, and he simply could not catch it! There! maybe that... It slid away again.

Kostya came out on the main street. The one where the windows shone. How fine! The city at night – how splendid it all was... Everyone asleep and dreaming one common dream. In that dream Kostya walks through the great city at night.

"What can I do," Kostya thinks, "to do it differently. So that I wouldn't dream any more filthy dreams. So that my breath wouldn't reek every morning from this foul tobacco. So that I wouldn't have these rotten stylish pointy-toed shoes. So that my heart would be truly light. Truly pure..."

1960

Andrei Bitov, born in 1937 in Leningrad, is recognized in Russia as one of the most important writers of his generation. His work is marked with subtle psychological insights and profound philosophical thoughts. He has established himself in the 1960s as a writer to whom conventional labels do not apply and his writing continues to remain outside any formal grouping. Much of Bitov's writing is excessively intellectual and deliberately mystifying. He is more literary than most other writers of his generation who tend to be more social.

His hero is usually given to self-doubt and even occasional self-loathing. He is often lonely and tormented over a search for his true identity. Although Bitov's stories are not strictly autobiographical his hero is usually a person who resembles the author himself. He is puzzled by the shifting dividing line between good and evil, real and unreal, which leads him to constant soul-searching. His writing invites a variety of interpretations.

Winner of many literary prizes, including the Pushkin and the State Prizes, Bitov has been widely published around the world in Russian and in translation. Most of his works are available in English from Harvill Press in the UK and from Farrar, Straus & Giroux in the US. His best known novels are: *Pushkin House* and *A Captive of the Caucasus*.

In this issue of *Glas* we offer the first English translations of two of his early stories.

Andrei PLATONOV

Nikita

*Translated by Robert and Elizabeth Chandler
& Angela Livingstone*

Andrei Platonov

Early in the morning the mother would leave home to go and work in the fields. There was no father in the family; the father had gone away long ago to the most important work – the war – and had not come back. Every day the mother expected the father to come back, but there was still no sign of him.

Five-year-old Nikita was left on his own, master of the house and the whole yard. As she left, his mother would tell him not to burn the house down, to collect any eggs the hens laid beneath the fence or in the sheds, not to let any other cocks come and attack their own cock, and to have the bread and milk she had put on the table for lunch, and in the evening she would come back and make him a hot supper.

"You haven't got a father, Nikitushka, so don't get up to mischief," his mother would say. "You're a clever boy now, and what's in the house and yard is all we have."

"I'm clever, this is all we have, and I haven't got a father," Nikita would say. "But come back soon, Mummy, or I'll get frightened."

"What's there to be frightened of? The sun's shining in the sky, there are people round about in the fields. Don't be frightened, you'll be all right on your own."

"But the sun's a long way away," Nikita would say, "and it will get covered over by a cloud."

When his mother left, Nikita went round the whole quiet house – the main room, then the other room with its Russian stove – and went out into the entrance. Big fat flies were buzzing there, a spider was dozing in the corner in the middle of his web, and a sparrow had crossed the threshold on foot and was looking for a grain or two inside the house, on the earthern floor. Nikita knew every one of them: the sparrows, and the spiders, and the flies, and the hens outside; he had had enough of them, they bored him. He wanted now to learn something he did not know. So Nikita went further out into the yard and came to the shed, where there was an empty barrel standing in the darkness. There was probably someone living in it, some little man or other; in the daytime he slept, but at night he came

Nikita

out, ate bread, drank water and did some thinking, and then in the morning he would hide inside the barrel again and go to sleep.

"I know you, you live in there," said Nikita. He was standing on tip-toe and speaking down into the dark, resonant barrel. Then he gave it a knock with his fist to make sure. "Get up, you lazy bones, and stop sleeping! What are you going to eat in winter? Go and weed the millet, they'll put it down as a work-day!"

Nikita listened. It was quiet inside the barrel. "Maybe he's dead!" Nikita thought. But there was a squeak from the wood, and Nikita got out of harm's way. He thought that whoever lived there must have turned over onto his side, or else was about to get up and chase after him.

But what was he like – this man in the barrel? Nikita pictured him at once in his mind. He was someone small but lively. He had a long beard which reached right down to the ground when he walked about at night. He didn't mean it to, but his beard swept away the litter and straw, leaving clean paths on the floor of the shed.

His mother had lost her scissors not long ago. He must have taken the scissors himself, to trim his beard.

"Give us back our scissors!" Nikita asked quietly. "When father comes home from the war, he'll take them back anyway. He's not frightened of you. Give them back!"

The barrel remained silent. In the forest, far beyond the village, someone gave a hoot, and the little man in the barrel answered in his strange black voice: "I'm here!"

Nikita ran out of the shed into the yard. The kind sun was shining in the sky, there were no clouds in the way, and Nikita looked at the sun in fear, hoping it would defend him.

"There's someone there – living in a barrel!" said Nikita, looking at the sky.

The kind sun went on shining in the sky, looking back at him in return with its warm face. Nikita saw that the sun was like his dead grandfather, who had always smiled and been

25

Andrei Platonov

nice to him while he was alive and still able to look at him. Nikita thought that his grandfather had gone to live on the sun now.

"Grandpa, where are you? Are you living there?" asked Nikita. "You live there, but I'll stay here, I'll stay with Mummy."

Beyond the vegetable plot, in a clump of burdock and nettles, there was a well. They had not taken water from it for a long time, because another well had been dug in the collective farm and it had sweet water.

Deep down in this dead well, in its underground darkness, lay bright water with a clear sky and clouds passing beneath the sun. Nikita leaned over the well-frame and asked: "What are you up to down there?"

Down there on the bottom, he thought, lived small water-people. He knew what they were like, he had seen them in dreams and wanted to catch them, but they had run away from him over the grass into the well, back to their home. They were the size of sparrows, but they were fat and hairless, damp and dangerous. Nikita knew they wanted to drink up his eyes while he was asleep.

"I'll teach you!" Nikita said into the well. "What are you doing living down there?"

The water in the well suddenly went cloudy, and somebody champed their jaws. Nikita opened his mouth to scream, but nothing came out, he had lost his voice from fear; his heart trembled and missed a beat.

"A giant and his children live here too!" Nikita realized. "Grandpa!" he shouted out loud, looking at the sun. "Are you there, Grandpa?" And Nikita ran back towards his home.

Beside the shed he came to his senses. Beneath its wattle wall there were two burrows in the earth. They too had their secret inhabitants. But who were they? They might be snakes! They would creep out at night, steal into the house and bite his mother while she was asleep, and his mother would die.

Nikita ran quickly back inside, took two bits of bread from the table and carried them out. He put one piece by each burrow

Nikita

and said to the snakes: "Eat up the bread, snakes, and don't bother us at night."

Nikita looked round. There was an old tree-stump in the vegetable plot. When he looked at it, Nikita realized it was the head of a man. The stump had eyes, a nose and a mouth, and the stump was quietly smiling at Nikita.

"Do you live here too?" the boy asked. "Climb out and join us in the village. You can plough the earth."

The stump quacked out an answer, and its face turned angry.

"All right then, don't climb out!" said Nikita, taking fright. "Stay where you are!"

It had gone quiet everywhere in the village, there was not a sound. His mother was far away in the fields, he would never get to her in time. Nikita left the angry tree-stump and went back into the house. He was not afraid there, it was not long since his mother had been there. It was hot now in the house. Nikita wanted to drink the milk his mother had left him, but when he looked at the table he saw the table was a person too, only it had four legs and no arms.

Nikita went out onto the porch. Far beyond the vegetable garden and the well stood the old bath-hut. It was black inside from having no chimney, and his mother said that his grandfather had liked to wash there when he was alive.

The bath-hut was old and covered in moss: it was a miserable little hut.

"It's our grandmother, she didn't die, she turned into a hut!" Nikita thought in terror. "She's alive, she's alive; that's her head − not a chimney, a head; and that's her gap-toothed mouth; she's only pretending to be a bath-hut, really she's still a woman, I can see it!"

Someone else's cockerel came in off the street. Its face was like the face of the thin shepherd with the short beard who had drowned in the river last spring; he had wanted to go and have fun at a wedding in another village and had tried to swim across the river when it was in full spate.

Nikita decided that the shepherd had felt like coming alive

27

Andrei Platonov

again and had become a cock; so this cock was a man – a secret man. Everywhere there were people, only they seemed not to be people.

Nikita bent down over a yellow flower. Who was it? Gazing into the flower, Nikita saw its little round face gradually take on a human expression, and then he could see little eyes, a nose and a moist open mouth that smelt of living breath.

"And I thought you really were a flower!" said Nikita. "Let me see what's inside you, do you have guts?"

Nikita broke the stem – the body of the flower – and saw some milk inside it.

"You were a baby, you were sucking your mother!" said Nikita in astonishment.

He went to the old bath-hut.

"Grandma!" Nikita said to her quietly. But Grandma's pock-marked face bared its teeth at him furiously, as if he were a stranger.

"You're not Grandma, you're someone else!" thought Nikita.

The stakes looked out at Nikita from the fence like the faces of a crowd of people he did not know. And every face was unfamiliar and did not love him: one was smirking angrily, another was thinking something spiteful about him, while a third stake was pushing against the fence with the withered branches that were its arms, about to climb out of the fence and chase Nikita.

"What are you doing here?" asked Nikita. "This is our yard!"

But on every side there were strange, angry faces, looking fixedly and piercingly at Nikita. He looked at the burdocks – they must be kind. But now even the burdocks were sullenly shaking their big heads and not loving him.

Nikita lay down on the ground and pressed his face to it. Voices were humming within the earth, yes, there were a lot of people living there in the cramped darkness and he could hear them scrabbling with their hands to climb out into the light of day. Nikita got up in terror; there were people living everywhere, strange eyes were looking at him from everywhere; if there was

Nikita

anyone who could not see him, they wanted to climb out after him from under the earth, from out of a burrow, from under the black eaves of the shed. He turned to the house. The house was looking at him like an old woman passing through on her way from some far-off village; it was whispering to him: "Oo-ooh, you useless children, there are too many of you in the world – eating good wheat bread for free."

"Come home, Mummy!" Nikita begged his far-away mother. "Let them just put you down for half a work-day. Our home's full of strangers. They're living here. Make them go away!"

The mother did not hear her son. Nikita went behind the shed, he wanted to see if the tree-stump-head was climbing out of the earth. The tree-stump had a big mouth, it would eat all the cabbage on their plot, and then how would his mother be able to make cabbage-soup in the winter?

Nikita looked timidly from a distance at the tree-stump in the vegetable plot. A gloomy, unfriendly face, overgrown with wrinkly bark, looked back at Nikita with unblinking eyes.

And far away, from the forest on the other side of the village, someone shouted in a loud voice: "Maxim, where are you?"

"In the earth!" the tree-stump-that-was-a-head answered in a muffled voice.

Nikita turned round to run to his mother in the field, but he fell over. He went numb with fear. His legs had become like strangers and did not obey him. Then he crept along on his stomach as if he were still little and could not walk.

"Grandpa!" Nikita whispered, looking at the kind sun in the sky.

A cloud covered the light, and there was no sun to be seen.

"Grandpa, come back and live with us again!"

Grandpa-sun appeared from behind the cloud, as if his grandfather had straight away taken the dark shadow off his face in order to see his enfeebled grandson creeping along the earth. His grandfather was looking at him now; Nikita thought his grandfather could see him, and he got up onto his feet and ran towards his mother.

Andrei Platonov

He ran for a long time. He ran all the way through the village along the empty, dusty road; then he felt tired out and sat down in the shade of an outlying barn.

Nikita sat down – for a moment. Without meaning to, however, he laid his head on the ground and fell asleep, and he did not wake up until evening. The new shepherd was driving the collective-farm sheep. Nikita would have gone on further, to look for his mother in the field, but the shepherd told him it was late and that his mother had long ago left the field and gone home.

When he got home, Nikita saw his mother sitting at the table and gazing at an old soldier who was eating bread and drinking milk.

The soldier looked at Nikita, then got up from the bench and took him in his arms. The soldier smelt warm, he smelt of something good and peaceful, of bread and earth. Nikita felt shy and kept quiet.

"Hello, Nikita," said the soldier. "You forgot me a long time ago, you were just a baby when I gave you a kiss and went off to the war. But I remember you. Once I was nearly dying and I still remembered you."

"It's your father, Nikitushka, he's come home," said the mother, wiping the tears from her face with her apron.

Nikita took a good look at his father – at his face, his hands, the medal on his chest – and touched the bright buttons on his shirt.

"And you won't leave us again?"

"No," said the father. "Now I'll stay with you forever. We've destroyed the enemy, now it's time to think about you and your mother."

In the morning Nikita went out into the yard and said out loud to everyone who lived there – to the burdocks, and the shed, and the stakes in the fence, and the tree-stump-that-was-a-head in the vegetable plot, and to grandfather's bath-hut: "Father's come home. He's going to stay with us forever."

Everyone in the yard was silent – evidently they were all

30

Nikita

afraid of a father who was a soldier — and it was quiet underground too; no one was scrabbling to try and get out into the light.

"Come here, Nikita. Who is it you're talking to out there?"

His father was in the shed. He was having a look at the tools and testing them with his hands: axes, spades, a saw, a plane, vices, a bench and all the other bits and pieces he owned.

When he had finished, the father took Nikita by the hand and went round the yard with him, seeing what was where, what was in good shape and what had rotted, what was needed and what was not.

Just as he had done the day before, Nikita looked into the face of every creature in the yard, but now he could not see a hidden person in any of them; not one of them had eyes, a nose, a mouth or a spiteful life of its own. The fencing stakes were thick, dried-up sticks, blind and dead, and grandfather's bath-hut was a little hut that had rotted and was slipping away into the earth from old age. Now Nikita even felt sorry for the bath-hut: it was dying and soon there would be nothing left of it.

His father went into the shed for an axe and began chopping up the old tree-stump in the vegetable plot to make firewood. The stump began to fall apart at once, it had rotted all the way through, and from underneath his father's axe its dry dust rose into the air like smoke.

When there was nothing left of the tree-stump-that-was-a-head, Nikita said to his father: "But when you weren't here, he said words, he was alive. He's got legs under the ground, and a belly."

The father led his son back into the house.

"No,", he said, "it died a long time ago. It's you — you've got a kind heart and so you want to make everything alive. Even a stone seems alive to you, and old grandma's living again on the moon."

"And grandpa on the sun!" said Nikita.

In the afternoon the father was planing boards in the shed,

31

Andrei Platonov

to make a new floor for the house, and he gave Nikita some work too — straightening the crooked nails with a little hammer.

Nikita got down to work with a will, just like a grown-up. When he had straightened the first nail, he saw a kind-hearted little man in it, smiling at him from underneath his little iron hat. He showed it to his father and said to him: "Why were all the others cross? The burdock was cross, and the tree-stump, and the water-people, but this man's kind."

The father stroked his son's fair hair and answered, "They were all people you thought up, Nikita. They're not really there, they're not solid, that's what makes them cross. But it was your own labour that made the little nail-man — that's why he's kind."

Nikita started to think.

"Let's make everything by our own labour, and then everything will come alive."

"Yes, let's!" agreed the father.

Andrei Platonov (1899-1951), a unique and extraordinary writer, has emerged from obscurity to assume his rightful place as one of the major authors of the century. His work was barred from publication during his life but all serious readers in Russia knew him and there is hardly any Russian writer today who has not been influenced by his deliberately incongruous prose.

"Nikita" is representative of his later, much simplified style. Platonov's great novel *The Foundation Pit* is published, in translation by Robert Chandler and Geoffrey Smith, by the Harvill Press. A selection of Platonov's stories, *The Return*, translated by Robert and Elizabeth Chandler and Angela Livingstone, will be published by Harvill in 1998.

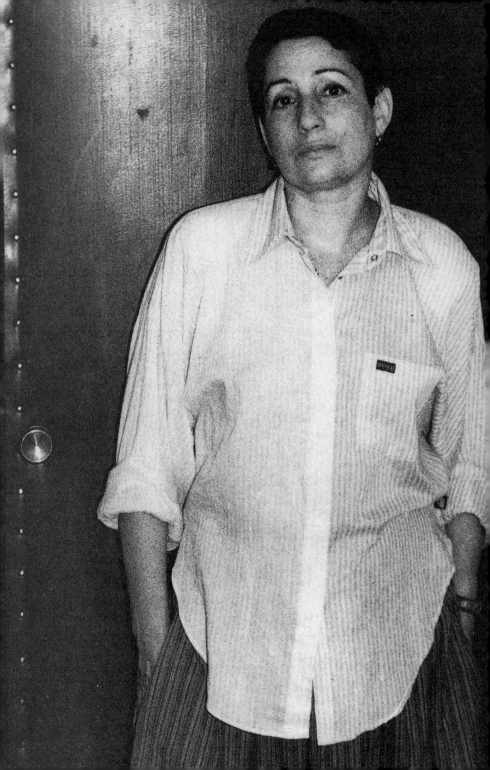

Ludmilla
ULITSKAYA
The Foundling

Translated by Alla Zbinovsky

Ludmilla Ulitskaya

Modern science claims that the emotional life of a human being begins while still in the womb, and much more ancient sources also attest to this in an oblique way: according to the book of Genesis, the sons of Rebecca, began fighting while still inside their mother's womb.

Nobody will ever know at which particular moment — in her pre-natal or post-natal life — Victoria first felt irritated by her twin sister Gayane.

Their perspicacious Armenian granny Emma Ashotovna could have ignored these minor infant squabbles had she not noted very early on the disparity in the personalities of the twins, and thanks to her largesse, her wing always covered the one whose legs were thinner and whose cheeks were not as rosy. That didn't mean that she couldn't also admire the strength of the other granddaughter.

The father was smitten by them both. The babies' crying was such a tortuous ordeal for him that he would sweep up the sobbing child (namely Gayane) in a suffocating embrace; he was ready to moo like a calf, bleat like a sheep or crow like a rooster, just so the child would calm down.

The smart little Victoria realized early on that the stormy love duet between her father and her sobbing sister put a real damper on the pleasure she got from oppressing Gayane, and so she stopped picking on her sister in the presence of her father.

In all fairness, it should be noted that the most dreadful punishment for Victoria was being separated from her sister into different rooms. When Gayane was taken into her mother's room and the door slid firmly shut down the narrow metal rail, Victoria would mournfully sit out her forgiveness near the single tracks for hours on end, as if waiting at the train station.

The mother did not intervene in the girls' relationship, and in general she didn't get involved in any family matters. The role she played in the household was one of a divine being — she sat in her narrow room on a high armchair, with her silver tinted braids crowning her head, which granny would comb out every morning for a long time. Twice a day the girls would come

The Foundling

and tell her, "Good morning, mamochka" and "Good night, mamochka," and she would smile weakly at them.

Sometimes Granny would bring them in to play on the rug near their mother's thin legs, wrapped in thick knit socks of the same design as the rug, but when the girls began to argue and cry, she would wince fearfully and press her hands to her ears.

Until the age of three, Victoria's encroachments were strictly limited to the material realm: she would take away her sister's toys, candy, socks and scarves. Gayane protested to the best of her ability and felt bitterly hurt. However, some time in their fourth year, an event occurred which at first glance seemed insignificant, but it marked an even higher level in Victoria's pretensions. An old doctor came to the house to treat the girls' colds. Yuli Solomonovich was from the category of long extinct doctors whose mere presence could calm down patients, the sound of their voices could bring down fevers, and sometimes even unknown to them, a drop of ancient sorcery was mixed into their art of healing.

The ritual of Yuli Solomonovich's visits had been established during Margarita's childhood. Strange as it may seem, he was already then a very old doctor, which suggested some sort of magic at play.

First they served him tea, always in the presence of the patient. Emma Ashotovna, just as thirty years before, brought in a tray with a glass in an ample holder, two teapots and a basket of nut biscuits. He chatted quietly with Emma Ashotovna, jingled his spoon, praised the biscuits, and pretended not to pay the least bit of attention to the girls. Then Emma Ashotovna brought in a basin, a pitcher with warm water and an extremely long towel. The doctor rubbed his pink hands for a long time, as if about to perform surgery, then earnestly dried his splayed fingers. By now the girls' eyes were glued to him.

The doctor majestically donned a crisp white robe and hung rubber tubes with berry-like metal tips on his wide flat chest. The gold frame of his glasses shone in his bushy eyebrows, and his bald head cast a reddish glow. Without realizing it, the girls

Ludmilla Ulitskaya

had long ago been transformed into spectators, sitting in the first row of the pit and enjoying the performance.

"And what are our young ladies' names?" he would inquire politely while bending over them.

He asked this question every time, but they were so young that the freshness of this question had not yet been exhausted.

"Gayane," answered the shy Gayane, and he shook her weightless hand in his big palm.

"Gayane, Gayane, wonderful," the doctor admired the name.

"And you, beautiful lady?" he asked Victoria. Victoria thought for a while — what she was thinking about, even Freud wouldn't have had a clue — and answered slyly:

"Gayane."

The real Gayane's feelings were hurt and tears rolled down her cheeks:

"I'm, I'm Gayane..."

The doctor thoughtfully stroked his shiny chin. He did know that these little creatures were quite complex, and he resolved to deal with the difficult problem at hand by self-deprecation.

Victoria glanced over triumphantly: not the plush teddy bear, not the rag rabbit — this time she had managed to grab her sister's own name and she rejoiced in her unprecedented victory.

"Well, well, well," the doctor slowly repeated, like a ticking clock. "Gayane... very good...." He looked at one girl and then the other, and then sadly and seriously turned to the abductor:

"Then where is Victoria? Victoria gone?"

Victoria breathed heavily through her stuffed-up nose. She wanted to be Victoria and Gayane at the same time, but to disclaim a name just like that, your own or another's, was also impossible.

"I'm Victoria," she finally sighed, and Gayane immediately calmed down.

And while the girls were fretting over the unsuccessful attempt to steal the name, the old man managed to examine both of them: he listened to them, drummed on their chests with

The Foundling

hard fingers and felt along all their lymph nodes, all the while smiling tightly with his closed lips.

Emma Ashotovna feasted her eyes on the doctor's artistic movements, mistakenly attributing his smile to the exceptional charms of her granddaughters. She was wrong – he was smiling to himself about his weak-sighted Biblical forefather, fooled a long time ago by his sons in exactly the same way.

From that time onward, the renaming drama was played out quite regularly on Tverskoi Boulevard, where their nanny Fenya took the girls for walks. Fenya had one weakness – an irrational love of striking up new friendships. Even though she knew most of the grandmothers, nannies and children who came here, she still somehow managed constantly to enrich her collection. It's entirely possible that Fenya inherited this passion from her mother who had worked as a wet nurse in a wealthy merchant's home, serving there to her dying day and raising Fenya under the wing of her kind master. Or perhaps it was the shadow of Yogel, the dancing-master and fashionable matchmaker, who had once lived here, somewhere to the left of Pushkin's monument spotted with pigeons' droppings, still hovering over the linden trees on Tverskoi Boulevard, and blessing the social life of nannies and their charges. At any rate, the proud Fenya would occasionally announce her acquisitions to Emma Ashotovna:

"Today we met new children, the admiral's children!" or,

"We met two girls today, like ours, but a year apart, Vertinsky girls, the actor's."

But what Fenya didn't know was that every time she struck up a new friendship, the same little scenario was reenacted – Victoria called herself by her sister's name, and Gayane, pouting and turning red, didn't call herself anything, which was why half the children called both sisters Gayane.

Fenya didn't pay any mind to these psychological games. Beyond socializing, she had other major tasks: to keep her well-dressed charges out of the dirty sandbox and the puddles, to see they didn't fall down, hurt themselves, or break out into a

Ludmilla Ulitskaya

sweat from too much running around. In this way, the over-protective Fenya condemned them to solely verbal amusements.

In her small circle of privileged children, Victoria was famous for telling her own versions of popular fairytales and stories of her own invention. Gayane was the silent observer, storing in her memory other people's ribbons, brooches, insignificant events and dropped words. Her favorite amusement until the age of ten was preparing "little secrets," that is arrangements of leaves, flowers, candy wrappers and pieces of foil under a piece of glass. Even in the summer, at their dacha, where the girls had a lot more freedom, Gayane preferred this solitary and sedentary amusement best of all, while Victoria rode on her bike, swung on the swings and played ball with the proper (from Fenya's point of view) children from the neighbouring dachas.

It was here, at the Kratovo dacha, during the last summer before beginning school, that Gayane was put to her first serious test. Gypsies had appeared in the area. First, four gypsy women with dozens of fidgety, roguish children appeared at the wide crossroads, where kerosene was dispensed from a barrel and the local old women sold tight bunches of white-nosed radishes and cucumbers that were as prickly as cacti. Then a classic lame gypsy man in an enormous greatcoat, covered with medals almost all the way to his belt, rode in on a cart harnessed to a classic gypsy horse.

There weren't any rug covered wagons or silk shirts in sight. Neither was there a lone striking beauty usually found among the ragged dark-skinned gypsy women of indeterminate ages. What's more, one of them was definitely an ugly old hag. They spent the night right in the middle of the square – in the cart or under it, nobody could tell for sure. In the morning, after Fenya went for milk, she told Emma Ashotovna about them, and the girls were forbidden to go outside the gate on their own.

"They steal children," Victoria whispered to her sister, and while Gayane contemplated this new danger in her life, Victoria had already let her imagination loose: "They've already stolen two children from our settlement!"

The Foundling

Meanwhile, the gypsy women went about their usual business, which was bothering passersby, to read some interesting news from their past or future lives off their palms, in exchange for a crumpled ruble.

Their business was fair to middling, so at midday the gypsies decided to go out to the dachas. The girls had been playing at the Karasik's place near the crossroads since morning, and they could see very well through the sparse fence. They saw a gypsy kid playing with a whip and the lame man scolding him in an incomprehensible language. Gayane was afraid to get up close to the fence, but Victoria, on the other hand, hung on the gate and stared daringly at the strange and lawless life.

At lunchtime, Emma Ashotovna came and took the girls home. About then, the younger gypsy women dispersed and all that was left of the camp was the hobbled horse, grazing along the side of the road on the dusty grass, the old gypsy man asleep under the cart, and an old woman, who flourished her colorful skirts as she blocked Emma Ashotovna's way and wailed:

"Oh, what I see, I see... Oh, look, misfortune is on its way, give me your hand, let me have a look..."

Emma Ashotovna pushed the woman away in disgust with her haughty hand, laden with large old coral rings, exactly the same kind that were on the dry, dirty hand of the gypsy woman, and glared at her with her fierce, dark eyes. The gypsy woman blew off like a gust of wind, and it was only after Emma Ashotovna turned away that she cried out after her:

"Go, go your own way, may your water be salty, and your food bitter!"

Victoria bravely stuck out her long raspberry-colored tongue at the gypsy, for which she was immediately reprimanded on the crown of her head by Granny's hard finger. Gayane clung tightly to the silk hem of Granny's new dress, the large polka dots of which were much rougher to the touch than the sky blue background.

The girls had lunch on the terrace, and then Granny allowed

Ludmilla Ulitskaya

them to sleep outside in the summer house, because of the heat. Fenya unfolded the cots and left, and then Victoria announced the following secret to her sister: the old gypsy woman was a real witch, and could turn herself into anyone she chose, and she also turned children into whomever she wanted. And their hobbled horse was not a horse at all, but two stolen boys called Vic and Shurik, whose parents had long been searching for them, but would never find them.

They spoke in whispers.

"If she wants to, she could turn into Granny..."

"Into our Granny?" asked Gayane, horrified.

"Uh-huh. And if she wants to, into Papa as well..." threatened Victoria. "Over there, look, there they are..."

And she waved her hand in the direction of the dacha's fence. An interesting plan was taking shape in her clever little head.

It was the beginning of June. Thick bunches of lilac were climbing into the summer house and their smell was very strong, like hot food on a plate. A bumblebee slowly pulled a bass note and the cicadas answered with their violin voices from the warm grass. Life was so young and so frightening.

"Don't be afraid," Victoria took pity on her frightened sister. "I'll hide you."

"Where?" asked Gayane in a voice full of hopelessness.

"In the woodshed. They will never find you there," said Victoria, soothingly.

"And what about you?"

"I'll hit her with a stick!" said Victoria sternly and Gayane didn't have any doubt that she would. Hit her she would.

Barefoot, clad just in their cotton shorts with large pockets on their stomachs, they stole their way to the woodshed. Victoria lifted the latch and let her sister inside.

"Sit in here and don't look out. And when they leave, I'll let you out."

The latch shut from the outside. Gayane was sure she was now out of danger.

The Foundling

Victoria glided back to the summer house and covered herself from head to toe with a sheet. She imagined how scared stupid Gayane must be now and she herself felt a bit scared as well. But she also thought it was all pretty funny, and she fell asleep with a smile on her face.

Emma Ashotovna woke her up around six and asked where Gayane was. Victoria didn't remember right away, and when she did, she got worried. Their granny got even more anxious, began to rush about their large plot of land, first running to the outhouse, where the girls were forbidden to go by themselves, then to the raspberry patch, then down, to the bottom of the hill to the neglected wasteland, enclosed by an ancient fence. The girl was nowhere to be found.

"Gayane! Gayane!" yelled Emma Ashotovna, but there was no answer.

This long yell, the sound of her name, with a dent in the middle and a wide tail at the end, was absorbed unanswered into the fresh foliage, which hadn't yet completely unfurled into its full glory.

These were the first hot days, when the resin was beginning to sublimate, and when the first summer calm collected over the earth, following the rush of springtime growth of various grasses and leaves, and Emma Ashotovna's yells somehow obscenely spoiled the decency of the day, which was already bowing toward evening.

Victoria crawled up to the woodshed and lifted the latch.

"Come out!" she whispered loudly into the shed. "Come out, Granny's calling you!"

Gayane sat between an old barrel and a stack of firewood, pressed to the wall with her petrified spine. Her eyes were open, but she didn't see Victoria. Without even seeing her face, Victoria understood, and she was beside herself. Having endured a fright so enormous that it could not fit into her seven-year-old body, Gayane now found herself beyond its unknown limits.

Stuck into the airless half-darkness of the shed by her sister, Gayane dozed off, but then she woke up from some slight

43

Ludmilla Ulitskaya

movement near her temples, and suddenly found herself in a completely strange place – strokes of fiery yellow light cut through the space from all sides, she felt as if she was confined to a luminous cage, slightly rocking in the gray-brown darkness. It appeared to poor Gayane that some supernatural force had already kidnapped her, together with the shed, a stack of birch wood, the barrels, an old steel bed standing on end, and a pile of gardening tools, which hadn't been used since her grandfather's death. She had been cruelly kidnapped, together with time, stretched like a piece of old rubber band, whose beginning and end had been lost. And this movement, running airily past her temple, also had a relationship to the fact that time as she knew it had dissolved and disappeared somewhere, and this new thing moved along with her in a nauseating and endless circle.

"It's even worse than being kidnapped," thought Gayane, "they've forgotten all about me in some awful place."

The tip of her nose was numb with fright, icy goose bumps crawled on her back and a dark whirlpool slowly lifted her and twirled her and threw her into such depths that she could only guess that she was dying.

"Gayane! Gayane!" a loud modulating voice called her from afar, similar to her granny's, but she understood, that it wasn't her granny calling her, it wasn't even the gypsy who had turned herself into her granny, but someone else, even more frightening and inhuman.

"Gayane, come on out!" She heard the real whisper of her sister. "The Gypsies are gone, they're gone. Granny is looking for you!"

The horrible place turned back into the shed. Thin rays of light shone through the cracks between the boards, and everything was again simple and wonderful at the Kratovo dacha, and Granny in her blue polka dot dress was already coming to the shed, to finally find her lost grandchild, and Gayane, slowly coming to, wondered at the smallness and goodness of this world, in comparison with the enormity and boundlessness of that which

The Foundling

had surged over her there, in the woodshed, at the start of summer, in the seventh year of her life.

She flung herself at her sister with cries of "Victoria! Victoria! Don't leave me!" and clasped her in her arms. Victoria stroked Gayane on her cold back, kissed her coarse braids, ear, and shoulder, whispering:

"It's all right, it's all right, dear! There's nothing to be afraid of!"

It seemed to Victoria that at that moment, she was really protecting her nice and fearful sister from the danger, hiding behind the gates.

From that day onward, the day which Gayane remembered so clearly and Victoria completely forgot, an unusual sensitivity to everything dark and disturbing awakened in Gayane. It was a special feeling toward darkness, and she felt it even when opening the door to her dress closet. There, in the darkness, where you could not switch on the light, something nameless was lurking, something revealed to her back then, in the darkness of the woodshed. Even the small, cozy bit of darkness which was created by closing the sliding lid of her pencil case made her apprehensive. She had a similar disturbing sensation when she went to her sick mother. Her mother's illness appeared to her with a blotch of darkness, and she could even sketch that part of her head, neck and chest in which she felt the darkness to be concentrated.

Her sister's fears, guessed by Victoria, encouraged her to play even more cruel jokes: she hid her sister's notebooks in the most inaccessible corners of the flat, forcing her to crawl into the darkest crevices; she would shove a dead beetle into the dangerous dark space of her pencil case, in order to imbue her with the uncertainty of terrible reality. And when Gayane shrieked and threw her pencil case, Victoria would save her, hold her close and smile at her condescendingly:

"What is it, you silly thing, what scared you so?"

Victoria derived great pleasure from controlling her sister's fears. Their love for one another at those moments when comfort was needed was great indeed; they themselves were too young then to realize what dangerous and hostile elements could be thrown in to the mix of human love.

Emma Ashotovna, made vulnerable by tragic love and the illness of her daughter, understood a great deal about the madness and cruelty of love, but was not in the least bit interested in the girls' relationship and the nature of their mutual attachment. She was the only one in the family who would have had enough sensitivity and the ability to deal with the twins, had she not imposed a strict and very eastern hierarchy: if it wasn't a matter of life and death, then the main event in her life was dinner, and never ever children's squabbles.

Emma Ashotovna hastily got through the fuss of morning with the prolonged combing of four long-maned heads – her own, her daughter's and her granddaughters'. She braided their dark braids and dressed everyone in linen smelling of an overheated iron of cast-iron, prepared a quick breakfast, did some light cleaning and got down to the preparation of dinner, with all of its baked eggplants, stuffed tomatoes, spicy beans and unleavened bread.

Even though she came from a wealthy Armenian family, she spent her childhood and youth in Tiflis and so her cooking was more Georgian, that is to say more complex and diverse, than Armenian. She kept count of the nuts and eggs, coriander seeds and pea peppers, and her hands at the same time completely independently made fine and exact movements. She enjoyed cooking, in the same way as a musician enjoys the music created by his fingers.

Usually at half past six, Sergo would get home from work. The table would already be set and blazing with aromas. Sergo would wash his hands and bring his wife out to the table. She walked with the tiny steps of a wind-up doll, smiling weakly. This room was dusky and windowless, lit by a yellowish electric light, and her face took on the hue of old porcelain. They would seat her in a chair next to her husband. The girls sat on either side of their parents, but on the long sides of the table. Emma

The Foundling

Ashotovna sat formally on the other side of the table, and Fenya would open the door with her knee, bring in a pink soup tureen, the size of which was considerably greater than the needs of the family. Placing the soup tureen next to the left elbow of the mistress of the house, Fenya would disappear – she would dine in the kitchen and would not agree for anything to sit at this grand manorial table, where the plates were changed about three times, and the food was doled out with a small spoon.

A bit of soup was poured into the bottom of Margarita's bowl, she took a thin spoon into her thin hand and slowly lowered it into the bowl. The meal was purely symbolic – she only ate at night, alone: two pieces of black bread with cheese and an apple. Any other type of food – from the first year of her illness, when her mother tried to feed her something more nourishing – she took into her mouth but couldn't swallow.

This evening, as always, Emma Ashotovna took the plates into the kitchen and, putting on dirty glasses and a clean apron, began the washing up. She was indulging Fenya, who guarded her honor before her neighbours and never tired of reminding them:

"I'm not a cook, I take care of the children."

Sergo would take Margarita to her room and sit next to the old radio receiver, turning its ribbed knobs.

Alone with his wife, Sergo would talk. One couldn't say that he talked with her. But it wasn't exactly like talking with himself. This was a strange conversation between two follies: Margarita wordlessly addressed her beloved husband with a long-rusted reproach, almost not noticing the corpulent gray-haired man, whom Sergo had turned into during the years of her illness; and he, retelling and making comments about the evening radio broadcast, hopelessly tried to get through to the current Margarita with the help of this shaky auditory bridge, the Margarita still focused on the unfortunate events of long ago. They leaned on one another with their eyes, missing each other by decades, and continued their wild dialogue.

"Where is Gayane?" asked Margarita suddenly, in a distinct voice.

"Gayane?" It was as if Sergo had hit a telephone pole head on. "Gayane?" he reiterated, stunned that his wife had asked him a question for the first time in some years.

"They're doing their lessons," he quietly answered Margarita, taking her by the hand. Her hand was like glass, only it didn't clink.

"Where is Gayane?" Margarita asked again, insistently.

Sergo got up and glanced behind the partition. Victoria sat with her back to him scratching away with her pen. She pressed down very hard and moved her elbow around when she wrote, and her writing was fraught with smudges.

"Where is Gayane?" asked father.

Victoria jerked her shoulder and an ink tear leaked out of the bottom of her pen.

"How should I know? I'm not her keeper," answered Victoria, not turning around.

Victoria wasn't quoting. It's just that her whole little life wanted to become a quotation, and it floundered, not finding the proper context.

Sergo, all worked up because his wife had talked to him, mechanically looked for Gayane in the flat. He went out into the hallway, jerked the door of the bathroom, but there wasn't anyone in there at that moment. He went into the kitchen, where Emma Ashotovna was rubbing the shiny backs of plates and, perplexed, asked his mother-in-law:

"Margarita has just asked me, 'Where is Gayane?'"

Emma Ashotovna froze, as if her inner clock had just stopped:

"Margarita has just asked you?"

"Where is Gayane..." he finished.

She carefully put the plate down and, her chest and sides heaving, almost ran to her daughter. Propping the door to her room open, she asked from the threshold:

"Margarita, how are you feeling?"

The Foundling

"Fine, Mama," answered Margarita quietly, without even moving her eyelashes, "but where is Gayane?" she again asked and Emma Ashotovna finally understood the meaning of the question.

Gayane was gone. Not only was she nowhere to be found, but her new fur coat was not on its hanger, and her little boots with the fake shearling trimming were not in their usual place under the hanger. Her sunken, empty galoshes stood alone, each in its own drying puddle.

"So where is Gayane, Victoria?" asked Granny.

"How should I know... we were sitting, sitting, and then she left," answered Victoria.

"How long ago? Where? Why didn't you ask where she was going?" exploded Granny with a barrage of questions.

"I don't know. Didn't see. About ten minutes, or forty minutes ago. How should I know..." answered Victoria, still not ripping herself away from her notebook. She drew a large ink picture on the cover of her notebook with false enthusiasm.

Emma Ashotovna rushed out to find Fenya, but a steel lock hung on the door to her room – it was Saturday, Fenya hadn't yet returned from the evening church service.

It was twenty past eight, a thick humid darkness lay outside, like the kind during a winter thaw.

Not putting anything on, Sergo rushed out onto the street, ran around the round stone courtyard and stopped at the gate. He didn't know where to go now. Emma Ashotovna called around to the parents of the girls' school friends. Gayane was nowhere to be found...

The stage for this evening's disappearance had been set a month prior. The girls were both at home, recuperating from tonsillitis. Through two doors, Victoria smelled fresh meat balls, and made her way to the kitchen. The meat balls were big and honest ones, with garlic and fresh herbs, and so artfully made that it seemed they had a long and happy life in front of them. It was still a long way until dinner, but Victoria got one – a brown one with a shiny crust, barely holding in the pressure of the juices and fat. Victoria bit a piece off and wiggled her tongue, noisily sucking in air to cool it off.

Usually Emma Ashotovna did not allow such pre-dinner indulgences, but the girl was recuperating after an illness, and this was the first time she had asked for something to eat in a week.

Chewing enthusiastically, she eavesdropped on a conversation between the neighbours. Maria Timofeevna, shaking her gaunt head, discussed a terrible occurrence with Fenya – that morning a dead newborn infant had been found in the trash bin in the courtyard.

"I'm telling you, Fenya, it's either someone from the eighth, or from the twelfth entrance, in our's nobody was expecting," said Maria Timofeevna, promoting her own patriotic version of events.

"You just never know," grumbled Fenya, who had a very low opinion of humankind. They could've just laced themselves up, and you'd never see."

In spite of her virginity, she was very well informed about the practical consequences of the carnal sin, and she felt a strong revulsion toward it.

The conversation veered in a dangerous direction, and Emma Ashotovna, with her face all red from the heat of the frying pan, bid Victoria to return to her room. Filled up with the warm meat and the awful news, Victoria went down the corridor and thought about the poor newborn. First, she imagined it in a white lace blanket, like the one left over from the times of their mother's infancy and now covering their doll called Slava. Then she imagined this dead baby found on the trash heap as their curly-haired doll Slava. But somehow, this didn't satisfy her – she didn't pity Slava, nor did she pity the baby. She wanted something else, something more passionate. Then Victoria imagined the baby as very tiny and pink, like the hairless kitten from the communal cat called Marusya, but with little hands and feet instead of paws, and with Slava's pinky-yellow

The Foundling

hair. But this picture didn't quite satisfy Victoria's greedy imagination either.

She touched the bronze knob of her door with her greasy fingers and suddenly stopped in her tracks. Oh, if only Gayane was that imagined baby in the trash bin!

Victoria was breathless with excitement. Of course, someone close to them, secretly evil, steals little Gayane, kills her and throws her away... Victoria opened the door and everything disintegrated when it hit boring reality. There was Gayane, with a pink scarf around her neck, sitting at the table and biting the end of her long braid, reading an old, worn out copy of *Robinson Crusoe*.

Victoria went into the nursery and stood at the window. The trash bin in the courtyard was a large wooden crate, it wasn't visible from here, it was blocked by a two story outbuilding. She fixed her gaze on the chipping, yellow side of this building. Her father's engineering abilities had somehow been passed on to her in an intricate way: it was also vital to her that each wheel was connected to another, the connecting rod should press on a crankshaft, and in the end, that the machine should move. She wasn't at all satisfied with that dead baby. She needed a live one, thrown out onto the trash heap, and she needed it to be Gayane.

Victoria's eyebrows were almost connected, they arched, and at her temples they almost began to bend upward again. When she was deep in thought, her eyebrows involuntarily moved up and down, just like her father's.

Perhaps it was like this? Early in the morning, Granny goes out with a trash bucket and finds a girl on the trash heap. She thinks she's dead, but she's really alive. She brings her home and tells Mama – feed her, she's only three days old. But Mama has me, and I'm also three days old... And again the story's constructive defect becomes obvious: who is this scoundrel, who throws the baby away in the dumpster?

The police had already asked everyone willing to say anything about the criminal finding; they collected several fantastic versions, in which filthy lucre, sorcery and passion for informing

Ludmilla Ulitskaya

were mixed in an engaging fashion, and the courtyard, always living by the unbending, like eternity, law of the present, put the event aside into history, dooming it to oblivion, similarly to those stories of the great antediluvian civilizations. The investigator shelved yet another case of unsolved murder, which wasn't really considered to be a murder at all.

Only Victoria was tortured by her still premature plot. The thorny intrigue wouldn't let go of her, and she kept searching for the hypothetical mother of the baby discarded into the dumpster, who had turned into her sister Gayane thanks to her artistic license and wicked imagination.

On the third day of Victoria's creative torments, she found her long sought-for personage as she walked past a door in her entryway, which led to the half-basement caretaker's communal flat. The Becker woman, who lived in the corner room, was horrible to look at. She was very tall, even by male standards, she had a masculine haircut, her whitish face was as worn out as her clothes. She was said to be a drunkard, even though nobody ever saw her drunk. But she really was a drunk, in her own way. She drank every day, always by herself, locked away in her wretched little room. She would drink exactly one bottle of red wine, starting with a quick glass and then stretching the leftover half-bottle over two hours. Then she would go to sleep on a mattress, covered with a sheet from the hospital where she worked.

The sun rose whenever it pleased, depending on the time of year, but the Becker woman always rose at half-past five. Barely ungluing her eyes, she drank down whatever wine was left over from the previous night – two finger widths from the bottom... Another person would have gone to pot long ago, but what kept her together was the constancy and devotion to her routine. Regaining consciousness after her very deep sleep, she would go to work at the hospital, waving her mop. The other cleaners and hospital attendants didn't like her for her apathetic silence, lupine glances and zealous work. Nobody, except for the head doctor Markelova, who had hired her, knew what a

The Foundling

competent medical attendant and dependable assistant Tania Becker had been in the pre-war, pre-terror era.

Having slaved for twelve hours — two and a half shifts — she just managed to buy her nightly bottle on the way home and by eight she would hide away in her little hole. She would take off her boots and leather jacket, sit on the mattress and put her beloved bottle on a stool, serving her as a dining table. It was warm outside and in a few minutes, she knew, it would be warm inside, and she lingered because she cherished and extended this happy moment.

The people in the neighbourhood took an instant dislike to her because of her pride, which they shrewdly detected in her. The children were afraid of her and ran away when her long figure appeared in the thick stone gateway. They nicknamed her the "Corpse-cutter," since someone had started a rumour, that she worked in a morgue. But this wasn't true, she only cleaned in two of the most difficult departments of the hospital — purulent surgery and neurology.

Victoria began to prepare for battle. She gathered around her an assortment of rumpled girls, and, shaking the blue and red pompon on her knitted hat, told the story of how corpses are first soaked in large glass jars, and then they are sorted, legs separately, arms separately, heads separately, and it was the Becker woman who did this job.

Victoria's stories were frightening and enticing. The youngest of the group of girls, Lena Zenkova, would cover her ears with her mittens, but you couldn't drag her away for anything; even what seeped through her wet mittens wasn't lacking in mysterious charm. In addition, Victoria chose interesting places for such discussions: in the dark triangular space under the stairwell, in the storeroom between the wood sheds, on the sixth, top floor, on the narrow short staircase leading to the attic. Darkness, half-darkness, and indistinct knocks accompanied the performance every time, Victoria ended up a slave to her own fantasies, and had to think up something new, more far-fetched, more and more...

Ludmilla Ulitskaya

She fully coped with her role as the teller of offbeat horror stories which made all kinds of twists and turns, but the constant factor was the terrible Becker woman, who was always the centre of the story.

These sessions were very popular, but from the very beginning of the series the sensitive Gayane always tried to slip away, refusing to go out on the pretext of a runny nose or a headache. The performances would be postponed to a later time, when Gayane had no choice but to be right next to the storyteller.

Strictly speaking, the stories about severed limbs, black sheets and corpses coming back to life were not original. They were in keeping with their youthful ages, time and place. Undoubtedly, Victoria was a talented storyteller, and Gayane was the most impressionable of everyone in the audience. Gayane dimly sensed a certain troubling purposefulness in these stories about the nightly relations between the defamed Becker woman, and the even more defamed dead patients in the old city hospital.

These three steps downward, into the half-basement flat, seemed to Gayane the entryway to the underworld, and she, her feet almost not touching the floor, would fly up to the second floor at one go.

Returning to that memorable evening, they sat doing their lessons later than usual, because it was Monday, and on Mondays they had music lessons, and the day somehow had two humps. They sat at Margarita's old desk, across from one another. Victoria sat with one of her legs tucked in, which was strictly forbidden by their granny, and dumped rumpled notebooks and bitten-up pencils onto the table. Gayane stuck her hand into her bag and took out a brown envelope.

"Oh!" said Gayane, since she didn't know how the envelope got into her school bag.

"What's that you've got?" asked Victoria, lifting her curious eyebrows while the puzzled Gayane examined the envelope with the widely separated red letters, square and large, that said "Gayane. Personal."

The Foundling

"It's some sort of envelope. A letter," muttered Gayane. She held the envelope in both hands, and the letters, spread apart like stringy inky blood vessels, seemed alive and bloody.

"What's inside?" asked Victoria, almost indifferently. Gayane placed the letter on the edge of the table, as if contemplating if it was worth opening. With her sensitive inner being she understood that nothing good would come of it. The envelope lay on the corner of the table, smelling strongly of glue, pretending it had ended up there entirely by chance. Gayane lowered her hand to her school bag and took out her neat notebooks, a pink handwriting notebook with double and slanted lines, and a yellow arithmetic notebook with a reassuring grid. Gayane buried herself in this notebook.

"A letter for you, right?" Victoria couldn't resist, while trying to make out she wasn't at all interested.

Gayane turned over the envelope on its back, crudely glued together with still-wet glue. She ran her finger down the wet seam and answered her sister:

"I'll read it later."

Victoria twirled the end of her braid on her finger and stared at her notebook – things weren't going according to plan. The letter lay on the table unread, Granny could walk in at any moment, and Gayane, as if nothing had happened, was writing in her shiny notebook. Gayane's demeanor was serene, but in actual fact she was consumed by a nasty premonition and was completely focused on the unopened letter.

"Get away from here, get out. Just get lost," she tried to exorcise the impending moment. It didn't even occur to her that she could throw the letter away unread.

Victoria was tired of waiting and placed her hand on the envelope:

"Then I'll read it myself!"

Gayane awakened:

"No. It's my letter." And then she opened it.

"Gayane! The time has come for you to know the whole truth. Everyone calls me the Becker woman, and I am your real

55

mother. I gave birth to you and abandoned you, because I couldn't take you with me. This is a secret. I'll tell you all about it later. Soon I'll come, tell everyone about the truth and take you away with me, my daughter. We'll live together. Your mother, the Becker woman."

Initially it took Gayane awhile to figure out what the tiny, slanted letters said. The word "daughter" was written in large, fat letters. It took her a long time to comprehend what that word meant. Victoria patiently waited out the necessary pause, and finally asked:

"Who's it from?"

Gayane silently handed her the sheet of notebook paper. Victoria took pleasure in the text: it was good. She especially liked the beginning: The time has come for you to know...

Oh, this had happened before, before... Time stretched out like a weak rubber band, without a beginning and an end, and the strange movement along the nauseating endless circle, the feeling of a terrible theft, the sensation of darkness...

This resurfaced memory validated that this letter, terrible just to look at, told of a no less terrible truth: the frightening Becker woman was her mother.

"Don't be afraid," Victoria promised magnanimously, "Nobody will give you back to your mother."

"What, you've known all along?" asked the again terrified Gayane. Someone else's knowing aggravated this whole terror.

Victoria jerked her shoulder, threw her braid to the side and soothed her sister:

"Don't you worry so much. Of course I've known. Everyone knows."

"Fenya knows?" asked Gayane with dumb hopefulness.

"Of course, Fenya knows. I'm telling you, everyone knows."

The next round of evildoing was purely impromptu. Victoria was not an especially bad girl. An evil thought just took possession of her, and, as it is with talented people, it developed in a talented way.

"So what do you think made our mother ill? Granny brought

The Foundling

you from the trash bin and tells her: here, feed her! Do you think that was pleasant for her?"

"And then she got ill?" Gayane asked her sister again.

"What do you think? She says, 'I don't want to,' and Granny orders her... that's how she took ill."

"And you?" asked Gayane, trying to repair her world, which had come crashing down.

"What about me? I'm her real daughter, and you are a foundling."

"From which trash bin?" asked Gayane, as if this detail was very important.

"Which one? From ours, the green one in the backyard," said Victoria, brilliantly connecting geography to biography, and in this very moment feeling the utmost artistic fulfillment. The taste of the warm meat ball, the terrible news and the smell of floor polish, which was being spread in the corridor, she experienced all this as well in this moment.

"A-a-a..." Gayane responded weakly, and Victoria, sensing this weakness, suddenly doubted the success of her cunning joke – it wasn't turning out as cheerfully as she had hoped. And so, she stuck her nose into her textbook, searching for the necessary number of the problem and at the same time wondering how to liven up the situation.

When she lifted her head up from her book, her sister was not in the room. The carefully opened envelope and letter lay on the edge of the table.

"Sobbing in the hall," supposed Victoria. She planned on letting her sister sob for awhile, and then confessing to her prank.

And then their father walked into the room and asked:

"Where is Gayane?"

Gayane had gone very far away from her home, so far she had never ventured before on her own. All the way to Presnya. She stood at the entrance to the zoo, in the empty gate, where the degenerate gods of extinct peoples guarded the animal tribes

Ludmilla Ulitskaya

in captivity. Some sort of melancholy animal, or, perhaps, a night bird, emitted long, hoarse wails. A snowfall was starting, and the sky got lighter. Balls of golden, scattered light glowed around the street lamps, and slow, heavy snowflakes glittered, silvery and moonlike there, where the electricity didn't reach. At this moment, everything was new and untried: loneliness, and being faraway from home, these sad wails, and even the smell of the snow, mixed in with the smells of the stables and monkey house.

It seemed to her that an eternity had passed since she left her home, or several eternities. This was the eternity of horror before the Becker woman and the eternity of guilt before her mother. She believed her sister immediately and unshakably. Her whole life now made sense: the subtle uneasiness, anxiety, dark premonitions and abstract fears, all were now fully justified. Of course, she was the stranger in the family, and the terrible Becker woman was her real mother, and only Victoria had full rights to Granny, Papa, Fenya, to mother's pale morning kisses, and she, Gayane, would be taken into the basement by the evil yellow-toothed Becker woman.

The thought of her likeness to her sister, obvious to her from early childhood, didn't at all interfere with the general picture of the unfolding catastrophe. This thought was too petty to be considered in these very exceptional circumstances.

If her real mother was the Becker woman and she, Gayane was responsible for the illness of her poor, not-real mother Margarita, then everyone would be better off if she just died. The thought of death brought her an unexpected feeling of relief. She didn't at all think about the technical details of suicide, this also would have been too petty. It seemed to her it was enough to find a secluded spot, curl herself up into a little ball, and her passionate desire alone to cease existing would be enough in order to never wake up.

She walked along the side of the zoo, on a snowed-over road with no people, and she noticed from afar a dark figure, pushing his way through the slightly bent bars of a fence. Yukov,

The Foundling

the night watchman, was off on his usual nightly journey, carrying off a portion of second-rate beef which he felt entitled to, the meat allotted to the gaunt predators. He darted past the girl and disappeared in an adjoining courtyard. His girlfriend lived there. This was how the meat was stolen twice: first from the tiger and then from Yukov's family.

Gayane waited until the person disappeared from view, and then easily slipped through the bars of the fence. Here, in the zoo, it was wonderful, and not at all frightening. The sad wails of the night animal stopped, although from time to time there were some sort of mysterious loud sighs, rumbles and grunts. In the light emptiness of the evening, she went past the snow-covered pond to the cages, which were emptied some time ago because the animals had been transferred to warmer quarters.

A large wooden dustbin stood in the passageway between two high wire walls, it looked very similar to that green trashbin which stood in their courtyard. On the side of the bin were some briquettes of pressed hay, covered with snow. Gayane swept the snow away with her mittens, dragged out one bale of hay and turned it upside down. It smelled sadly of summer, the dacha, and all of her past life. She sat on the bale as if it was a low bench near Granny's legs, covered her knees with the scattered hay, screwed up her eyes and fell fast asleep, absolutely certain that she would never wake up in this world of evil and incorrigible justice.

Victoria shoved the letter and the envelope with red ink into her pants. In the bathroom, she tore it into small pieces and flushed it down the toilet. Mistrust for the trashbin hung in the air in these mean times.

Emma Ashotovna interrogated Victoria between calls to the morgue and the police station. Victoria answered with honest eyes – she didn't need to lie. She really didn't know where her sister had gone.

Emma Ashotovna was not Sherlock Holmes, so she didn't

notice the suspicious red spot on her grandchild's ring-finger, nor Gayane's notebook, which had been abandoned in mid-sentence, witnessing to the fact of the suddenness of her disappearance. By the way, Doctor Watson's deductive methods were not yet in fashion then, and other, current ones were completely unacceptable for Emma Ashotovna.

As a result of the confluence of these two circumstances, Victoria was sent off to bed, and Sergo was sent to the local police station for further inquiries, Sergo with his cast-iron hypertensive neck and his beet-red face, caused by all the blood rushing to his head.

The unhappy Victoria lay down in her sister's bed, bewailing the terrible fate of the vanished Gayane and at the same time pondering a clever plan of revenge against the Becker woman, who was at fault for everything that had happened.

In the second hour of the night, the satiated Yukov, having satisfied his physical and in some way spiritual needs at the expense of the starving tiger, again shoved his contented body through the bars of the gate. He intended to walk around the zoo and then stop by the manager's office, where his friend Vasin was on duty. Between two empty cages, near a large wooden bin, he found a sleeping girl. A small cupola stuck out of her head where the snow had fallen on her pompon; the snow, not melting, lay on her eyelashes. But she wasn't frozen, she was warm and breathing. He was surprised he hadn't noticed her earlier, he slapped her on the cheeks, but she didn't wake up. Then he swept the snow off her, picked her up and carried her to the manager's office.

Vasin was surprised to see him with such an unexpected find. They sat her on a chair, but she continued to sleep.

"Look what we have here, a sleeping beauty! How the devil did she get in," Yukov grumbled.

"Maybe she just stayed behind after closing time," conjectured Vasin.

"No, she wasn't there when I took up my post. I guess we

The Foundling

should call the police. Or maybe we should wait until she wakes up," reasoned Yukov.

"The police were just here. They might still be standing over by the gates. Go have a look," said Vasin.

Indeed, the police car hadn't driven off yet. Vasin brought over the lieutenant on duty. He also tried to rouse the girl, unsuccessfully. He stood her up on her legs, but her legs were bent at the knees and didn't straighten.

"Something's not right here," decided the lieutenant, and drove the sleeping child to the Filatov Hospital.

By the time the admission of the strange patient was processed, by the time the police lieutenant completed his rounds and finally returned to his station to make a report about the sleeping find, it was already the sixth hour of the morning.

Nobody went to sleep in the house on Merzlyakovsky Lane. Sergo lay on the couch, with a pink scarf tied around his head, Emma Ashotovna sat in an armchair, pale and stone-faced. Every so often, Margarita's pitiful exclamations could be heard from the room:

"And where is Gayane?"

Her question went unanswered.

Only Victoria slept, in her sister's bed, hugging the tear-soaked pillow, and lying with her knees pulled up to her stomach, in the same position in which Gayane slept in the isolation ward of the hospital, where they had placed her so they could determine who she was and what was wrong with her.

When the phone rang and Emma Ashotovna was told that she should go to the Filatov Hospital where, most likely, her vanished granddaughter was, Sergo began to sob loudly, and Emma Ashotovna had to give him a big dose of valerian before he got into his thick padded coat. For the first time in his life, he walked arm in arm with his mother-in-law, they struggled through the deep night snow, not yet shoveled into piles by the caretakers, he led her, in her proud fur coat, in her fur hat with a silk bow shaped like a propeller in the back, through Nikitskaya

Ludmilla Ulitskaya

to Spiridonovka, crossing over the Garden Ring, soon entering the calm of the reception ward of the Filatov Hospital.

Emma Ashotovna was showed the sleeping girl through a glass door of the isolation ward, but they didn't let her go in to see her. The doctors said that although the girl was whole and unharmed, there was something not quite right with her, and in the morning the neuropathologists and other specialists would examine her, since she slept without waking and even in the warm bath, where they had placed her, she didn't change the position, in which she'd been found: knees bent and arms crossed over her chest. By the way, she was sleeping calmly and had no temperature.

Upon hearing all this, Sergo fainted, he got very pale and fell into a heap on a chair that happened to be nearby. They gave him some smelling salts to smell and he came to. Then it was Emma Ashotovna who led her son-in-law across the Garden Ring, along Spiridonovka, through Nikitskaya to their home on Merzlyakovsky Lane. The caretakers had already cleared the sidewalks, it was already light, and the workers rushed to work on the jingling trams.

Both of them were silent. They had hardly talked since he returned from the war. Yes, you could say that in this family only the girls talked, or were talked to. The adults – Margarita, Sergo, Emma Ashotovna, spoke constantly only in their inner monologues. This was the sad music of a family's madness, the unresolved reproach of the women and the stubbornness of the man, just as insoluble.

But their mutual silence today was not filled with discord, both of them didn't understand what on earth had happened to their child, and this mutual incomprehension, and the strange night they had lived through, brought them closer together.

"Sergo, what on earth do you think happened to her, eh?"

"God only knows, Mama. I don't understand anything: the girl has everything."

They had looked the same age for quite awhile, the fifty-year-old Sergo and the sixty-year-old Emma Ashotovna.

The Foundling

When they came up to the house, they saw a sparse crowd at their entryway and an ambulance. It was just as if the ambulance had materialized from all the previous night's terrors, but their spiritual energy was completely sapped, and that was why Emma Ashotovna didn't care to find out for whom the emergency service had been called.

It had been sent for the Becker woman. Early in the morning her neighbour, one of the caretakers, Kovaleva, not hearing any of the usual morning preparatory sounds and not seeing her neighbour at the kitchen sink, pushed her door open, called to her, and not getting a response, pushed the door open all the way with her shoulder. The hook flew off and Kovaleva found the Becker woman, her face buried in a thin pillow and her legs lowered on the floor. It was as if she had been sitting, and then had fallen with her face forward into the print of the hospital pillowcase. The Becker woman had succumbed very suddenly to acute heart failure, and there were two finger widths of red wine left untouched.

Fenya said, "She's paying for her sins." But there are no sins to deserve such an end. And nobody could figure out why Tania Becker's cruel fate sent her to the prison camps because of her German great-grandfather, recruited as a Petersburg shipbuilder in Peter the Great's times, and then in a methodically mundane fashion took her husband, mother, sister and three-year-old daughter, and then in the end turned her into a horrible scarecrow to a ten-year-old girl whom she'd never even known.

Victoria was not awakened for school, so she slept peacefully. On the other hand, Margarita got up. Combed and dressed, she stood on a chair placed on the middle of the dining table, and wiped the crystal icicles on the chandelier with a damp cloth.

"So what's with Gayane?" she asked from up above. The glass rods continued to tinkle.

"Everything's fine. She's sleeping," Emma Ashotovna answered carefully.

"I almost lost my mind," Margarita said quietly. "Mamochka, make some pilaf for dinner."

Emma Ashotovna, in a state of shock, gracefully lowered herself to the ottoman. Then Margarita raised her eyes to her husband, who had entered the room and addressed him for the first time in many years:

"Sergo, help me get down. I saw that the chandelier was very dusty."

Victoria, who was already awake, heard all this from her room. She yawned, and stretched her arms and legs.

"What a little fool Gayane is. I'll give her my American doggy," she decided magnanimously. She climbed out of bed, searched for the stuffed animal and put it on her sister's pillow. A plush witness to an uneasy conscience.

At this very same moment Gayane also woke up. She straightened her numb legs. She didn't have catalepsy, which is what the doctors had surmised. She looked around. She didn't like the dream with the windows smeared with white paint, so she closed her eyes again.

When she awoke again, her granny sat next to her on a chair, her diamond earrings sparkling, smiling happily with painted red lips, and it was because of some lipstick smudged on her yellowish front teeth that Gayane understood she wasn't dreaming. And also, from behind her granny's back, his doctor's smock rustling, was Yuli Solomonovich. He, a famous doctor, was allowed to take away this patient, and he was rubbing his rosy, very dry hands, so that he wouldn't chill the warm child's body with the coldness of the street that had penetrated his old gloves.

Ludmilla Ulitskaya, born 1938, a biologist by training, has been writing all her life but only in her early fifties, already in the post-Soviet years, did she manage to get published in Russia, although her stories had been appearing in emigre periodicals in the USA and Israel and translated into many languages. In 1993 her short novel *Sonechka* was shortlisted for the Booker Russian Novel Prize and two years later received the prestigious Medici Prize for foreign fiction in France. This year *Sonechka* was awarded the Penn Prize in Italy. Her latest novel *Medea and her Children* was also shortlisted for the Booker Russian Novel Prize.

"There has never been a heroine in literature who were less heroic while at the same time being so striking and psychologically precise."
—Gallimard Publishers

See also Ulitskaya's stories in *Glas* 6 and 7, her first appearance in English translation.

Zufar
GAREEV
The Holidays

Translated by Arch Tait

Zufar Gareev

Oleg! I remember again the instant I wake up. It is a long time till evening, though. It's going to be a long wait. As always in the mornings Grandfather is already out of bed and sitting bolt upright on his narrow couch staring out the window. He has a hacking cough. My parents want to get rid of him. I have heard them talking about it several times but don't really believe it. What would they say? How could they put it to him? Grandad, actually we thought we'd take you off now to the old folks' home. They've got proper nursing staff and all that and you'd be much better off there, and anyway we're out at work all day. He might just not want to go though. How do you cope with something like that?

My mother's cousin is called Valentine. On Sundays when he comes for lunch he's always criticizing:

"I say it to your face, it really is your own silly faults you live as wretchedly as you do. Admit it."

"Or else..." my father always answers shortly.

"Get shot of him, buy yourselves some decent furniture for this room. You'd be doing the boy a favour at the same time. He ought to be seeing people his own age now, pals, a girl-friend..." At the mention of a girlfriend he sniggers. "Is there a lady in that heart of yours, eh, Nikolai?.. It's all over for the old man, time he let other people have a life. I don't mind talking to him if you can't bring yourselves to do it."

"You've lost all conscience, Valentine!" Mother exclaims, pushing her plate away. "Have you forgotten how we got this flat? Jumped the waiting list for a phone? Got a good television? And then you think we should just turn round and send him off to the poorhouse?"

"You Krasikovs are just having me on. You think I don't see the seething resentment? Come on, I'll put it to him."

"Well, you're no better than a thief!" my father shouts, thumping his fist on the table so that the plates jump. "A thief and a scoundrel! Heaven knows how much stuff you've stolen at work. Do you think everyone's like you?"

"Yes, as a matter of fact I do. Only some don't get the chance."

The Holidays

Uncle is feeling sure of himself and carries on eating his meal imperturbably. His plump little finger is extended, his fork glints, he breaks his bread into little pieces. He's certainly no hypocrite. He looks at father derisively:

"Don't get so worked up. You have been jealous of me all your life. You think I'm a scoundrel? Well maybe I am, but all your life you've been ever so ever so wanting to do things and haven't dared to because mumsy wumsy said you mustn't. I can't be bothered with people like you. A man's either flint or he's... And if he's neither one thing nor the other, if he fancies doing something but he lets something hold him back... Well, we know all about people like that. Go on, Irina, say something!"

"Valentine, he's my father. How can you talk like that!"

"He's my father, he's my father..." Uncle jumps to his feet. "What's wrong with you? Do you think life lasts forever? When are you going to have a life of your own? Great... You must be completely stupid! First it's father, then it's the kids, then it'll be the grandchildren... and when do you get to live yourself? No, thank you very much..." Uncle angrily finishes his repast. "Or you could rent the room out. Fifty roubles a month would be better than a poke in the eye with a sharp stick. You're not millionaires exactly..."

He has forgotten me again. He pulls out his handkerchief, wipes his lips, gives a deep, resounding belch, gets up, pulls on his coat and hat, and leaves.

My deaf grandfather looks as though he's been eavesdropping on my thoughts and heard what uncle said. He sits still as a mouse, as if he is petrified, staring out the window, through the clear panes where the ice has partly thawed. His little grey head seems to hover in the air, pinned in place by his hearing aid. After breakfast he and I go out to the shop to get his war veteran's grocery rations. They issue them from a different shop each time, but the queues are always the same, never dying, never killed off by time, and on each occasion some old woman's name has been missed off the list. The sales assistant runs her nail down the paper and keeps shouting in her ear, "It's not

69

there! There's nothing under 'B'!" Sometimes I think grandfather will get missed off the list some day and then they won't issue us the buckwheat or the good Kuban sausage. I just wouldn't be prepared to go pleading with them that he should be on it. Neither would he. Right there in the shop hefty old women with dyed hair are paying over the odds to get some of the old men to sell them their special rations, and packing them away in huge shopping bags. Let's just get out of this place! I want to seize Grandad's lousy ration book and stamp on it and destroy it, and never see these queues again or those old women's frightened, darting eyes. They're afraid the food is going to run out, or that they're going to be told to come back tomorrow, or preferably never, to a different address between two and five in the afternoon, and it's bound to be in a courtyard in a poky basement, round on the left, in some alcove, And they'll only issue war pensioners' rations if you prove you qualify by bringing the actual round gold-coloured medals. Come back another time, in other words, or preferably never...

Only after dinner will there be Oleg! Now I have something in my life to think about too. I wait for evening when I will see him. When it is evening I come out of the flats. Igor and Sveta are by the entrance already. Ah, Nicholas, *m'sieu Nicolas*, hello, *salut*. Sveta is just as plain as Oleg's Natasha. Then Oleg and Natasha are coming. We're going to the cinema, Igor says, how about you? Oh, we're not doing anything in particular, Natasha says, but if there are tickets going get us some too. Which one are you going to, the Sophia or the May Day? Igor and Sveta go off. He pushes her around boisterously in the archway. Actually he treats her pretty casually, he knows he's got the upper hand. Igor is always playing to the gallery, Natasha says. We stand there on and on, I tell them about my poor grandfather, Natasha not listening very carefully. Oleg is looking away too, as if expecting someone to come along any minute. He picks at the snow with his toecap, and I think he may actually be listening very carefully indeed, only he doesn't want to let on to Natasha. What's the film anyway? Natasha asks. Oh, it's some French

The Holidays

film, I say casually. About Belmondo. Oleg picks up on the irony but doesn't let on, maybe because my irony has turned out to be directed at her too, although I didn't specially mean it to be. He has understood, though: we are sharing a secret, but I am still the gooseberry. Even so, I don't want to leave. If I do I'll just keep wishing I was back here, I've been waiting all day for this after all. Well, and what did your grandfather say? Natasha asks. She may not really care, but has to ask something, she can't very well just come straight out and say, push off, can't you see we want to be alone, just the two of us, we want to walk around together, we like being just the two of us. He didn't say anything, I tell her, he's deaf, he can hardly hear a thing, it's beginning to look as if his mind's going. Surely he must know everybody's sick and tired of him, Natasha says, blowing on her hand through her mitten and putting her head on Oleg's shoulder. It's time they were all dead and buried, she says, blowing in the mitten again. But they want to live, I say, drowning in a sea of compassion. Suddenly Igor comes back, without Sveta. No tickets, he says, what can you expect, it's Saturday, busier than the black hole of Calcutta. Sveta freaked out, he says, spitting on the ground, she's pushed off home. He doesn't give a damn either, then. If she can do without him, he can do without her. There are four of us now, it doesn't seem odd my being there, as though I'm dogging them, begging for something. Although I wasn't begging for anything anyway, and never would. We're just out together, like any other group of friends. Let us be seated a moment, Comrades, Igor says when we come out at Izmailovo Boulevard by the Theatre of Mime and Gesture, and he points to a bench. We pile on to it. The film is off, Igor says, but behold I have a magic potion, and he pulls it out. I light a match, fluffy snow on untouched railings. Boys often do that, I have noticed, light matches, throw catch phrases around, and the snow melts and melts. Igor finishes opening the bottle. He wears his scarf very loose around his neck. I like that. Let's celebrate, he says. I shrug, I have tried drinking several times and hated it, but if I say no Igor won't have anything to talk

Zufar Gareev

to me about and through him Oleg will probably find me a drag too. Then he'll starting laughing at me again, *Ah, m'sieu Nicolas.* Right, I say as enthusiastically as I can manage. Boys, you must be crazy, Natasha says, we're right next to the police station. Now it's for Oleg to decide. We do need one glass at least, Oleg says, but not very definitely; he probably doesn't want to drink all that much either. Got a glass, Igor? Let's just drink straight from the bottle. Natasha miffed, just don't take too long about it. She blows in her mitten and says, I'll keep look out for you, any trouble I'll whistle, and she goes off towards the light. We drink the wine in turn, Igor, me, Oleg. We're not enjoying it all that much, but Igor puts a brave face on it, let's go to town, Comrade Communists! He starts telling us all about this French film but Oleg suddenly says, Igor, turn off the verbal diarrhoea will you. Why do you keep on and on all the time about girls? Igor says, you can't quite tell whether he's joking or not, it's all right for you, *m'sieu*, with respect, you already have a grand passion in your life, but *m'sieu Nicolas* and I are bereft, *n'est-ce pas, m'sieu Nicolas*? We are starvelings. That's not the point, Oleg says, do you want us to start sharing girls or what? You've got Sveta, I say to Igor, you're just going through a rough patch with her at the moment. She's pathetic, Igor frowns, she drags me down, you can have her if you like. I say, I don't like. And why not indeed, he enquires archly, as if he were the girl he is offering me, there's even a love-nest thrown in. Say yes, Krasikov, my folks have gone to Velikii Ustiug for the holiday. Sixteen are we? Time, my friend, to sample all manner of delights. Cut it out, Igor, Oleg interrupts, pulls out a cigarette and passes it to me. I splutter and cough, tears come to my eyes, Igor boisterously thumps me on the back. I decide Oleg doesn't much care either for all this silly talk about girls. It's all put on. Always playing to the gallery, Igor is. Oleg and I know that, it's a secret we are sharing. I am very, very grateful to Oleg but can't raise my eyes to his face in order to thank him unnoticed, they have become very heavy, I'm afraid that in my gratitude I may seem to be presuming. I raise them anyway.

The Holidays

His eyes are grey, beautiful and even, the way skin is beautiful and even on cool, matt hands which don't have the veins standing out on them. They are even and lively and the heart beneath his skin must beat steadily, thud-thud-thud, the blood not coursing through his veins in sudden surges... Igor starts whistling, whee-whew, you can tell he is a bit put out by Oleg. Natasha calls, finished yet? I say, still half a bottle to go. People are passing by behind our backs, turning to look. Want some? I shout to Natasha. Are you out of your skull, Krasikov, she answers, I've never drunk shit like that in my life. Is that my wine you're calling shit? Igor whistling again, whee-whew. Whose do you think? Natasha asks with the hint of a sneer. Oleg smoking in silence, looking away, intent, as if he's expecting someone to join us any minute. She's joking, Igor, Oleg says, but you can't tell whether he's peace-making or just looking for something to say. We drink some more, me first, it catches disgustingly in my throat, I even gag. Igor grabs the bottle from me, hand it over, *Nicolas*, come on, old workhorse, let's have it, Comrade Communist, he takes a swig himself then holds it out to Oleg. I can see Oleg doesn't really want to drink, he's forcing himself, like me. Let's finish it off in the cellar, Igor says and shouts to Natasha, all done! Natasha comes back, blowing in her mitten, evidently a habit. She plonks herself down where there isn't enough space between Oleg and Igor, giving Oleg's shoulder a demonstrative poke to say, shove over, will you. Oleg demonstratively pushes her fur hat over her eyes, she laughs, ooh, Oleg, don't, ooh, stop it. Igor says, guys, we ought to have a piss in front of the lot of them now, he whispers in my ear, that would be a hoot, eh? And he's reeking of wine. Silly! Natasha says, her head on Oleg's shoulder, nuzzling his face, her eyes hidden under the hat pushed over her face. Oleg half smiling at Igor. He has probably forgotten me for the moment. It probably feels good not to have the sense of owing me anything, not to feel the cautious web of my eyes on his hands, or his face, or his eyelashes. Down in the cellar we finish Igor's bottle off and he pushes a candle in it. We watch the candle weeping as its life melts away, every tear that falls means it has less and less of its life here left. What a fate! If it wants to exist it mustn't spend itself but stay quietly in the dark not wasting its tears, but if it wants to live it has to burn and weep so clearly.

How did they get on to us? In comes the beat policeman first, with a law and order volunteer in a fox fur hat close behind. The volunteer has glasses with thin gold rims, the candle flame reflects in them in an odd, remote, somehow disagreeable way. More of them up there in the doorway. Come on out, four eyes says sourly. He shouts up the steps, why has this cellar been left unsecured, Margarita Ivanovna? But we aren't doing anything wrong, Igor says, just looking at this candle. What are you doing then, having a prayer meeting? the policeman asks. No, just sitting here, Igor replies. Couldn't have chosen a lovelier spot, could you? The policeman runs his torch over the walls, fox fur runs his over the floor. There are empty bottles lying about, bits of glass, some old paper. Vodka session? he asks. No, we are just sitting here, I say. All right, kiddies, out you come. He shouts up the steps again, your Oleg's down here, Marina Yevgenievna, how about that? I know his mother a bit, she's some academic bigwig, I think. We're going to stay here a bit, Igor says, digging his heels in, what law are we breaking? Oh, really know your rights, don't you, four eyes answers, catching Igor's sleeve and trying to pull him up, hissing at him, are you right in the head, laddy? And you stop shoving me about, Igor says pulling himself free and sitting down again. They've had a skinful, the four-eyed creep says, smell like a brewery, the whole of Izmailovo can smell it. We're just leaving, Natasha says nicely and stands up. Come on, Oleg, let's be going. Oleg looks away, and stays put. Stay here, Oleg, Igor says, what business have they got trying to kick us out, as if we weren't good Communists. Natasha tugs at Oleg's sleeve and suddenly starts blubbing. She yells at Igor, shut up, do, Igor, don't go trying to drag Oleg into your idiotic escapades! Just because you are a clown, she yells, just because you are a complete fool don't think everybody else is too. Perhaps we should go, Igor, Oleg

The Holidays

says dully, this is silly. You're a toad, Igor says to Natasha and she suddenly starts thumping him in a fit of rage. You're a strait-laced toad, you're a really sad person. Natasha yells at him, I don't even want to talk to you, you're just nothing, you're a rubbishy, useless idiot, I've always told Oleg that. Toad, ha-ha, shop assistant's daughter, Igor groans, as if the full impact of her words has only now hit him. Natasha is already outside, Oleg standing by the door, brooding, intent. There is no telling how he is taking all this fuss. Then he gestures dismissively, come on, guys, that's enough drama, let's go. Don't try reasoning with him, Natasha shouts from upstairs, he's just an idiot who's always making trouble. He's a complete fool, he's just a clown who doesn't know when to keep his mouth shut! Four eyes is now confidently hauling Igor towards the door, Igor suddenly gives up resisting and says coolly, let's go, then, friends, to the police station or what? Go home, four eyes says dusting down his coat, sleep it off, you're too keen on your rights. Oh, sleep it off, eh, Igor yells, dancing right in front of him in the snow. Sleep it off! His scarf is flying free, completely adrift from his donkey jacket. I go back and rescue Oleg's cigarettes. Natasha is blubbing in front of Oleg's mum, pleading. Forgive me, Marina Yevgenievna, that half-wit dragged us down here. You do forgive me, don't you? she wheedles. I'll talk to you at home, Marina Yevgenievna says, turning to Oleg. He suddenly explodes: Mo-ther! Natasha is wittering on and on: You do forgive me, don't you?

I get home, but I'm still thinking I've got to give Oleg his cigarettes back. I'm also thinking, what if everything turns out the way it can do sometimes, for some people, somewhere, the way you see it in films. I would ask him, perhaps I could come round to see you sometimes? And he would answer me, sure, whenever. I would lean against the wall, hands casually in my pockets, no fear, no tension, and I would say, perhaps I'm making a nuisance of myself, you're busy, you've got your own life to live, and I... He is standing by the wall too, directly opposite me, we have been standing there a long time, almost an eternity, our hands in our pockets, our legs crossed...

Zufar Gareev

No, that's okay, he replies, I wasn't doing anything special, just listening to Pink Floyd and looking out the window. At first snow was falling outside the window, then the leaves turned green, then they fell, it rained, then it was snowing again...

Well, and so on. We talk, really just throwing catch phrases around, not too animated, not too involved, but mostly we say nothing, just look out the window. At first it snows, then the leaves fall, then it rains, then it is snowing again...

I put on my coat and fur hat and boots and go out. While I am still far away I can already see there is no light in his windows. I think, they must still be out there together, he and Natasha, that is. I have come closer and stopped under a tree, gazing, gazing. Suddenly Natasha comes out the entrance, from the distance I can't see whether she is looking pleased or indifferent. She is just going to turn the corner to cut across the grass and go between two blocks of flats to the bus stop but I call out, Natasha. She looks round. Oh, Krasikov, what are you doing here? Just out for a walk, I say. I saw there was no light in Oleg's windows, thought I would stick around a bit, maybe see the two of you by the entrance when you came back. I look into her beady eyes and hold my breath. Any minute she is going to yell right in my face, what's it to you whether his light is on or not, what business is it of yours, anyway what is it you want from Oleg? Clear off, stop getting under our feet, go somewhere you're wanted, because you're not wanted here, go away, just go away. I'm yelling this straight at your ridiculous head, I, Natasha, am yelling at you, you pathetic...

O-oh, Natasha says, he's got a sore head, he's gone to bed. I almost jump for joy. It's all that Igor's fault, she says, he's forever getting Oleg drunk, you've seen him at it. Wine just depresses him. Have you got a ciggie, she asks after a moment's pause. Yes, of course. I take a couple from Oleg's pack and we light up. She is still worked up about Igor: He'll never amount to anything, he has the mentality of an underachiever, he's a complete fool, a clown! Still, that's enough about that, she says, I am probably boring you. She has gone off to the bus stop,

The Holidays

waved to me. I go up the stairs, I have stopped at his door. I squeeze the cigarettes in my pocket. If I give him them today it will seem fair enough, by tomorrow it would seem a bit weird, even if I just did it when I bump into him. It would seem odd, too, *too* considerate. Suddenly I hear someone coming up the stairs. What am I doing hanging around his door at this late hour? It's his mother, probably, back from the local law and order office. I try to think what to say. The cigarettes? No, she'll disapprove. I've got a little thing I have to give Oleg. She will say suspiciously, well, give it to me then, young man, and I will pass it on to him in the morning. Then I say it's something very important, I need to give him it personally. Very well, she will reply rather curtly, and then sarcastically tell Oleg, "Your pal has brought you something terribly important, he wants to give you it personally. You'd better take my microscope, it is very important, but unfortunately quite tiny. No, it is not his mother, somebody else: click goes a key one floor down. So his father will open the door, he is hardly going to start prying. I ring the bell, Oleg opens the door himself, he has a towel over his shoulder. You weren't sleeping? I say. No, he replies, I've just washed my face in cold water, I had a bit of a headache. I hold out the cigarettes. Look, you forgot these, I was just passing and thought I'd drop them in. Oh, he says, thanks, but why bother? I go cold. I say, what do you mean? It's stupid, I can't win. Why did I bother disturbing him over nothing and why am I bothering to start clarifying nuances in the middle of the night? He says, I just meant, bringing the cigarettes back. I'd forgotten all about them, you should just have kept them, he throws them down in a chair. I say, your mum'll see them. He says, she and my dad know I smoke, my dad smokes Java too, so does she, so they won't know whose they are anyway. Well, I'll be off now, I say after a pause. Right, he says, so long. Perhaps we'll see each other tomorrow, I don't have anything on tomorrow... Suddenly he says, will you be down in the courtyard tomorrow? Tomorrow? I ask him. Yes, sure I will. He gives a smile with just the corners of his mouth, a hint of a smile. My heart leaps!

Just a hint, no more, I don't need more than that, anything more would be fake and I only want the truth. There will be more tomorrow, and the day after that, and I have many, many more days ahead for hoping. It will be a thousand years before at last we meet and smile at each other. See you tomorrow then, he says, and looks at me evenly with his beautiful grey eyes. I don't hear, I push the door, run down the stairs, rippling echoes in my breast ringing ding-a-ding-ding. His mother is coming upstairs. "Hello!" and down, down, down... I am walking along the street. The ice has partly thawed on the windows of the houses, they are so clear, the trees for New Year are lit up, everything is somehow magical... it is the snow, fluffy as cotton wool, I have only just noticed what a lot of it there is. Oh, to be born again, and know nothing, and remember nothing, like this snow. And nobody remembering you yet either. You walk along, and nobody's eyes have made you tawdry and shopsoiled yet, nobody's sleepy, cantankerous, suspicious thoughts have made you thumbed and dog-eared. I try to tread on the snow very carefully. A single clumsy movement and everything will be back to normal, the mood will go, everything will disappear, the snow will sink and blacken, the buses come back out on to the streets, morning will break and the eyes re-appear, bleary, prickly, indifferent, as if everything that was to happen in the world has already taken place and now there will never be anything ever again...

I would if I could have breathed that white world in till my lungs were ready to burst... while it was all still so happy and unusual. I would have breathed it in, and closed my eyes, and held the air inside me for a long, long time until all life's ills had passed overhead and I could gulp in the next deep breath...

Zufar Gareev, born in 1955 in Bashkiria, spent his childhood and youth in a small Bashkir town. In the army he served as a prison guard and later worked at a timber factory in Siberia, then started publishing his literary attempts in the local press, and finally came to Moscow a mature writer with a distinctive voice all his own. He has published several stories and two books. The critic Sally Laird said about his novel *Multiprose*: "Gareev is notable for his linguistic virtuosity... His prose displays an extraordinary dynamism and presents, in a cartoon-like effect, snatched scenes and conversations, banal and fantastic, run through in a kind of hilarious fast-forward."
See also Gareev's stories in *Glas* 1, 4 and 7.

Leonid

LATYNIN

The Bear Fight

Translated by Kate Cook

Chapter One

Emelya slept.

In his den.

Deep in the Moscow forest.

Beside his father, the Bear.

Who was warm. Shaggy. Brown. His own kith and kin.

The mixture of bear and human blood in Emelya circulated in the enclosed space of his body more slowly than in humans, and had not come out yet to puzzle people. He slept, giving no thought to his second father, Volos, whom Emelya had left at the place of his execution in the holy city of Suzdal, entwisted and entwined in the numerous rubbery roots of the sacred oak tree, he slept unaware that Volos had long since seeped drop by drop, with the spring sap, into the crown of the oak and was living there near the top, taking the place of new branches, and regretting that he could not go down, waiting, rocking, stirring, rustling, and muttering a prayer with his green lips, waiting to see if Emelya would return, stand below and talk to his father.

And Leta, Emelya's mother, burned at the stake, drifted as a cloud above Moscow, like a puff of smoke unlost in the sky, and gazed down, searching for her son and his sacrificial fathers, regretting that only Gord was still alive and rejoicing that at least Gord remained. The happiest, and consequently the most vital of them was the Bear, sleeping the bear's usual, earthly, winter sleep of dormant nature. Yet without disturbing winter or hurrying spring, nature was awakening slowly the way the body of a swimmer leaves the sky and enters the water, the way the snow falls into fire and is extinguished, like wind touches the sea and whips up the waves, the way a star drops to earth and is burnt up, the way night turns into morning yet does not cease to be night and, finally, the way grain buried in the ground rises to heaven as ears of corn. Still, praise be to God, following laws unknown to man.

The Bear Fight

For Emelya, however, the Divine Night was ending as the festival of the Awakening Bear approached, heralding the Divine Day. Unlike nature, Emelya did not possess the gift of natural transformation and he could not wake up, as he should have deemed necessary and understood clearly and obviously. Yet again he was dreaming the same dream, on the other side of human transformation. Reproducing himself, splitting up, dividing and multiplying, like the meander round the collar of his shirt, like the refrain after a solo, like the ritual movements of dancers circling clockwise round a bonfire on the day of the Awakening Bear. The faces blurred, flashed past and reemerged in this round dance, one after another, sometimes forming a single countenance, sometimes splitting into a myriad visages.

Their movements, voices and bodies kept dividing and merging, and whether there were four of them or forty times four, no one could tell, even if the tellers were more skilled at counting than Euclid, Lobachevsky or King Solomon, no one could tell how many people had passed through the earth since man was created.

The Moscow forest was quiet.

The den breathed with their double steam, Emelya's and the Bear's.

Meanwhile Prince Boris's huntsmen roamed through the snowdrifts, their caps catching the fir branches, as the wild beasts fled, flew, cantered and crawled away from the human noise into the wildernesses of future streets: Petrovka, Yakimanka, Sretenka, Tverskaya, to go on living their measured, calm, unconstrained lives.

The first to follow in Prince Boris's tracks was Chang Shi.

In the preceding year of 11008 in the month of March on the 21st day Chang Shi, the nephew of Lin Ben, who ruled the province of Tsin, was still in the village of Chaotsiun never dreaming that fate would part him from his teacher Se Chen, the brother of the famous Se Bao, both pupils of Din De Sun, himself the disciple of the famous Chou Tun, who in turn had learnt precision blows from Li Yun, the pupil of Men Kan, a monk of ruined Shaoling and one of the few in whom the school of Shaoling lived on in all its precision and truth to the models of the school.

The reason why Chang Shi unexpectedly found himself in the retinue of twenty-year-old Prince Boris of Rostov, the son of Prince Vladimir and the Greek princess Anna, and had ventured into the Moscow wilds on this bear hunt, was both simple and highly reprehensible.

When his father's murderer Yu Yung, son of the provincial ruler Shandung, spat contemptuously in his face in public, Chang Shi broke the basic rule of Shaoling. Instead of begging Yu Yung's pardon and retiring with the words: "Forgive me for getting in the way of your spit", he cracked Yu Yung's chest open with one blow of his palm, tore out his warm and beating heart, and flung it down before Yu Yung fell to the ground.

After this Chang Shi was struck off the list of names of the Shaoling school which links the age of Sung and the age of Ming so strongly, as if since the day of the destruction and the revival of Shaoling not a single day had passed, not a single event taken place and not a single tactic defiled the image. Chang Shi had committed more than a sin. He had violated not only an external tactic, but also an inner law of the life of a pupil of the Shaoling school, and had therefore to flee not only from Chaotsiun, but also from the Celestial Empire: from the village because he had killed a man, and from the Celestial Empire itself for he had killed God.

Which explains why Chang Shi, now in the retinue of Prince Boris of Rostov, fought more often, morosely and eagerly than the prince's other bondsmen. He wished to blind his soul with blood and evil, so that it would not see him kill God. And Emelya, who had been chased out of the den by the dogs after the Bear, was for him a means of attaining if not purification, then oblivion and distraction. Although at first the early spring March morning had made even him, Chang Shi, feel less morose than usual.

The Bear Fight

He had slept soundly in the house of Gord, Prince Boris's man and Emelya's sacrificial father, who had built his dwelling a mile from the temple of Veles and the Moscow River where another tribe already lived and where Gord was now a stranger, but the spot was dear to him and the memory of Leta drew him there, like a crazed horse its rider, and Gord went home, albeit only once a year, usually in summer, on the day of his sacrificial wife's death.

The Bear's den was on the spot where the Church of the Holy Apostle and Evangelist John the Divine now stands in Bogoslovsky Lane, where it crosses Bronnaya Street, just opposite Post Office No. 103104.

Chang Shi smiled out of the corner of his mind at the sight of Emelya, confused and sleepy, who had been chased out of the den by the dogs a minute later during which time four dogs, black, white, red and yellow, sank their teeth into his Father Bear's fur and then, dragging his intestines across the snow and staining it with blood, began their farewell chorus, while the Bear, who now looked like a hedgehog with a dozen arrows sticking out of him, collapsed in the snow and closed his wise bear's eyes.

So, driven out of the den Emelya stood there, rubbing his eyes and squinting at the sunlight, seeing neither the snow and the fir trees nor his Father Bear lying in the snow, waiting for the world to grow clear and distinct, not possessing the gift of transforming nature nor having learnt the art of transforming man.

Sleep still clawed faintly at his memory and muttered mockingly: "Tell your son Ivan that the world is bogged down in deceit which is why every large and small matter ends in war", and the new era had already raised its pen to inscribe a row of dots and divide his forest life of a free beast from the life of a warrior, bondsman, bodyguard or slave, or however it is given to a man to see, sense and call it, like the life of Chang Shi standing opposite him in the sun.

Chang Shi could have strode up to Emelya, drawing two

Leonid Latynin

knives from his belt, as the Invincible Cobra was to do later, falling upon a German platoon and killing half of them. He could have picked up two whips like Hu Yang Cho's octagonal, finely carved, with twelve thongs in the left hand and thirteen in the right. He could also have taken the cudgel wielded so expertly by Yu Sun, who with his bare hands had killed a tiger with bulging eyes and a white spot on its forehead in the Tsin Yang Gang pass.

But Emelya, who had crawled out of the den yawning and rubbing his eyes, although tall and stalwart and clearly of remarkable strength, was no more of a threat to him than a year-old bull to a toreador, or a rider on horseback to a machine gunner, or a boy on a bicycle to a soldier in a tank. At least so thought Chang Shi, and he was undoubtedly right within the logic of the school of Shaoling, and he was also right when, dealing a few light blows to the head, shoulder and stomach of the ever battle-ready Emelya and running over Emelya's pain points like a pianist over the keys, he realised that his opponent possessed the bear style, which he himself knew, loved and practised and was, therefore, protected against this style more than against others.

Chang Shi was inwardly reassured, and at that very moment received a blow from Emelya's elbow, collapsed, burying his face in the Bear's blood-streaked fur, and rose grimly to his feet, now with a different attitude to Emelya.

The elbow blow was not part of the bear style, so he had to find out whether it was unexpected, accidental or another school which deserved to be studied and, like a jazz improviser, produce his own version of this borrowed tactic.

This was not hard, for Chang Shi controlled his body no less than Yoka Sato the bow and strings of her violin, so he made a few easy and graceful movements within this blow and sent Emelya face down in the Bear's blood, noting that after his fall Emelya got up somewhat more quickly than he, Chang Shi, master of the secret blow, who could catch the power of the earth's revolutions, turn it into the movement of his hips and

The Bear Fight

through the tips of his fingers cast the whole earth upon his victim as he grunted all the air from his lungs.

Herein lay the enigma, for no one ever got up after this blow.

Yet he had the feeling that the earth's power sent through him into Emelya had been extinguished by the movement Emelya made as he pushed himself off with his hands from the Bear's warm, kindred, still living body. Like a grasshopper claps its legs, resembling two lovers lying in a meadow, and flies up in the air. The power of the blow by his two feet on Chang Shi's chest was so great that only the snow, the Russian snow, stopped Chang Shi from ever regaining consciousness.

Prince Boris and Gord, who did not know yet that the man before him was his sacrificial son, and the other seventeen bondsmen clapped their mittens of soft embroidered deerskin.

They were glad that at last the morose and invincible Chang Shi had for the first time received a blow that would take him down a peg and knock out of him at least some of the scorn and contempt that he felt for his fellow bondsmen. Whereas for eastern and southern people deceit is valour, the basis of combat, renown and heroism, for the ordinary northerner it is base, foul and demeaning. Since Chang Shi always came out on top in any skirmish, it followed that baseness had the advantage over valour, and this was not only indisputable, but invariable and obvious.

Now Emelya's direct spring blow had changed their attitude to these qualities. It was not that in watching the fight they had felt any sympathy for Emelya, but because they did not like Chang Shi they were glad that he too could be humiliated.

Chang Shi immediately pulled out two knives, and the mill turned its sparkling circles in the March sun, but soon the circles grew dull as Emelya's blood separated the steel and the sun. The wounds were painful, but not dangerous.

Boris's retinue was bored, the Prince also. This was the work of a butcher.

It became clear that Emelya had no more than a minute to live. This was obvious to everyone except Emelya and, of course,

Leonid Latynin

Chang Shi. Emelya's movements resembled everybody else's and yet were never repeated, just as the motion of flames in a fire or of waves in the ocean or clouds in the sky is never repeated. Emelya did not have a school in the Shaoling sense, but his blows contained an animal element with a human finish and vice versa, and you could never make out where one movement ended and another began.

What is more, something happened that made Chang Shi shudder. He could easily, particularly with knives in his hands, have fought a dozen of Prince Boris's men and not necessarily have perished. He could easily have overcome his opponent, who, well-versed in the Shaoling technique, was now reproducing himself into two, three and four and could have reproduced himself any number of times, but, being a multiple person, he remained similar in his knowledge and movement and law to the original. Yet here something happened of which Chang Shi knew very little.

It was a miraculous vision of the god Fukuruma, who is known to every Russian from the tale of Koshchei the Deathless, whose fate is in a coffer, and in the coffer is a hare, and in the hare is a duck, and in the duck is an egg, and in the egg is a needle in the tip of which is the end of the wicked king's immortality. Known from the embroidery on an ordinary towel which shows Bereginya (the protectress) in her house, and inside Bereginya is a smaller house with a smaller Bereginya in it, and inside the smaller Bereginya is an even smaller house with an even smaller Bereginya... and so on ad infinitum, like candles placed between two mirrors during fortune-telling are reflected endlessly, or like each matryoshka doll contains a smaller matryoshka in the endless line of which Bereginya is immortal.

Now a mass of little bears, each one smaller than the one before, sprang up around Chang Shi, from a Emelya who looked like a grown-up bear to a Emelya the size of Tom Thumb who was about as big as a bullet, and they all revolved in a circle round Chang Shi.

But the whole of Emelya stared at this broad cheek-boned

The Bear Fight

squint-eyed face and reflected that although he had fought many a dragon, wolf, stag, wild boar and bear at the Bear's behest, he had never fought a man, and fighting a man turned out to be more interesting than a wild beast, because a beast's range of movements was restricted by instinct and habit. They were predictable, and easily too. But a man was formless. Although in Chang Shi there was both a system and restrictedness, they were quite different from those in an animal, and herein lay Chang Shi's vulnerability.

You could not learn anything from any of the Emelyas, because none of Emelya's movements were repeated. Each Emelya was the same as the combat and also slightly different. By standing above himself and observing the combat, Emelya became invulnerable for Chang Shi. Nevertheless the combat would have continued for a long time due to Emelya's insatiable curiosity had not an inadvertent blow from the biggest Emelya's left heel landed on Chang Shi's neck, causing the latter to collapse onto the Bear and both his knives to sink into the Bear's first shuddering, then motionless body.

This decided the outcome. Peace retreated, giving way to myth. The lightest Emelya rose into the air, and the bare heels of the almost invisible Emelya, who was more like a bullet than a human being, began to dive down.

These calloused heels with their sharp stony spurs were intended to pierce Chang Shi's back to the right and left of his backbone and stop within a millimetre of the skin on his chest on the inside.

But on its way this blow encountered the resistance of the Bear's behest, his first behest which Emelya repeated in the morning at sunrise: that a murdered man's death lives on in his killer.

And the second behest, which he repeated when the sun was at its height, that a murdered man's pain lives on in his killer, softened Emelya's blow.

And the third behest arrested the blow at the very beginning of the movement. Emelya repeated this behest when the sun was sinking into the nether regions of the earth and streaming along the horizon like spilt blood: that today's enemy is always yesterday's or tomorrow's friend.

As a result, the Emelya who was the size of a bullet turned aside, barely touching Chang Shi's back, and gave way to the medium-sized Emelya, who did a somersault and, falling down on him from both sides, with the sides of his hands directed the weight of the heavens merged with the weight of Emelya's body into Chang Shi's head and brought his hands down to the right and the left of his temple so hard that Chang Shi's Spirit shot out like toothpaste from a tube, leaving the live Chang Shi on the snow with his face pressed into the Bear's fur. After this blow all through the 21st day of March Chang Shi's spirit and reason existed separately from his head, which was carried together with his body into Gord's house and left by the warm stove on the floor, next to the spot where Emelya swaddled in the prince's strength was also to sleep. But that comes later.

For the moment Chang Shi's spirit flew off over the whole of Moscow and what would later be Vyatka, crossing the Urals which divide the alien West from the native East and the alien south west from the native south east, then over Siberia and Lake Baikal, to his native village of Chaotsiun, remembering on the way not the battle that had just taken place, not Yu Yung, his father's murderer, and not that for some strange reason Emelya's spirit had proved to be stronger than the Spirit of Chang Shi, but, of course, how lucky he had been that day when, drugged by a potion, he lay on the chopping table in the inn of Dai Hei and the man-eater Sun Er Nian, preparing to become minced meat for Yu Tsian or to be baked into pie fritters and sold in the markets of Tzin region, when Sun Fu, the future pupil of Dzin De Sun, had recognised Chang Shi and saved him, thereby enabling him to take vengeance on his father's murderer Yu Yung, and as a result of this Chang Shi's Spirit eventually received the right to return for one day to his gods and relatives in his native province, and when he was flying over Siberia it seemed as short to him as the space between the dots in omission

The Bear Fight

points or as the distance in an instant from the age of Sung to the age of Ming.

Thus into a body similar to that of the Apostle Matthias, who took the twelfth place vacated by Judas Iscariot on the ninth day of August in the year 10063 after Judas was stoned in Jerusalem, into the body of Chang Shi, which lay next to the Russian stove, on the floor, returned the new, revived spirit of Chang Shi, the future devoted friend of Emelya, having visited his native land by Emelya's will and power.

Emelya stood there, leaning against the knotted trunk of the oak tree, warm compared to the snow, his loyal friend of today, and vented on it the boredom which he felt each autumn before withdrawing to the den and becoming a sleeper destined to wake when the time comes.

The string of little bears inside Emelya that had toppled out before Chang Shi's eyes in all their different shapes and sizes, now slipped back invisibly into the one big, shaggy, beast-like Emelya, who walked slowly up to his Father Bear and looked into his eyes. The Bear's eyes opened slowly, goggling and red, reflecting Emelya's face, and were slowly extinguished, ceasing to see life ever again.

Emelya pulled Chang Shi, like a wet shirt, away from the Bear's blood-stained fur, put his arms round the Bear and buried the Bear's blood in the blood of his father, weeping, or rather howling long, quietly and hopelessly, as Veles's grandsons had once wept, the brothers Rus, Varangian and Sloven, who loved war more than heaven and earth, in their house in Bel Grad over the body of their father Troyan, who was as huge as the Bear, and as shaggy as the Bear, and as strong as the Bear, and as tough as the Bear when he led his men to the slaughter, and was stabbed to death on the night of the 24th of March in the year 10621 by four bondsmen on the orders of his middle son, the accursed Kii, when Rus, Varangian and Sloven were sailing to the Greeks. And the next year Prince Boris standing here now opposite Emelya would also have wept over his father Vladimir, on his death in the city of Kiev, if it were not for

Leonid Latynin

Boris's brother Svyatopolk, who had Boris murdered by four assassins, one of whom was Torchin, and the second Putsha, who are now standing at Boris's right hand and looking at Emelya, and the hands of each of them reach for their belts on which hang swords, the blades buried in the snow, because Torchin has an average sized sword, and Torchin himself is small, whereas Putsha himself is average, but his sword is too large for his height. It is not his own sword. Putsha took it from a dead Greek.

But Emelya does not see Prince Boris, or the Hungarian Gergy, whose head Putsha will cut off so as to take from his neck the gold pendant now glittering in the rays of the March morning sun. Nor does he see Dan, or Boris, or Putsha, or Gergy, because...

Emelya has already begun to live a new life without his last father, although of course Gord, his sacrificial father, has already recognised Emelya by the scar on his left shoulder and, bending down to Prince Boris, explained to the prince that Emelya is Volos's long-lost son, and his own son also, and that Gord would make a warrior of him fit to adorn the prince's retinue with his strength.

How and where they carried Emelya, he neither heard nor saw. His memory abandoned him, so as not to interfere with his grief, not to sap his strength for this futile activity.

The sun had already turned its gaze from the top of the ancient Moscow fir trees to the middle and, its eyes still not touching the ground, spread warmth over a shaggy fir branch on which a blue tit was singing and turning its head, taking no notice of the humans' vain doings and thankfully stretching its neck towards the sun's gaze.

The morning passed, and the battle, which continued until midday, struck its six hours out of the quiet, calm, slow, measured, smooth-running chaos and the now peaceful life of the remote Moscow forest that once lived at the intersection of Bogoslovsky Lane and Great Bronnaya Street, which became shorter than Little Bronnaya Street after the various reshapings

The Bear Fight

of the former forest and subsequent capital city, that in time was to wipe the forest here from the face of the earth, just as a ruler with one stroke of the pen obliterates human names and tribes from life, and time, and memory, and history, and only human memory does not notice this power and this authority and this right and this endeavour, as the ocean does not notice the cliffs, or the shallows, or the ships which are inside and outside it and are of no concern to it, and it would be easier to move a mountain, or quench thirst with imaginary water, or stop an elephant in heat, than change this divine immutable law.

Chapter Two

A pace behind Prince Boris came his bondsman Perse, from the town of Kyata, flowing from the tips of the toes on his left foot through his body into his right heel.

Twelve years had passed since the time when Perse, after the Shah of Khoresm Abu Abdallah, whom he served loyally for a full five years, passed through friendship with Mamun, who took Abu Abdallah's power and life in Kyata, fell out of favour with Mamun and fled with the help of friends of his friend Ishak ibn Sherif Abdul Kasim Mansur.

Then, after learning by heart the first few chapters of Ishak ibn Sherif Abdul Kasim Mansur's Shahnameh, he quarrelled with him as well one day and, like a leaf driven by the wind, fled on until he came to Prince Boris's retinue, where he learnt to speak Russian reasonably, received the nickname of Perse, and served the prince sadly and indifferently, saved from total indifference, in other words, death, by the names of his family which included Bizurdzhimirkh who composed the Vamik and the Asra, and even Bakhramgur himself.

There is not nor can there be in the south, which is called the east by people of the west and the south by people of the north, anyone who does not know the story of Bakhramgur and his beloved Dilaram who, replying to her beloved slowly and

Leonid Latynin

rhythmically in converse, revealed the beauty of harmony at the end of a phrase. Many years later this was called rhyme.

The birch trees, and the fields, and the endless forests, the forests of Suzdal, and Moscow, and Tver, and Vladimir, and Novgorod, were alien to Perse. He would not have survived in this beautiful white and green northern land, were it not for the names of his native parts, towns and rivers, which he put into his strange prayers. Before he went to sleep, sometimes all night, he would repeat them, bowing, nodding his head and rocking.

When he repeated them the sounds evoked visions and mirages, and Perse wandered at length and in detail along the streets of Sheikh Abbas Veli, together with Abu Abdallah, then gazed hard and long at the black waters of the Polvan Ata and repeated to himself in an order which only he understood:

> *Hazevat shah abat*
> *Yarmysh ilych niyaz,*
> *Bai yangi bazar aba,*
> *Mangyt yarna yan su taldyk.*

His invisible hands touched the invisible leaves of the giddi, the chingil, the kendyr and the turang and, casting his eyes over the yellow waters of the Magyt Yarny, and the brown Shah Abat, and the black Yarmysh, he repeated aloud these words, sharp as the tip of his curved knife with its four grooves for blood to run down and just as cutting, and began slowly to fall asleep, sailing away from the white, cold and alien Russian shore, where the only thing that saved him, a stranger, was the fact that all strangers in Russia were welcome, whereas all Russians were treated as strangers.

The other thing that saved him was his skilful blows and his courage, which was indifference to life, but was seen as indifference to death.

Striding step by step after the prince, Perse, eyes cast down, saw not the prince's red leather boots and not the pitted March snow melting in the March midday sun, but a green field on

The Bear Fight

the feast day of Navruz, another name for the New Year, which was today, because it was the twenty-second day of the month of March. And in the Moscow land it was the year 11010, whereas in Kyata it was the first day of the sowing, the coppers were steaming, the meat was stewing and there was a fragrant smell from the freshly baked flat bread that lay on an earthenware dish decorated around the edge with flowers and leaves of which there was such an abundance.

The whole field, covered with carpets and brightly coloured dresses and kerchiefs, was singing and dancing to the jingling of silver beads, earrings and necklaces, the sound of the zurna and the banging of the drums.

But here there was snow, fir trees, silence, the back of beyond. Moscow. He wore mittens on his hands and a green quilted coat on his shoulders bound by a strong red belt bearing black swastikas along the full length of the narrow path that ran round him, a silent spell against disasters on a long journey, in which Perse felt like a horse constricted by a belly-band far less comfortable than a normal sash.

Perse dreamed and watched Navruz and listened to its voices, while Boris's huntsmen drove the Bear out of his den and pierced him with arrows and a birch stake which now lay, in clots of still unfrozen blood, on the snow next to the Bear, who lay on his right side with his paws drawn up, like a child in its mother's womb, preparing to come out into the light of day, like Tsar Pavel of Russia on the bloody-red carpet, edged with a black meander, who was bludgeoned to death by four assassins on the mute orders of his son who at that moment became an ordinary patricide or degenerate, to be more precise.

Perse came to only when Boris tapped him on the shoulder. The prince had noticed that the longer Perse served him, the more frequently he returned in his thoughts to his former life and that he came back only when a big fight was about to begin.

Perse started up and saw Emelya standing in the snow. The sun was shining over Emelya's head, there was a birch tree

behind his back, a knife in his hands, and Zhdana's white shirt
on his shoulders, with a red ornament round the collar, hem
and cuffs to stop evil spirits from entering Emelya's body.
Emelya's bare feet shone in the sunlight on the pitted, thin-
crusted, heavy March snow.

Perse drew out his knife and walked over to Emelya taking
his time, the way a master goes to the fold for a lamb to cut
its throat with a knife and, after bleeding it, hands it over to
his sons to skin it and carve up the fresh meat properly and
zealously.

Perse walked over to Emelya, not even allowing the thought
to enter his thoughtful other-worldly head that this lamb was
capable of anything except Russian combat. For twenty-two years
Emelya had spent each spring, summer and autumn in movement,
striking, defense and licking his wounds: the latter forms part
of Russian combat, as bone forms part of the body and the soul
part of bone.

Of course, Emelya knew each tree in the Moscow forest by
name, knew which day, hour and month the spring current rose
in the trees, which his hands and skin could sense. And every
creature on earth and every bird in the sky answered his call
and voice.

When you live for a long time in the forest, as in the country,
each other creature is either a friend or an enemy, and every
third a relative, but everyone knows one another and even at
night everyone can recognise everyone else, for each beast, bird,
tree and flower has its own smell, just as each man has his own
name.

But that is just life, not an occupation or a profession,
whereas Russian combat is a different matter. His Father Bear
had instructed him for many years, it was like collecting water
in a bucket drop by drop. Eleven years had passed, and the
bucket was now full. When he was sleeping in the Den in winter
he had hardly any other dreams. As long as the dream lasted
Emelya would run up the trunk of the oak tree, as a bear does,
up to the lowest branches, the oak tree which stood on the very

The Bear Fight

spot of the future Execution Place, jump from branch to branch until he reached the top, grasp the last branch and swing on it, then fall down, as if by accident.

He would slide down from the very top with relish, skilfully and surely, holding his body back slightly as he fell, as if resting on the branches that came under his fingers; then, breaking his fall by holding on to the last branch, lower himself gently to the ground, onto the green and yellow grass, as none of his other bear brothers could. This he repeated a hundred times a day until the yellow grass turned white, under an early snowfall, until, as in the case of his ancestors, it was the time of the Divine Night which follows the Divine Day, where the elders of Rosha recorded their secret sacred Vedas, which are as familiar and comprehensible to the initiated now as they were three thousand years ago.

It was then they discovered that when reality becomes part of the Divine winter sleep it is multiplied, transformed and dissolved in the soul, memory and reason and, returning to wakefulness, makes a man more than a man, even a man who has the dark, heavy, viscous blood of a wild beast flowing in his veins.

From his Father Bear Emelya received the knowledge that Russian combat skill, which outwardly was nothing but running, jumping, crawling and striking, defence, flexibility, resourceful-ness, agility and alertness, is polished and whetted and becomes reality only during the long divine sleep. Like a grain goes to sleep in the ground and wakes above it as an ear of corn, and bread, and life, so a jump, and a blow, and a leap are made in sleep in the manner of Russian combat, and the sleep may last 33 years or even longer, depending on the length of life in store for them.

For it is in sleep, and in sleep alone, that the miracle of transformation takes place. Thus a master transforms a piece of marble into Venus de Milo with the face of a man and the body of a woman, making it impossible for even a musician to divine her sex and meaning, Venus, languishing there in the alien lower

Leonid Latynin

hall of the Louvre, blind and naked before the blind who walk past her. Only in sleep is human experience forgotten and memory handed over not to the mind, thought and logic, but to blood, breath and motion.

Only in the long and too frequently repeated Russian divine sleep of the night do running, and jumping, and movement become what the world calls Russian combat, which has neither logic nor system, just as the sea does not, shifting in variously-shaped live waves from shore to shore and splashing on the shore, nor can there be any resistance to it, and which is as simple as the steel that the Persians tempered in the blood of captive youths, plunging the blade into their live bodies.

Sleep, and sleep alone, makes Russian combat such that the warrior who has mastered it lives in a different dimension and barely comes into contact with a warrior who deals him a blow. So fine weapons and excellent techniques are helpless in the face of Russian combat because it has no desire to kill and resist, Russian combat born of sleep, desires to travel from the Elbe to Alaska, to teach the earth its language and its song, its patience and its sleep, its fear and its love, and to build houses on this earth that have no roofs or walls, but have a glimmering and a looking out into the always, and have support and all that can replace walls, a roof and a floor when there is cold, hunger and strife outside, that is to say, they have the way to go and the reason why to go, and the way always, and this is the very essence of Russian combat for the ear of the initiated and the ear of the listener for whom such infidel questions as "What is to be done?" and "Who is guilty?" do not exist, just the one and only universal question – "When?" and the one and only answer – "Always".

Always – in pain, and fear, and joy, and sacrifice, and tenderness, and rapture, and faith, and madness, and power, and revolt, and freedom, and dirt, and prattling and outrage and, the endless "and", in which you can fit as easily as a rabbit in a cage, a dog in a kennel, a hand in a pocket, or a cork in the neck of a bottle, all human life and all human immortality,

The Bear Fight

which have their end and beginning neither here nor there, but outside here and outside there.

At that moment Emelya started up too, either at the crunch of Perse's footsteps or from the sun which had appeared over his head, and the first straight, almost perpendicular rays of the midday sun stared into his eyes. The fur coat on the prince's shoulders was of white sheepskin, his beard and moustache were not as fine as Emelya's, but thick, broad, trimmed and touched with frost.

Emelya stretched and smiled. He was enjoying the first rays of the sun, the air and the paws of the fir trees, furry as a bumble bee. A man who lives above the Arctic Circle, where the Divine Day lasts for six months and the Divine Night for the other six, has the same feelings on his main feast day, the first sunrise after the Divine Night.

At this moment Emelya's thoughts and words seemed to freeze, as if a bird, resting on air, had ceased to flap its wings so as not to prevent its eyes from seeing: for movement always prevents us from seeing what is there and shows us only that there is movement, which is quite unlike what is there.

Then Emelya's eyes stopped smiling at the sun and the trees, for apart from firs, sun and snow they could now see his Father Bear lying on the ground and the blood on his brown fur, and although his hand immediately grasped his knife, Emelya was not ready for battle. Parallel to the observation of reality by the eye and mind, his body itself performed some inner movements as if touching the keys of each muscle in his hips, arms, legs, back and stomach to test them.

The muscles responded to the touch of strength inside, and the music of his body was light and harmonious, as the Bear had said it should be, his body was indeed always ready for Russian combat, and now the strength which was testing its co-warriors inside Emelya returned to his mind, and everything – mind, strength and experience – came together in Emelya, like military commanders assemble before a battle.

The commander in charge of arms persuaded Emelya to put

away his knife because it occupied his hands. Today's battle, in accordance with the law of future causes, would be short, and the knife would have nothing to do, so it could rest. Emelya stuck the knife back in his belt in its home-made leather case embroidered by Zhdana of the forest, who had given him the case last autumn, without recognising him in the forest or understanding why, impelled only by a forgotten memory of their love.

The commanders went off to their posts again, and as always, Emelya turned into many different Emelyas, although there had been just the two of them together, the man and the bear.

At the sight of Emelya putting his knife away, Perse laughed. Placing his legs apart and hunching slightly, he turned the blade of his knife downwards. The March sun touched the steel and flowed onto the snow.

Emelya heard a sunbeam ring quietly along the blade.

He too hunched his shoulders, slightly less than Perse, and spread out his arms like a bear about to get down on all fours.

Perse leapt at him, lifting his knife. Emelya took an invisible step backwards.

Perse lost his balance and fell in the snow. His knife plunged into the back of the prostrate Bear. The Bear jerked. Although blinded, he could still feel pain.

Perse pulled out the knife and got up. Blood ran from the blade. There was no sun on it now. Each of them took a few steps. Perse's steps were easy to calculate. They either corresponded to his thinking or were opposed to it, but not asymmetrical. Thinking played hardly any part in Emelya's movements. Now only the commanders, each one separately, were busy with their charges, but there was still no perfection in their movement. One of the blows from Perse's knife struck Emelya's shoulder, ripping his shirt. The blood gushed out, mixing with the Bear's. The retinue cheered. They approved of Perse. So did the prince.

Emelya hunched even more. His bare foot trod on something

The Bear Fight

sharp under the snow. Emelya moved his foot, and at that moment his thinking saw Perse's movement and, moving his foot away, Emelya placed it simultaneously like that, just there, and moving his body slightly he put one arm just below the other and one shoulder just above the other, as if he had wound up a spring and found it hard to keep it in position so that he could use it when he began moving.

When a boat is carried along in the current, it need only be properly directed, and no movement is necessary to increase its speed. In the same way Emelya, having allowed Perse to get within an inch of him, used the movement of the spring and directed this force through his fingers. The fingers of his left hand lay obediently and accurately on Perse's long black hair that had escaped from his cap when it slipped off as Perse fell to the ground, and simultaneously the fingers of his right hand tightened the taut belt round Perse's waist. Using his strength, the natural movement of the spring, and merging with the force of Perse's fall, Emelya's hands redirected this movement, helping Perse's body to fly over Emelya's head and turning its movement into flight towards the trunk of the oak tree which stood by the prostrate Bear, sending it not crosswise, as the Bear might have done, but along the trunk, so as not to break the body.

Perse went limp and dropped his knife. The hem of his coat caught on a sharp branch and he hung there upside down, like a pendulum on a clock that has stopped.

Like the Apostle Peter, who became first among equals and was crucified upside down in Rome by Nero in the year 10064 on the 29th day of June to atone for denying his teacher, in whose name Emelya was christened with Volos in the year 10988 in the northern capital of Russia, the Great Novgorod, or New Town, by his uncle Dobrynya.

Silence fell.

You could hear a woodpecker working away monotonously with its beak.

The spot where Perse had fallen and where the sacrificial oak stood was exactly half-way between the future wooden

Leonid Latynin

Church of the Great Ascension, which lies on the Tsarina's Road from Moscow to Novgorod and was burnt down on the 22nd day of the month of March in the year 11629. Fifty years later Natalia Nikolayevna Naryshkina was to build a stone church on this spot, and the cathedral by Bazhenov and Kazakov was erected a century later. The second point which was the same distance from the sacrificial oak was Grenade Yard, which burnt down a century before 11812 after an explosion and which would be clumsily resurrected on easy money by masters from Suzdal on the eve of the one hundred and twenty first century.

The Moscow sun peered curiously into the open eyes of the stunned Perse, dividing into two reflections. His knife lay beside him in the snow blade upwards, his left leg was twisted, the right one also, and out of his nose and mouth trickled two thin streams of black blood, barely visible amid his beard and moustache.

Perse now looked more like Psayev who would have his throat cut in the Chechen mountains five versts from Shali by the Cossack's son, Esaul Danila, who killed him to avenge his father, also an Esaul and also Danila, who had been killed by Psayev, before he himself fell onto the damp earth on the sacrificial day of 20th July in the year 11995 pierced by the shot of Psayev's brother like a partridge on a spit.

Emelya straightened up. The commanders dozed. Who could say how long they would have to go on serving, so even a moment of respite was welcome.

His thoughts turned to the prince and his suite. And this was the moment, the dividing line, beyond which lay a different, new life for Emelya, unlike his life in the forest, his new life in Boris's retinue right up to Boris's death. Emelya would be the first to see the already saintly Boris still alive, and Boris would be the last to be seen by Emelya, blinded with impotence and helplessness. But between these events lay many others, and the first one was taking place now.

"Get him," said Prince Boris.

A few seconds later ten men were pinning each of Emelya's

The Bear Fight

arms. Emelya was tied and bound and thrown crosswise onto the saddle of Boris's horse. And the half mile from the future Church of the Great Ascension by the Nikitsky Gate to the house of Gord, Emelya's sacrificial father, which was next to the future Patriarchs' Ponds, in the future Yermolayev Lane, later Zheltovsky Street, near the future palace, designed by Zheltovsky, a copy of an Italian palazzo dating back almost to Emelya's time.

So, Emelya travelled this half mile in a role in which he had lived during his apprenticeship, bound to a tree with ropes, but unlike his apprenticeship, he was not touched by wolves' fangs, so life was quite bearable, and the new always evoked surprise and curiosity in Emelya.

The technology of friendship was simple, or so it appeared to the bondsmen. For forty days Emelya was starved. He was kept in a barn with strong doors and no windows. The prince himself came to bring him food and drink, while the others watched through a narrow window, spat at him and pointed at him mockingly.

In reply Emelya only looked at them curiously. Fairly soon he understood what was being offered to him: hatred of everyone and loyal devotion to the prince.

Outwardly he subjected himself to this. And when he was let out and dressed as a bondsman, Emelya knew each member of the retinue inside out and saw not only their actions, but also their motives and the variations of their behaviour as clearly as we see the sun and moon above us or the movement of fish in a crystal clear aquarium.

Thus a man, finding himself in the castle of Franz Kafka, who has long been lying in a cemetery under a thick layer of gravel made smooth by water and time and brought to the grave by his living admirers in accordance with the old superstition, having mastered, absorbed, and digested the task of penetrating the labyrinth of the castle and ascertained the triviality, mediocrity and tedium of the castle's dead routine, doomed and calculated for a hundred years ahead, − if he still retains albeit a grain of honour, wit, talent and life itself, and, finally, if he lifts up his eyes and does not see but at least feels the handle of the door which will take him away from there, and, having at last, thank the Lord, escaped from the confines of the castle, meets others who are hurrying to the place he has left, sees and understands down to the finest nuance how people live there, by what they are guided and by what they themselves and their motions are determined.

During his period of taming and training this understanding was mostly instinctive, of course, but at the time when Emelya made these events the text of a book, the ritual, routine and mechanism of the castle were as easy as pie for him or, I repeat, as clear as the sun and moon in good weather.

He also understood the measure of the prince's patience and goodness against the background of even Gord's ritual spite, which was in fact, − for Gord had recognised him from the scar in the middle of his solar plexus, on the second day, − a way of helping Emelya to survive in the retinue.

This understanding was more important than Emelya's love for Boris. The whole retinue and the prince taught Emelya primitive loyalty -- it was the easiest thing in the world to please them and persuade them that their eternal ritualistic methods were right and effective.

Although in fact Emelya continued to live his own independent life, the retinue and the prince saw the effect of their training on him and were perfectly content with these good results. In time Emelya actually forgot what Prince Boris was really like then.

When Emelya, living in a monastery after the murder of Boris by Svyatopolk the Accursed, was to write about the prince, about his meekness and mildness, his piety and goodness, he would not be lying, for the prince was indeed warm-hearted and forgiving.

For in the course of a man's lifetime memory changes shape as often as the lines on a man's hand or the roots of a tree as it grows, and in the same way a man's soul also changes shape.

The Bear Fight

For the soul and memory always change: in some because of time, in others because of a chance encounter, while in others the transformation takes place irrespective of people, ideas and time. This is inevitable, for future saints were just ordinary people at one time. Each person has the right to be transformed, although many do not make use of it, and some use it to their own detriment.

So with his new future soul transformed Boris was meek and devout, whereas with his present soul of an ordinary prince, he was the embodiment of power. Father Bear had always taught Emelya: submit to the power that is stronger than you and master the power that is weaker, and your soul will never be troubled. Boris was stronger than him, but each of his men was weaker than Emelya taken separately, and Emelya could only be mastered by Boris.

So Emelya became Boris's friend and the head of his retinue. But very occasionally he would go off into the forest again, walk along his path between the pine trees, listen to the birds singing while a thrush he knew perched on his shoulder, on his homespun shirt, and a squirrel took a ride on the other shoulder, holding on to his hair, and he experienced once more that forgotten feeling of unity with the forest, and with the birds, and with the sun, and with the grass, and sang his bear's song.

He sang that summer was fine, and autumn and spring were fine too, but in winter the wind blows and the snowstorms rage, so the king of the forest seeks out his den and sleeps until the day of the Awakening Bear, which men celebrate as the resurrection of their god and their hope that their affairs will prosper, that the harvest will be great, and that there will be increase in their families and in their flocks, and whenever this is – be it on 24 March, 11 September, 23 October or 1 May – is surely of no import.

Emelya had become a man but he could still see people only from the forest, from that freedom of greenery, birds, sky, clouds and air which were of one blood with him, the forest that smelt of fir and pine and in spring, if you notched the birch bark with a knife, out gushed the sweet juice that he liked to drink when he woke from his winter sleep, catching the transparent white birch blood in a birch-bark vessel, and the juice ran over his face burnt by the light, and the drops trickled down his blond hair onto the awakened earth of the melting Moscow spring forest, which with time men would cover with asphalt and stone, murdering the forest, the water and the air.

1996

Leonid Latynin, born in 1938 in a small town on the Volga, has several collections of poetry to his name. His highly original novels, *The Face-maker and the Muse, Sleeper at Harvest Time, Stavr and Sarah*, were only published in the post-Soviet times. *Sleeper at Harvest Time* also came out in translation in France and in the USA where it had an enthusiastic press. The hero of "The Bear Fight", Emelya, is the same Emelya who is also the hero of *Sleeper at Harvest Time*, half-boy half-bear, born of a sorceress and a bear in the deep pagan past. "His incantations possess a magic power... This is a pagan Genesis," said *Magazine Litteraire* about *Sleeper*.
See also Latynin's stories in *Glas* 1 and 6.

Alan
CHERCHESOV
Requiem for the Living

Translated by James Meek

Could it be that Time as such does not exist at all, and there is only an endless web of endless stories, drawing patterns in the deafening silence of Eternity? Could it be that Time is simply a means by which these stories may be told and heard? Could it be that it is not stories which grow out of Time, but Time which grows out of them?

I do remember, of course I do, how could I forget! I was already fifteen when he left the village. He was certainly not ordinary. And if he was, well, it could only have been for the first ten years or the shortest time more. His father and mother were caught in a mudslide, together with his father's brother who survived, though he lost his voice, and with his voice his reason, all of it, to the last drop. They say his legs were paralysed from the fear as well, except I do not know exactly and do not remember, since I was born twenty years later. But if they say so, it means something like that did happen to my father's brother, that uncle of Alone's. At any rate when the whole family fled the village they lashed the uncle with traces to their buffalo, back to back, as if his own weight was too much for him to sit up. He was fat, they say, like a three-year-old boar, he ate and ate all the time, as if in place of his voice and his sense the gods had given him two stomachs in addition to the one he had to begin with, and the first worked no worse than the others, probably even better, because as they say even with three stomachs you would not have the strength to gather so much fat. So they fitted his carcass to the hump of the buffalo, the elder mother with the daughters-in-law and the children were put in the wagon, and the old man and the two other sons set out on horses, three of the five they had stolen, the best in the whole river-gorge. And they say that when they fled nobody said a word, so as not to sin against their own tongues and ears, they just watched them to the very bend in the road, as the dawn allowed. Then they went to their homes and began to wait.

And after several hours of waiting they met ten horsemen in the yard, five of them brothers, who had in a single night

Requiem for the Living

not only lost their horses but gone fifteen miles on foot, and then galloped the same distance back up the mountain on borrowed mares. And I think that in that moment, looking at them and having read the doom in their eyes, our people envied the others, the ones who had fled. Honest people often envy thieves, especially such lucky ones, although they do not admit it to themselves, putting contempt in place of envy. Only contempt and envy are one, like meat and salt, a common enough thing. So when they said they already had blood enemies beyond the pass, everyone envied those who had fled, for they were lucky thieves. And let them throw away their home and their land, as my grandfather said − as real sacrifices go, this was nothing. For a real sacrifice, he said, something must be lost, and they got horses in exchange, the best horses in the river-gorge. And besides the land was such that if you dropped a felt cloak on it you would hide the entire holding. So there was no loss, and if there was, the smell of it would be blown away by the wind on the road. The wind always blows on the back of a thief.

That was what my grandfather said. And it seems they were lucky thieves. I worked that out for myself.

And the hatred our people began to feel towards the thieves then was worse than they had felt at first, in the morning, and this new hatred was more bitter than the silence with which they had seen them off, though certainly no stronger than that with which the riders looked down on our people from those mares which were not their own, stupefied by all the useless miles they had travelled and by having their helplessness witnessed by others, by our people, into the bargain. And so this second hatred, from silent men on borrowed mares, was more dangerous than our own, doused by jealousy and sustained by the desire to conceal, to ignore, to reject − to renounce the jealousy, I mean, along with all the other parts of a deed born and realized in the most unlikely place, where none of our people had stolen before or even thought you could get away with it, let alone so easily, the way it was supposed to be done, skilfully and without punishment. And in order to head it off, this danger, and in the

Alan Cherchesov

final reckoning the jealousy and the acknowledgement of it too, a step was needed, an action, a word, something which would at least look harmless, if not useful. Not noble. That would almost have seemed like cowardice. But the main thing was that a step should be taken. At that time the elder Khanjeri called the riders into his house, protecting our people by means of custom and turning ten embittered men first into ten tired travellers and then into ten pacified guests.

And there it would all have ended. Not for them, of course, not for the outsiders, but for our people, with the village buying itself out, since Khanjeri told them straight away, those ten, about the land and the house, he said by rights they belonged to the guests now, hardly to the village and even less to the previous owners. He said we may not be rich in land, but we will respect the laws and what is fair. He said none of them, the thieves, even had relatives here, so that there was no-one in the village to answer for them, just their own walls and holding. He said that the all-high would punish the villains and that man must put his trust in heaven – in fact he said all that there was no need to say, that had been clear since the sun came up, and by now it was already dusk. And anyone could have told you what was to happen next, from a senile old man to an infant child, if only the gods had not deprived the first of memory, and had provided the second with the power of speech. I could have said what would happen myself, even though I was born fifteen years later, as long as I am a son of my father and a grandson of my grandfather, as long as half the blood of one and one quarter the blood of the other flows in me, because a drop of it would have been enough to have predicted what would happen.

Now they should have got up and left, having refused the invitation to spend the night and having offered thanks for the hospitality and the food. And they should have mounted their borrowed mares again, five of them, and made another journey of fifteen miles to their homes so as to return before dark the next day, with tools and a cart, to load up and carry away the

Requiem for the Living

flagstones from another family's khadzar, working instead of nursing the blood-feud and turning their hands away from trouble. That was how it should have been, and everyone thought that was how it would be. And the ten of them were already set to get up and leave. They had already turned down the invitation to stay, and had already spoken the last toast, and even emptied the drinking horns, when it happened.

No, I do not want to say that anyone had forgotten his being an orphan, or did not think of it. On the contrary our people remembered it all the time, which is probably why it had not come into their minds since the very moment the cavalcade with the whole family had vanished in the silence beyond the bend in the road. But they remembered now, in an instant, as soon as they saw him in Khanjeri's yard with his hands held twisted up behind his back, covered in the dust from the road, hardly taller than his own shadow on the trampled earth. And the fear in his eyes was broader than that shadow, and himself, and brighter than the scar left in the sky from where the mountains had cut the sun. And once they had remembered, no-one needed to explain where he had been found and why he had come back. Where else could they have found him except at the graves, and why else should he have come back, except for that? So the reason became clear almost straight away.

The only thing which was not clear was where he had hidden the horse. But this too was soon sorted out, although the boy, they say, would not admit it, he was stubborn in his thieving and half mad from fear. And when Khanjeri's son tracked the horse down in the twilight beyond the bend in the road and brought it saddled to the yard and gave the bridle to the elder of the ten, and the elder mounted it, a horse stolen twice in less than a day and a night, though not lost in the end, they bound the boy to one of the mares, free now, and took him away with them, promising to kill him in three days unless the other four were returned and everything went back to how it had been in the beginning. Only Khanjeri told them straight away he could not allow it, he said the thieves were not going to fall into

111

someone's trap, or be caught at all. He said he is an orphan, that one, he is not responsible, and the son of a good father, and almost younger than his years and hardly smarter than the wit he has, and in the end – it is true he did not want to, but he did bring back one of the stolen horses, so you should let him go. And the elder of the riders did not agree. He also protected himself with custom, as Khanjeri had done a couple of hours before, except this was already a different custom, no need to explain which one. Customs in matters like this are only there for protection, like a jacket protects against the wind. You wrap it round you and shout out from within.

In general our people did not stand up for the boy. And of course few believed that they would kill him or, as it was laid down, mutilate an ear. Most people were inclined to think he would end up as a dogsbody or a labourer. Everyone was sure, naturally, that he would stay there, in the other village – that was how it was bound to happen, whatever turn events took. So it seemed the story would end there – for our village and for them too, the others. But I have already said he was not ordinary. This was the moment when all that was ordinary in him wore out, you could say, like old clothes. Or as if time itself had aged. That is how it happens: you live and you breathe and all of a sudden you feel that a certain time has just that moment gone, moved away, torn you away from yourself and even made you see yourself from outside, whether you want to or not, making you watch your past self from the side, and there is nothing you can do about it. A certain time grows tired and worn out, departing of its own free will into the past, and a new time comes to take its place, sniffing around you short-sightedly with greedy nostrils. That is how it happens, you see, whether it is for one man, or for all men – rarely to be sure for one and all men together. But after three days that was exactly what did happen, a time which touched one and all men, because after three days the boy came back, with a knife instead of a dagger and a little basket of food, and settled into the empty khadzar, a place where even the cats did not go prowling any more.

Requiem for the Living

It was the elder of the ten riders himself who brought him back, on the very cart which had been working away to strip the flagstones and the superstructure from the khadzar. It seems that he, the elder, had no special faith in miracles either. More likely he saw sooner than the rest how time had shed one of its old skins and over three days he had accepted this or, at least, come up against the new time which had grown to replace the old. Then one of them – the boy or him, the elder – decided to finally share the old and new, and harness the mule to the cart, and cover those many, many miles they had travelled I do not know how many times already, for the sole reason of finishing with it all; that is, to make a new beginning. So the worn-out end came in a way the village had never thought or expected, and the fresh beginning was quite different from what our people were counting on then, watching in silence as the boy nodded to them and strolled into the empty yard and from there into the empty khadzar.

It had already turned mouldy. It was blotched with damp and it was not ready for this at all, not that the village was either, astonished and clutching in vain at a slippery strip of peeled-away time. Then, before an hour had passed, everyone was gawking at how the boy came out of the yard and went to the neighbours', that is to our place. He called my grandfather out and started talking about a gun without lead or powder, and his harvest, and grandfather just looked at him to begin with, not saying anything, and eventually of course he could not hold himself back any longer and asked him: What for, he said.

And the other one, hardly taller than his own shadow in his grandfather's boots, frowned and turned angry and threatened to make the proposition to someone else, someone more accommodating, and by now my grandfather scarcely hesitated, reckoning – he often used to tell us about this – how much six-sevenths of the boy's harvest would be worth. Never mind that it was not yet gathered in, it was already worth more than an old gun without any powder to go with it, it was even worth more than the shame of making an unfair bargain, and off he

Alan Cherchesov

went inside, and brought the weapon out, and the boy did not know how to hold it properly but took it and marched proudly back, not turning his head or answering the stares he got. And the next morning, almost with the sunrise, there he was again at our gate, calling my grandfather to tell him he had made a mistake. One eighth of the harvest, he said, I only need an eighth, not a seventh from every threshing. But for that I need straw mats too, and a sheepskin coat. And grandfather went into the house again, and again brought out the things, and the boy took them, not paying much attention to the state they were in, and disappeared behind his damp walls. Because, they say, they had not yet seen any smoke.

There was no smoke for six days, and for two of the six he left an untouched bowl of food on the lintel, and after that he still left the bowl, but in the evening this time, empty. And they say there was neither malice in his eyes, nor warmth. That was when they started calling him Alone, and the name caught on, displacing his real name, which few people had remembered even before: who remembers the name of every young boy? And when that which is ordinary comes to an end, names are not specially needed. Names are for other people, for normal people. But in six days he made them see that one name was not enough. And they came up with another way of naming him: Man-boy. Because after six days he appeared on the street with a knife at his belt and walked up through the village. He made straight for the council of elders and did not stop until he had come right up to them. The elders still did not understand. They say he had to greet them three times, and tell them the fire in his hearth had been rekindled (they had not noticed the smoke over his khadzar at first, and when at last they saw it and realized, they got up – the most senior elders of the village – and took him in, and pointed to a place of honour on a bench, and he sat down, and only after that – there was something! – only after that did the rest of them sit down. And they say none of them laughed, because the look in his eyes did not allow it, and I do not know if any of them laughed later.)

Requiem for the Living

That was when the name was born: Man-boy. Then our elders had to think things through and do some working-out. They worked out straight away that first it had been necessary to make him an orphan, and then to let half a year go by, while his second grandfather and uncles had not yet carried out their horse-thieving and fixed themselves up with the swiftest form of wealth, before saddling it up, this wealth of theirs, and saddling up their good fortune, and fleeing with it beyond the pass – there, where their pursuers already had blood enemies. And they also worked out that it had been necessary for the boy to steal one of the five horses himself, and gallop to the graveyard, so as to be caught there and to be left three days awaiting death; and then for him to be brought back, and to exchange almost his entire harvest for an unloaded gun, a sheepskin coat and a few straw mats. And that left six days which could in no way be accounted for, and some thinking was needed about this.

And the old men thought over the gun and the fire in the hearth, since it never occurred to anyone simply to ask, and how could they, since each of them was about fifty years older than the boy, and as many times more experienced. It hindered them, this experience of theirs, since what had just happened did not figure in it. But the new name – that very one, Man-boy – had already appeared, it had already been spoken out loud. Then one of them – perhaps it was Khanjeri, perhaps it was my grandfather, perhaps someone else – realized that he could be quietly divided into two, and the boy could be forgotten for the time being, so as to concentrate on the man, the more so since he – boy, man, riddle – duly came to the council every day and sat next to them on the bench with such an expression on his face that it never occurred to anyone to laugh, joke or protest. So there it was. He sat there not merely as the proprietor of a khadzar or a plot of land but as the head of an entire household, a whole clan, of which he was now the only representative. All the same, six days earlier, he had been waiting for something, he had been doing something, before lighting the fire in the hearth, fastening a knife to his belt for want of a dagger and coming here, to the council. Then they remembered the grave, and thought over the question of the gun, and they sent to the Blue Path to check, and when they had checked, it was confirmed, because there were indeed traces, and the grass was cropped by just as much as a horse would need – any horse, even the best in the river-gorge – for a whole night. And when they had thought it through and confirmed it, all they needed was to take everything else into account, and it became simpler than simple. Now it could be reckoned that not only had it been necessary to make him an orphan, for him to run with the thieves and for he himself to steal, and then to be condemned by the blood-feud, to avoid it, and return. He had needed to wait six more nights in the dark cemetery with an unloaded gun until one of them, one of the thieves, came to him and was made to believe that the gun was loaded, and could not persuade the boy to give himself up, and was obliged to leave forever, empty-handed, skulking off in the dawn, beaten and resigned to it. And only then had he – boy, man, mystery – been able to legalise his solitude and light the fire in the empty hearth with the rights of a proprietor, and fasten a knife to his belt for want of a dagger, and make the old men see the smoke, to recognise it and get up to greet him.

At the same time it was worked out that an eighth of the harvest would not be the last deal he did and, accordingly, not the last bargain my grandfather could get out of him. And it turned out that at the age of ten, or however old he was, even if they were years more man's than child's, he had set up house, a very solid house, the only household in the village with one owner and one member of the family, as if the thieving had been just what he needed, as if solitude had only helped him. Besides, an eighth part of the harvest, a harvest which a week earlier no-one had been reckoning up at all, was much more than he had been marked down for to begin with. His share added itself up against the needs of those who had abandoned theirs: the old head of the family, the two healthy men and the

Requiem for the Living

other one, their sick brother (lard wrapped in a coat, the belly-man with the greed of a three-year-old boar), and their children, and their wives, not counting the elder mother and those who had not yet been born. And it turned out that our family, for all it had won, had won less than him, and had in that way lost. "He hired us," my grandfather would tell me, looking wearily at the neighbouring fence while the sun quietly burned his bony shoulders and clotted his eyes with its brightness. "He was doing us a favour, but he still hired us. He gave us charity and for that demanded that we feed his solitude. He made us his labourers."

Because that was how it turned out, according to the deal: his share of every threshing was delivered straight to his barn, and all that was asked of him was to open the doors. So he ended up sitting in the council of elders longer than anyone else, through the very busiest harvest time and the very hardest labour, as if he was the richest of the rich or the laziest of the lazy. But he was not lazy, either. Our people understood that afterwards, when they saw what he had been preparing himself for. And that was later. He left after thirty years. In that time he got for himself not just sheep and a horse, not only excellent tools and a cart, but a coming of age and understanding that was all his own, unlike anyone else's, without expending one drop of the solitude which had brought it to him.

Yes, solitude made him what he was, setting him against us all and depriving him of whatever love he might have had from another. And it made him an outsider in the place where he had been born and grew up, and where he lived forty years, absent only once, when for three days he went to face his own death and then came back, having barely escaped. Yet solitude was preparing him for something else, all the same, and having prepared him, it sent him on his way. Of course I remember how he left. And I remember how everything began...

He fooled everyone again, you see − my grandfather first of all, since everyone, not just grandfather, was waiting for the next bargain to fall into their lap, and thought it was bound to be soon, since essentially Alone had nothing apart from an empty khadzar and a bit of land, unless you counted a gun without cartridges and a sheepskin coat for the winter. And this was precious little, even for a ten-year-old. And of course grandfather was the most impatient of all, torturing himself with the burden, like a pregnant woman with birth-pangs. And he even thought up an idea to bring him out, to force his hand. He went to the fort with a dozen ibex hides, and returned without them, and held himself back for a whole week, not saying anything to anyone. And as soon as his patience broke he called my father into the house and pulled a thin package out from under his bunk, and father understood immediately and trembled from the shame, because he sensed something unworthy, and it was as if he felt (he would assure me of this himself) that it would not work, that it would only bring disgrace. And grandfather unwrapped the package, took the thing out and handed it to father, and father used to tell me he had never seen a finer piece of work. He said he had seen greater beauty in the years that followed, but finer – no, he had never come across finer (and I think he had, but had just never held it in his hands) – and that it meant grandfather had gone off with something else besides the hides, and this something had all been spent on the tanning of them, and the sum of the deed now lit up the room so brightly that it left white spots in father's eyes, and the shame boiled up in him so thickly that his throat began to ache. And grandfather told him to take off the old one, and he took it off, and then fastened the new one to his belt, and grandfather said: "Walk about with it for a while. Let him see it. He doesn't have a dagger yet, does he." And father nodded and went out, and when he was moving up the street towards the council he kept thinking (he told me himself) that he would not be able to stand it, and at the same time that of course he would, and that this was the worst thing of all. And he thought (this is already me imagining it) that now he was just as much poisoned as my grandfather was, and that the whole village would never be cured of the infection, let alone himself. And perhaps it occurred to

Requiem for the Living

him – or he forced himself to think – that it would come out, that it would work and that the old man would turn out to have better judgement than his sons.

And, my father told me, he ended up having to march there and back past the council seven times, and there was just Alone sitting casting his short shadow, and he kept looking at father, frowning and not saying a word, and the sweat poured off father, all but dripping into his boots and squelching round his ankles, but Alone simply watched him and said nothing, as if a sick horse was being shown off in front of him, and my father used to say he would be damned if he had not been a sick horse, and an old one besides, all our family and all the family of horses together. And, father would say, it was not that the boy inside Alone did not cry out or become anxious, so much as that he barely even woke up while he watched how this horse paraded in front of him, bound with a simple rawhide strap and adorned with a silver hilt and scabbard. So it all went to the devil and nothing came of it, and the old man was left tearing his hair out again.

Then, father would tell me, your grandfather remembered we had a donkey. And he forced us to scrub and comb it as if it was a prince's charger. We did everything short of rubbing it with oil and cleaning its teeth. And afterwards, said father, each one of us, each of the brothers, would take turns to mount the donkey and three times a day ride to some distant bend in the river to water it, just so as to go past his khadzar and past the council where he might be sitting. And what was the point of the donkey, if the boy in him could not even rouse himself to look at a horse, father would say. What was the point of the donkey, when he did not notice half a pood of silver!

The next thing was the business of the sheep, and that had to be done quickly, because the harvest was almost gathered in, which meant the threshing was approaching, and it was vital to have things ready in time. And the old man picked out three sheep and began to fatten them up and pamper them as if he was preparing them for sacrifice. They brought them grass right

119

there in the yard so as not to lose any of their fat taking them out to pasture. But with the threshing over, Alone still had not been round. So grandfather sent my father's brother to him to invite him to supper. This time, my father told us, it was his brother's turn to sweat.

He deceived us again. And my father's brother came back and told the old man the whole conversation, word for word. To be more exact, it was hardly a conversation, just a speech, since the messenger had not managed to open his mouth and was only now able to start speaking. "He said he won't need the sheep till summer," said my father's brother. "I didn't get a word in, he started talking about the sheep himself. He said he'd get sheep by summertime without our help. And now, he said, he doesn't need anything. Then he asked when he should open the barn. And I didn't know what to say, I just watched how he was clenching his jaws and trying to hide a yawn. I stood there and didn't say anything." And at this, my father told me, the old man began to shake. He just sat there shaking, in full view of everyone, and not from laughter, that was clear. And once again my father thought: this is a bad business. Like a fever. And most likely he went on to think that this infection was more dangerous than any fever, already knowing he would not be able to stop himself either, since he had been poisoned no less, and his brother had been poisoned no less than him, and that none of them would be cured. But next morning they filled the sacks, and Alone had nothing more to do than open the door of his barn. So he was the winner again.

They say he would spend all his time sitting in the council, day after day, cleaning his nails with his knife and looking wordlessly around him, getting up only to add brushwood to the fire in his hearth. But at that time you would still have found people in our village ready to bet that his nature would reassert itself, that the child in him would reappear. And you would have found doubters, but no-one who would have been ready to doubt out loud. So they just had to wait – reckoning that the patience of old men, in the end, was bound to be greater. The truth of

Requiem for the Living

this was confirmed very soon, only not at all from the expected quarter. And, they say, from that moment there were few who were so stupid as to think that he would one day yield or lose to anyone, even if he wanted to.

And when that morning, limping and staggering, he dragged himself into the council, not only did they all hear and understand but, most likely, saw how it was, when he had yielded and lost, not trying to defend himself or even contemplating surrender, how he had been beaten, laid low and trampled on – and was all the same victorious. They had seen how their own grandsons, great-grandsons and sons had surrounded him in the middle of the road, and how he had kept on walking, not slowing down, not quickening his step, as if not noticing, and how he had come up against a living wall, but had not made a single movement to drive it back, to strike out or even to protect himself. And how he had not cried out once as he endured their blows and their fury, trying with all his strength not to fall. And how in the end he had fallen, collapsing to the ground, beaten by dozens of fists in a hostile storm of panting breaths. And how the breaths had become louder and hotter as the blows aimed at his stubborn silence fell too quickly and missed their target, and the breaths had exploded into frenzied shrieks from young throats, and how their frenzy had come first from astonishment, then from rage, and finally from terror alone, how none of the adults, frozen where they stood in shock and distress, had been able to say a word, let alone approach the boy or intervene for him, since at first it had been somehow too soon, because everyone had been waiting, and then suddenly, in an instant, it had become too late, and it became clear he had deceived them again – all of them: grandchildren and old men, sons and fathers – by not making a sound or making a move to defend himself. And when the warriors had become frightened of what they had done, left off and run away, when he had been left lying in the darkening dust in the red twilight, the adults had taken a good while to pull themselves together and shake themselves out of the shock. But they had hardly come close to him – the grubby little body lying in the midst of the black earth – when they were frozen to the spot. Because he was already standing, and then (they were hardly aware that they had stopped, that they were not moving any more, just observing) he had carried on walking towards his house, with an even, steady effort, powerful and inexorable, like a buffalo before the plough. A tiny little buffalo... It had been like a miracle, lasting no more than a moment: he lay, he stood, he walked on. As if they had dreamed it all, as if he had never been lying on his face in the middle of the road and had never even stopped...

And now, watching how he climbed up the street next morning, all of them in the council were obsessed with a single hope: that he would keep his mouth shut. But he did not stay quiet for long – just as long as it took him to get his breath back and wipe the perspiration off his forehead. And they heard: "That's the last time. It won't happen again." Then for a long time they heard nothing again until he said: "Tell them that in every crowd someone has to be first. Either the one who makes the first move, or the one who seems to have made it. Let them know, the first one and the other one who seems to be first, that it won't happen again. After that tell them you've seen my knife and that my knife has sworn that it was the last time." And they heard silence again. And, they say, on that day and the two days after not one of them let their children out on the street.

But once his wounds had healed and the scabs faded away he began going to the council as before. He did not do anything else, just basked in the sun as it cooled with each passing day and dug under his clean fingernails with the edge of his knife. And every morning, as before, he would fall on the bowl of food and jug of beer left on the doorstep and put them back towards evening, feeling neither malice, nor gratitude, nor scorn.

But as winter approached something changed. He was obviously bored. And he went to my grandfather again and asked: "How many cartridges does a rabbit cost? You know, how much does a rabbit usually cost if you count it in the things it

Requiem for the Living

takes to kill it with?" And grandfather was quiet for a bit and said: "It depends. Depends how many times you shoot the rabbit." And the boy nodded. "That's the reason I'm asking," he said. "It wouldn't be a bad idea to add up how many cartridges it would cost to go down the mountain, go into the woods, track down a rabbit, nab it and bring it back here to someone who hadn't gone down, hadn't tracked anything down and hadn't done any nabbing, who hadn't spent anything to have a dead rabbit in their hands, not even a minute of time, never mind any effort? Maybe you know?" Grandfather thought and said: "Maybe I could make a guess." And the boy asked: "What's your guess? Probably very dear?" And grandfather said: "I wouldn't say very. It's just you can do your adding up any way you want, but the cartridges'll be exactly the price of a rabbit, every time." And at that the boy screwed up his eyes and looked at grandfather as if he was weighing up how much the old man himself was worth. The only thing was, grandfather used to tell us, you could not make out what he was valuing me in: rabbits or cartridges.

But then the boy nodded and said: "Agreed. Name it." And my old grandfather called one of his sons and got him to bring lead and powder to make four cartridges, and when the things had been brought the boy's hand darted out and grandfather poured it all into his little palm, and the palm vanished, and then, grandfather would say, it appeared again, but empty already. And grandfather said: "Only if the rabbit stays in the woods, the one who didn't go down the mountain, didn't go hunting and didn't even do the missing of the target isn't going to get anything for not spending his time and effort. If the rabbit stays in the woods the one who didn't go down the mountain is going to remember straight away about the four cartridges and is going to want something in exchange. He'll be wanting another part of the next threshing, if you please." "Fine," said the boy. "Suits me. Just show me the way it has to be done." And grandfather showed him, and told him how to aim properly, and even oiled the weapon with marrow, to make the deal fair

123

and above board, because he already knew almost for certain that this time he had the boy, that this time it was going to work. And when a person knows for certain that a deal is going to come off, he likes it to be all fair and above board – at least from the outside, at least from a distance.

And when Alone had left, grandfather called father and said: "That'll do. Take it off. Put the old one on. It wasn't meant for you, was it? Or have you forgotten?" And father remembered, of course, he hadn't forgotten for a moment, so he took the dagger off without a word, only they say he flushed crimson all the same. "It was as if my moustache had been cut off," he told us. "As if half my years had been taken away, as if they were mocking me..." Anyway grandfather could not care less what father felt and how they were looking at him. And for two days, they say, the donkey was taken to be watered at the nearest riverbank, like it had been before, and grandfather did not notice and did not even look over the fence into our neighbour's yard, he was so confident in the outcome.

But one time grandfather went up to the council with something to say to the men sitting there, swaddling their old age in their cloaks. And when he came back you could see he had no more doubts, and in his eyes a gentle light was shining. And then, my father used to tell me, I began thinking for the first time about kindness and how it looked in men. Or, rather, I already knew what it looked like, I just still was not used to it. I was not used to thinking how insatiably kind your grandfather's eyes could look without his being ashamed of it. Only I never suspected, father would say, that there could be so much kindness in a man's eyes when the virtue behind them lay only in the certainty of victory. And at this I quickly told myself not to think about it any more.

And on the third day the old man ordered pies to be baked for lunch and waited meekly in the yard, watching the road and the drowsy sun above it. And by that time everyone had found out the substance of the few words he had composed to put things in their proper place before the council.

Requiem for the Living

He had said something to the effect that when two people are making a bargain, the third has to stand aside. He has to just stand aside and watch until the other two have finished. Because you see this third one, if he is one of us and remembers the law, will not let himself get into an argument over someone else's deal, even if he has something to sell himself. He will not get involved, because he really is one of us and would never be jealous of anyone. He is smart, of course, and at times like these he knows his smartness is always seen and valued, especially when both the two are pleased with their deal and have already shaken hands.

That is what he said. No more, I think, but hardly less either. And now grandfather sat in the yard and waited eagerly for the moment when the guest would come through the gate and would recognise for the first time that he had lost. And of course he was not the only one waiting, and we were not alone. There were enough eyes and ears in the village for others to be waiting. And when the boy finally appeared in the distance they already knew in the council, but the old man did not even get up to look, he was so sure. And we formed up nearby, my father would say, as if by command, although there was no command. And each of us tried not to look either, yet nor could we find it in ourselves to chat. So our eyes overcame us and we did look. Then, after we had looked and seen, we could not say anything any more, we could only look from the old man to the road and from the road to the old man, who was still without the slightest doubt. And, father would say, I felt nothing but shame and malicious joy. Except the shame quickly faded, and when Alone approached, only the malice remained, since we were all poisoned...

And the boy came up to our gate, pushed the wicket open and said to your grandfather: "You owe me another four cartridges." That was all he said, you see: you owe me four cartridges. And your grandfather sat there and tried with all his might not to believe it, and he was not shaking any more, like the last time. And then he silently nodded to me, and I took both rabbits from the quickly held out hand. And then your grandfather nodded again, and I went to get lead and powder, and the boy held out his hand and I poured them into it. Your grandfather looked him straight in the eye and struggled to say something, but instead of him it was the boy who spoke: "Next time you want a brace you'd be better paying in advance. Every time you want to buy a couple of rabbits just give me another eight cartridges." And the old man gave a sign, and I had to go back into the house again and fetch an advance for the boy. So now he had exactly one dozen cartridges with lead and powder. If, that is, he had spent the first four shooting the two rabbits, and you could not swear to that any more.

And when he opened our wicket again after several days, the old man bought all four rabbits, added half as much again to the original price and another sixteen bullets on top, together with a whole bag of powder. For the next hunt. And the boy stood in front of him, knitting his eyebrows and chewing his lip, flexing his fingers and stowing the counted-out cartridges in his pocket. The old man looked at him, spreading his arms out wide and leaning his head to one side, as if he was looking for something he could not find, as if he did not remember exactly what it was he was looking for. And it came about that these deals multiplied and increased in step with the number of dead rabbits in our yard, in a way they were never supposed to have done. Now it looked as if, for the sake of victory, grandfather had taken it upon himself to buy up all the rabbits from our wood, and a down payment on the ones from the next wood besides, even though no extra harvest imaginable from any plot of land in the village could be worth so much lead and powder.

And, of course, father would say, your grandfather understood this perfectly well, but was still unable to stop for another fortnight, the more so since no one tried to intervene: no-one forgot his speech in the council because no-one was inclined to forget it. So there was no one left to intervene except the boy himself (or us, if the whole family went out shooting rabbits from morning till night without once missing. But even then we

Requiem for the Living

would end up giving up our land, piece by piece, in exchange
for all the bullets and powder he had hoarded up). And father
told us how all this went into a kind of millstone, grinding our
lead and churning out rabbits' ears in exchange. And again
nobody knew when it would end, so once again, action gave way
to expectation.

But in a fortnight the state of expectation showed mercy
and yielded, extracting this thorn which had pierced the deep
flesh of our days and sending the boy to us again.

He dropped by towards evening, when the sun had shrivelled
away and your grandfather sat in the yard on a leather-covered
stump, gazing into space as usual from the side of the road. And
when the boy came the old man did not move, he did not blink,
as if tied to the lump of wood on which he had used to chop
meat and logs and which had for so many days now had the
skins laid on it with the sunrise. And the boy said: "I accept.
I'll give five back for every sheep. Only I won't need them till
summer." And grandfather did not budge or nod, and the boy
had to repeat his words: "Fifteen cartridges for three fattened
sheep. They can bring them to me when it gets warm. But I'll
pay you now. It'll be easier for you to sell than to buy. What
do you need so many rabbits for, anyway?" And grandfather
stared into space with his gummy eyes, not replying and not
moving an inch, as if he was not listening. Then the boy beckoned
with his finger, and I came up to him obediently and held out
both hands, and watched obediently how quickly he left and
how his shadow went jumping obediently after him. And afterwards I went back into the house, threw the bag in the corner
and drank for a long time from the water jug, and it tasted as
if I had been running for a long time. Your grandfather sat in
the yard with his back to the dusk and our pity, and it was like
his own wake, although we had not seen it yet. Yet everyone
knew he had admitted defeat, and it was hard to watch, like
dragging a heavy cart up a hill.

That was what my father used to tell us. And grandfather
would not take the story any further. So it was from my father

that I heard about the cards. That was a year later, when Alone went to the fort for the first time, borrowing a horse from Khanjeri and leaving his part of the threshing for security, though by this time he had other things he could have left. A few sacks of grain, say, or the eight ibex hides by which he had grown richer in summer, or even better – his place in our council, or his solitude, at least. Because nobody liked him, I have already said. And when he came back, it turned out he hadn't brought a single package with him, and this was strange, not like him at all, so yet again it was as if he had deceived us. Anyway he went up to the council in the morning and did not tell anyone anything, and of course no-one asked. Then he slipped his hand inside his beshmet coat and produced a pack of cards. But our people only watched and wondered. This thing was like the boy himself: small and beyond understanding, fragile and closed off and somehow more sly and quick than all the rest of them sitting there. So they said. Then he opened the pack, drew out several cards and laid them face up on the ground in front of the elders. And our people watched the cards, hiding their fingers, labouring over the reckoning of what he might exchange them for. But the cards' true purpose never entered anyone's head. And most likely at least one of them thought that this was a new kind of Russian money from the fort, much more valuable than any money they had ever seen or only heard about before. Then they were bound to think the boy was going to use these new things of his to buy or barter much more than even he had ever managed to get away with, and it even made them afraid, for my father told me later: it was as if they had shown us a strange beast, you understand, or our own ignorance. Something secret was shown without it being explained and even without it being said that it really was secret. As if there are things in the world created by human hands only to be looked at without being understood, and if you cannot think of anything else to do with them to guess how to pin them to your coat, if this is the first time you have ever come across them, after all...

Then the boy poked one of the cards with his finger and

Requiem for the Living

said: "Everyone pick a card. This one's mine." And he covered with a pebble a card with a red blot drawn on it. So then Khanjeri chose, and Soslan after him, and then Taimuraz, and then all the others. Your grandfather was the only one not to do any choosing, but even he could not bring himself to turn away. And the boy said: "Remember, so you don't get mixed up," and raked the cards into a heap, then shuffled them and laid down the pack, face down. After this he nodded to Taimuraz, and he turned the first card over. They turned cards over one after the other − all of them, except your grandfather − until old Aguz said, "That's mine." And the boy nodded and answered: "You've won." And Aguz asked: "What? What have I won?" And the boy shrugged and answered: "Nothing. You just won." Then they all went quiet, and, father told us, we'll all be damned if they didn't already know what Aguz was going to suggest next. And sure enough Aguz did: "Let the pebble be in place of something, something you can win. Anyone can be lucky, can't they?" And when they had agreed, Aguz said: "Let's make it a skinful of arrack." And they agreed again, but the boy said: "No, I don't have any arrack. I'll put down a quarter bag of flour." And they nodded, and passed the cards to everyone in turn to shuffle, and of course made the boy take the middle turn. Except that his card turned up first all the same. Then he said: "Now I'll put down a skin," and they shuffled them again and put the pile down at their feet and told the boy to draw the first card, and he drew it, and found his card straight away, and started to draw strokes in the dirt with the point of his knife. And your grandfather sat nearby, swallowing, and something twisted set in on his lips, something like a smile.

He did not play at all that day, just watched spellbound as the boy drew his strokes in the ground, and they say that for each full stroke of his the others would get half a stroke at best. And that same evening messengers were sent scurrying from yard to yard with burdens on their backs, and some had to resort to carts, while the boy alone took nothing from his house, not even the rubbish, though his gate stood open longer than anyone's, and all he had to do, as usual, was to open the door of the barn when they brought their sacks, or lead them to the storeroom if they had brought a wineskin.

After this nothing happened again for several days, and everyone bided their time, because he seemed to have forgotten about it, as if he had become bored again. But then they went and asked him, and he shrugged his shoulders and brought the cards, and they played again, for pots and pans and iron tools this time. Only our old man, father would say, had already stood aside, thank the gods. He just watched, a pale smile fixed to his face. And this was the second time in a week grandfather had been sitting so close yet been wise enough not to lose. He sat very close to the boy and followed his eyes, which showed not a trace of excitement, only a certain delicacy and boredom, even when he drew his strokes in the dirt.

So once again the messengers and their burdens began hurrying to and fro, and so many goods were piled up that the boy's home started to look like a warehouse. But it was as if this did not interest him, and for the next couple of days they did not see him in the council, although our people were waiting for him, fired up by the game and poisoned as never before. And, father told us, they secretly sent their sons to him to ask after his health, since it hurt their pride to end up in debt to the cards so easily. Then somehow everyone suddenly noticed that there were no more bowls of food left on the boy's doorstep, and no more jugs of beer, and realized they could not remember when the bowls and jugs had disappeared, and so could not remember when they had repudiated him. Yet for some reason no-one was able to talk about this, as about a common loss or a general sin, so perhaps now they even hated him. Not everyone, that is: there had to be something pleasing in it all for my grandfather, as if he and the village had changed places, as if now it was his turn to look on and laugh. But whichever way you look at it, grandfather was of the same clay as the rest, so he differed only in that he had chosen to stand aside, and in his pale (no darker than his bald patch, father said, that the

Requiem for the Living

sun never saw till the day of his funeral, when his hat lay by the coffin and the rain kept falling, you remember – the rain fell as if performing a second baptism, and his white scalp seemed to be covered by a cold sweat, and only then, said father, walking behind the coffin, did I remember his smile, or rather only then did I realize what it had resembled) taut (it stretched from his very cheekbones, and the sinews in his neck quivered with the tension, my father said) smile, not because his brain somehow worked differently. He thought the same way as everyone else – or almost the same – and the way they thought was not at all like the way of thinking of the one who had drubbed them all. It was even so very different that so far they had not predicted any of the boy's moves, not a single thought or desire, and, as a result, they were doomed.

And this was not bad luck (it was not bad luck alone, bad luck was not the point), it was something else, deeper and more ancient, than mere chance or someone else's good fortune. It was fate.

Alan Cherchesov is a young writer living in Vladikavkaz in the northern Caucasus where he teaches world literature at the local university. The above story of an orphan boy is an opening chapter from his first novel *Requiem for the Living* which was published in Moscow by Sabashnikov Publishers. It is a philosophical parable set in a mountain village where the hero's strangeness and alienation underscore the distinctive Caucasian culture and strict code of honour.

Anatoly PRISTAVKIN

Kukushkin Kids or the Cuckoos

Translated by Clive Liddiard

Anatoly Pristavkin

> *This story is set in the 1940s and is about a boy from a special orphanage for children of "enemies of the people".*

It was a tiny place. Once it was a village and then a railway junction. Most people worked on the railway. Then quite recently – since we had been around – a small factory making soldiers' uniforms had been set up. The half-ruined church, that used to be occupied by the waifs who had vandalized it now housed a metal works manufacturing barbed wire. We'd been taken there a few times to give them a hand. We'd even worked the machine that straightened out the wire. There were huge bales of barbed wire lying all over the churchyard, on the old graves and even at the railway station. We had no idea what it could possibly all be used for. They said it was needed for fencing. But there was so much of it you could have fenced off the Earth right around the equator. There were no perks available from that place, apart from the odd roll of wire, but at the sewing factory we were allowed to take the off-cuts to patch our clothes with. Sandra had even managed to make up a dress for herself out of the scraps.

I had a day off from the home to meet someone called Masha who claimed to be my aunt. We passed by the church and the factory and walked along by the railway line until we came to some sparse bushes and a field beyond them. We sat down on the grass between the embankment and an abandoned wooden barn. The sun was shining, it was nice and warm.

My aunt – although I could not bring myself to call her that – had on a short skirt and a white cardigan. She was young and seemed literally to shine. I had never realized that women could shine so. From her bag she took a towel and spread it on the grass. Then she brought out a can of German corned beef, a knife with a wooden handle, some onions, cucumbers, a few potatoes and hard-boiled eggs, and even some proper butter in

Kukushkin Kids or the Cuckoos

a glass jar. I had never tasted butter before, I had only seen it once in Hog's house – Hog is head of the special home. German canned food I had also seen only from a distance. The Cuckoos would be so envious when I told them what a feast I had had! I wondered whether to take an empty can as a memento. It smelled so wonderful that one sniff was enough for you to feel full. That's rubbish, naturally, it wasn't enough, of course you wanted a bite after a sniff.

I tried not to notice the way my aunt fussed around, cutting and scraping. She got out half a loaf of bread, and the smell of it all made my knees feel like jelly. My head swam. By not looking somehow I saw it all even more clearly; but there was one thing that I simply could not understand: why on earth all these delicacies had to be ruined by cutting. They would go down beautifully just as they were – bite and swallow... And I couldn't help wondering where all these goodies had come from. You couldn't pinch all this stuff at one go. Buy them at the market? You'd need a thousand roubles!

I was running out of patience, but dogged does it. Just then my aunt said:

"What are you thinking about, Sergei? Let's eat."

I don't know for how long we'd been eating, somehow it all went by so quickly that I could not say for sure. One thing I did notice, though: my aunt ate hardly anything at all. You could see straight away she had will-power. I munched away, though, and next thing I knew there was no more to munch. And then I noticed she was looking at me very closely, even with pity. It even seemed to me that her eyes were glistening, but it might have been the onions. I know I cry when I eat onions.

"Well, shall I tell you about your father?" she asked as she poured me a mug of sweet fizzy drink from a bottle.

"O.K." I said.

After all this food and drink it was the time for a story. Well, fair enough. She'd fed me, called herself my aunt, she'd been hanging on my every word – rather a nice feeling, anyone would agree.

"Anton Petrovich was thirty-five when we met. Your mummy was dead. He was all on his own, and you... Well, he managed to find you a place in a kindergarten. Are you listening to me?"

I nodded. I was listening. It was just a bit strange: all this seemed to be about me and yet not about me. Mummy, daddy, a kindergarten... What kindergarten? I'd been in care all my life! I'd like to shout in this lady's ear − right in the ear of my provider − that I had always lived in this special home. What kindergarten, for heaven's sake!

But I nodded obediently. By all means, let her spin her yarns. If her stories made her feel better, it was fine with me. When your belly's full it's nice to listen to a story. What other tricks had that daddy of mine got up to? While I was crawling about a kindergarten or whatever...

"Your dad, Anton Petrovich," the lady went on evenly, "was, well, how can I put it, a design engineer. Quite a big cheese! But in spite of that he was a kind, caring person."

"Aha, a good man!" I said recalling some remark I'd heard.

"Yes, a good man."

"I see." I nodded and started looking out over the field.

"Did you say something, Sergei?"

"No, just making sure I remember."

She nodded and went all thoughtful. The short fringe on her forehead and those enormous dark eyes. That supposed father of mine probably called this supposed aunt of mine simply Masha. Not half! My pretty auntie Masha! I daresay Anton Petrovich, the designer, had had a taste of that canned food and the dairy butter and he knew right away which side his bread was buttered on. I'd become a good man myself if they fed me these goodies.

"He was in the Design Bureau, or DB as it was known, building aeroplanes. I used to work in the same place, only in the sick bay. I'm a doctor, you see. Well, anyway, one day he came along to see me. He'd caught a cold at the aerodrome, watching a test flight. He'd had a temperature, but it was a military aircraft they had to test and pass. It was passed eventually and now they're all over the place at the front. R-5s they're called. Maybe you've heard of them."

Masha looked at me with pleading eyes. She really wanted me to know all about the planes and the man who invented them and tested and had a temperature.

I took pity on the lady because of the butter and corned beef. I nodded. Every boy knew, of course, about R-5 planes which the Germans called "Black Death". As for the story about my heroic daddy, I could have invented one just as good or even better. Back at the home pretty well every kid could make up some sort of a story about a hero-father, you'd listen with your mouth open. There was Talalikhin, the pilot, and Dovator, the cavalry general, and what not. Heroes all around, but there was no aircraft designer among them yet.

At that point I lost interest in the lady's story. Even before I had not been listening very hard. But when she gave me a claim to fame and started going on about this aircraft designer I stopped listening altogether. My mind wandered to more mundane things: the weather, work at the factory, and how it was the middle of August which meant the school term was coming. I might even have dozed off such was my blissful state of previously unknown repleteness. Somehow I missed the main point and was jerked into wakefulness by Masha's final words:

"He was accused of having sold his invention to the Germans, the drawings of the aircraft and all."

"Who?" I asked dully, like a complete dunderhead. "Anton Petrovoch? Sold the airplane?"

Masha stared at me in surprise.

"He's Anton Petrovich to me but he's Dad to you."

"But he sold it? That airplane?"

"Of course not!" Masha exclaimed. "That was what they accused him of."

"Who are they?"

Masha checked herself and fell silent. Then she glanced about her before asking:

"What's that across the road? Is that the river over there?"

"Yes," I replied. "But who accused him? The police?"

Masha heaved a sigh and gazed sadly at me.

"He was innocent. He was arrested. Then they sent for me. But I only admitted treating him as a patient. They asked me about those drawings and I told them about his cold. They spoke about enemies of the people and I told them about his temperature. They let me go. Not right away, three years later. I hadn't been his wife. Anyway, not an official wife. They took him away."

"Where?" I asked.

"I don't know. They call it 'deprived of the right of correspondence'. I tried to find out. I went around asking. And they would start questioning me if I were a relative or something and why I was so bothered about him. And I said I wasn't related to him but he had left a child behind and I would like to adopt him, that I was looking for the child, actually. Don't you worry, they would say, the child is well looked after without your assistance, and he'll be none the worse for that, so don't bother searching for him. Go home and relax, mind your own business. And so I did. With some difficulty I got fixed up as a medical orderly in a hospital. Later when the war broke out and there was a shortage of doctors, I was allowed to practise again. They hid you away so well that for ages I could not find any trace of you, particularly since you'd been given a different name: Kukushkin... Let's go down to the river," Masha suggested.

I had now started to think of her as Masha. But of course I didn't call her anything out loud: that would be going too far! I did agree to go to the river, though.

We crossed the railway. On the other side were the ruins of the old brick works. Through the field we went, along a path through the sorrel and the buttercups and other flowers whose names I did not know, down to the river called Pikhorka. It was neither broad nor deep, but there were no other rivers for me to compare it with, since I had only ever seen others in films or in pictures. We bathed in the deeper parts, diving in from a tree, and even did the overarm stroke in it.

Kukushkin Kids or the Cuckoos

I started telling Masha all about it but I could see that her mind was far from the river. She was still in a bit of a state after telling me about Anton Petrovich, and particularly how they came to take him away. Although, on the other hand, there were enemies and spies all around. You wouldn't find any in our village but you just had to watch films to see them doing their dirty job. In "Engineer Kochin's Mistake" they wanted to steal some invention of ours. And a little while before there was this film about miners. This actor Andreev and Ivan Kursky were mining coal. The local miner I know said it was very life-like except that nobody tried to blow up the mine where he had worked: because of the mismanagement you didn't need explosives for the coal faces to start caving in. In the film, though, there were two other men, one was always singing songs and playing his accordeon: "Bonny lass, with an eye made out of glass," or something of the sort. But then he had a go at Ivan Kursky to stop him overfulfilling the five-year plan and setting a record. And the other man kept hitting the props to make the mine cave in. But of course, the baddies were caught while the good guys set their record. Then at the end of the film they marched with their picks as heroes, singing a song. It was really fantastic.

We sat on the bank while I told Masha about the film. And she just sat there chewing a blade of grass in silence. Then all of a sudden she asked.

"Don't you remember anything at all? There was a river where we lived, too. A really big one, with bridges across it."

I pretended to be trying to remember the big river and the bridges. But I could not for the life of me remember anything. Moreover, I knew there wasn't anything to remember apart from the Pikhorka.

"Maybe the house... Or the tram? It ran by your house. No?"

I couldn't remember any tram either.

"Or maybe this?" suggested Masha."You and me and your Dad went for a walk to his airfield. It was Aviation Day. We

139

crawled under some barbed wire to get in. Your Dad laughed when you caught your pants on it."

I said nothing but something clicked. I did not yet know what.

"There were parachutes..."

"In a green field?" I asked out of the blue.

"Yes, in a green field."

"And there were plums."

"Plums?" repeated Masha in surprise. "What plums?"

"They were selling plums there. Or maybe they were not plums. And maybe they were not selling them."

"I don't know... Maybe there were." She tailed off. Then suddenly she exclaimed: "Yes, there were plums! Your dad bought some in a marquee for you and me."

I couldn't figure out where I had got the idea of plums from. I must have remembered the barbed wire and the plums, and also the parachutes. Or maybe there hadn't been any parachutes and plums, and I had simply seen it all in some film?

"But where did the plums come from?" I shouted.

"Your dad bought them," Masha reminded me.

"That's not what I mean."

"Then what do you mean, Sergei?"

"I don't know," I said. "I don't know! I don't know!"

And sure enough, I had no idea why I had got so worked up. It made no difference to me whether there had been any plums or not. But Masha was visibly in a state as I could see. There had been this Anton — what's his other name — Petrovich of hers, and she had been put in prison because he had been a spy, that is, an enemy of the people. But she still felt sorry for him as I could see clearly. And what had plums to do with it all? Plums and parachutes.

My head was aching from it all. So I told Masha I was going for a swim.

"Isn't it a bit too cold?" she asked.

I just laughed at the way she worried. There she was going off to the front. Didn't she know that we went swimming till the end of September. And the most daring of us even took a dip in October, on a bet.

I got undressed behind a bush for I did not have any trunks, and from there I asked Masha:

"Why do you think my birthday's in September?"

"How do you mean, why?" she asked in surprise without looking at me. "I was at your birthday party once."

"When was that?" I asked feigning indifference.

"It must have been... yes, your birthday's on the sixth, and in 1939 you turned six. A week later they took him away."

I couldn't say I was dying for a swim. It was not fun going swimming on your own, without the other Cuckoos. But in the first place I wanted to stay alone for a while, and in the second place I also wanted to be alone, and in the third place, too. Anything to stay away from that stranger Masha who went all weepy as soon as she mentioned her beloved Anton Petrovich.

While she'd been feeding me she was really beautiful, she seemed to shine, like the sun, giving off a lovely warm light. And she smelt nice, too. But when she started on about spies she became unpleasant and cold, and it even occurred to me that she might be a spy herself.

But then I thought about it and decided that she could not possibly be a spy. Spies were different. And come to think of it what would a spy want with our special home? Just feeding a starving waif butter and corned beef? In that case the more the better, who'd refuse food for free. We wouldn't give away any military secrets because we didn't know any. We had lots of tricksters around but that was hardly a secret. Perhaps only for Masha here.

I dived in and, holding my breath, clung to an underwater snag for as long as I could manage. I had this idea that when you're underwater you only have room for the one thought: how to get to the surface without swallowing any water. But even underwater I found all this nonsense about Anton Petrovich and

Anatoly Pristavkin

Masha nagging at the back of my mind. I clambered out and hopped up and down on one foot, shaking the water out of my ears. Then I hastily pulled on my pants.

As I was getting out, I noticed that Masha had gathered everything up and − damn! − had thrown the can deep into the reeds. No way of finding it there. She had smoked a cigarette while I was in the river, and from the bush I saw her throw the butt away, too. She said:

"Come here, Sergei, closer. You've cut your leg. We'll soon make that better."

Before I could protest she had whipped a bottle of iodine out of her bag, and in spite of my howls dabbed it skillfully on my knee.

Try as I might to break away and kick her, she succeeded in cauterizing the wound before letting me go.

"There now. It's just as well I carry my medicines wherever I go. Are you going to walk me to the station?"

"No!" I replied crossly.

"Why not?"

"My leg hurts."

I was having my revenge for the forced treatment. But in fact I was dying to go to the station, particularly since it would all be above board, under Masha's wing. We were strictly forbidden to go there on our own. Though, of course, we went anyway. If we were caught we were put in the cooler without food. The only thing you were punished more severely for was running away.

Of all of the "dens of iniquity" our village had to offer, the station was the most attractive to us, the urchins of the special home. Trains to and from Moscow steamed by, leaving all manner of apple cores, leftovers, cigarette ends, and even occasionally an empty box of chocolates, smelling so sweetly that we would take turns at sniffing it for at least a week.

I didn't bother telling Masha any of this. She wouldn't have understood.

We set off in the direction of the station. Not through the

142

village streets but along the track as most people did, as a shortcut.

Masha hopped nimbly over the sleepers so that I could hardly keep up with her. When we were walking side by side I asked her:

"How did you pick me out among all the others?"

I should have asked that a long time ago, back at the river. Then I wouldn't have this nagging doubt. I could just imagine her going away, leaving me ignorant of who I really was. And whether I dived underwater or not I would still be troubled by this thought. Better to be put out of my misery right away. So there I went, head first so to speak!

Masha made no reply. She walked along in silence. I decided she had not heard my question, but I didn't want to ask it again. Then all of a sudden she said:

"You know something, Sergei, I think I've probably told you too much already."

She heaved a great sigh as she said this, and I understood then that she was a very nice but unhappy person. I even started feeling sorry for her. If I felt out of sorts since she had started all this I could just imagine how she must have been feeling all these years. "I shouldn't have burdened you with all this."

"Oh, I don't know," I said.

"But I do. I told myself to hold my tongue. And now here you go again. Getting me excited."

"Alright, I won't." I turned away.

"Why won't you?" she snapped, suddenly angry. She stopped and her big dark eyes engulfed me. They were suspiciously moist. "Of course, I'll tell you. He's your father, after all. Your father, Sergei."

I said nothing.

"It was easy to pick you out. You're his spitting image."

"Whose?"

"Your father's, for Heaven's sake! I did not manage to have a good look at you first, I was so overcome. I just knew it was you. Just like pictures of him as a boy!"

That bothered me for some reason. Perhaps because I had never had any pictures of my own. Who needs them anyway?

"What was... he like?"

I couldn't bring myself to say this strange word "father".

Just then there came the whistle of a train from behind. We got down off the rails. As the train, loaded with trucks and tanks covered with tarpaulin, rumbled by, churning up the dust she tried to tell me about this man using her hands and gestures. She raised her hand to show how tall he was, then she flunged her arms to demonstrate how broad his shoulders were, then with her finger she described curls on his head. As she did her mime she made faces, which was rather funny – like watching a silent film. Once the train had gone by and the noise had died down to just the gentle pinging of the rails we got back onto the track and she asked:

"Well, did you understand anything?"

I nodded but there was one small puzzle, though: had this handsome man really been my father? If they combed my hair and took my picture perhaps I'd be just as handsome, both in length and width.

"Where is he now?"

She shrugged and turned away. I felt that she might burst into tears again, so I changed the subject.

"We'll come to the station soon," I said. "Do you mind if I collect cigarette ends? They are not for me, they're for a friend."

"Go ahead," she replied. "What about giving him a whole pack?"

"He's not used to that. Dirty stubs is all he needs."

Masha missed the humour.

"What's the difference?" she asked in surprise and produced an unopened pack of "Belomor" from her bag. Without a second thought she handed it to me. "Don't you smoke yourself? You must have tried it."

"I've tried, we've all tried, even Sandra."

"It was horrid, wasn't it?"

Kukushkin Kids or the Cuckoos

"Oh, I don't know."

"But I do. If it hadn't been for prison I wouldn't have started. Incidentally, your father did not smoke. He had a sweet tooth, though."

I found her remark quite silly. What an idiot this woman was: doesn't everybody have a sweet tooth? What's the point of a sweet tooth when you have no way of getting sweets? I wish she could tell me.

We reached the station and Masha told me to wait. She was away a long while, so I had plenty of time to gather a whole pile of cigarette ends plus an empty match box and a button off a uniform, too. At last she returned.

"I've done all I had to. I've got a ticket, so now we've got a bit of time. Would you like something to eat?"

This question was hardly less idiotic than the thing about sweet teeth. Just show me the idiot who wouldn't drop everything for something to eat. You can always find room for something to eat, except that no one ever offers you anything to eat. Once we came across some vegetable oil as we were rifling a storeroom. We guzzled it till it made us sick. But that had been a long time ago. We hadn't had a chance since for a good blow-up.

From my silence Masha realized just what a silly thing she had asked. She took me by the hand – even though it was uncomfortable and even awkward to walk like that, not to say embarrassing – and led me towards the restaurant.

"We'll sit in here till the train comes. O.K.?"

"O.K." I said hoarsely.

Of course I was thrilled as I crossed that sacred line barring us, the hungry rightless riff-raff, from that true paradise. That, at any rate, was the way we saw it. I followed Masha in and was taken aback at the size of the cool hall with its marble floors and pillars and at the numerous tables covered with snow-white tablecloths. There was all sorts of stuff on them but I was so frightened that I couldn't make out what it was. Then I saw the windows with heavy velvet curtains which prevented us, try as we might, from seeing anything from outside. There were tubs

145

Anatoly Pristavkin

with real trees in them and a huge painting on the wall. In fact, the whole of the wall was a painting, showing an almost real-life forest in the middle of which roamed some bears. My mouth fell open but I remembered where I was and covered it with my hand. I had never seen anything so beautiful before. If only the Cuckoos could have seen this they'd have stood gaping, too. But I'd tell them all about it, I memorized all the details – the sunlit pines, the single toppled tree, and the bear cub scrabbling about on the trunk while the other cubs were busy hunting. Just like us at the home. If they told me that the picture was called "The Urchins at Large" or "The Urchins Hunting" I'd believe them.

I could have stood there for hours watching the picture but Masha gently nudged me in the back. When I came back down to earth she said softly:

"Let's go and sit down at that table over there. You'll have a good view of the painting from there."

I sat down careful to avoid touching the tablecloth which was much too clean and therefore uncomfortable. I could see now that there was an empty vase on the table and some other little glass things containing, for some reason, salt and something else, and it was all free. Strangely, nobody stole them. At the home they'd have disappeared instantly.

A man in a white coat came running over to us. A funny fellow, short, noisy and with roguish eyes. I can spot a rogue at a glance, they have a special look about them.

From her bag Masha took out some coloured coupons. The man snipped off a few of them with his scissors, pointed to some dishes on the menue and disappeared. Then he came trotting back and set down really white plates in front of me and Masha. I had never eaten off plates like that, they probably broke easily. There was something on the plate that smelt good. Then the man set down two bits of metal by my plate. One of them was a knife and the other one Masha called a fork. I tested how sharp the knife was: not very good. But I liked the fork, though. You could stick someone with it the same as a decent knife. The

Kukushkin Kids or the Cuckoos

man came back again and this time set down a jug of red water and some tumblers which they called goblets.

"That's a fruit drink, it's sweet," Masha explained. "Let's have a drink and then eat."

It struck me that, what's his name, Anton Petrovich, must have had this sort of drink with her.

I picked up the tumbler with both hands and drained it, and then licked all around the rim as well as my lips. But there was no spoon to eat with. They hadn't given us any spoons! I didn't want to ask for it for fear they'd shout at me: "Have you pinched it already?" But just then the man appeared again behind my back and put down a spoon.

"There you are, Sir, you'll be more used to that."

Me – Sir! Just like in a film. He'd been quick to catch on that I needed a spoon, though.

It was all rather like a film where I wasn't myself but someone playing my part. It was funny to watch this someone playing me and at the same time know that it was really me sitting there, although it seemed much too incredible.

The Cuckoos would never believe it, nor would I myself when I thought back on it tomorrow. If only I could spend the rest of my life there, at that table! I'd hide the knife and fork under my shirt, so's nobody stole them, the glass bits and bobs too. I could even cope with carting my chair around.

Just then something else happened. Two men appeared by the potted tree in the corner. Nobody paid any attention to them for everyone was engrossed in their food. One of the men had rather a disjointed body and was wearing a military uniform without shoulder-straps. He lifted a fiddle to his chin and tapped his foot a couple of times. The other man, dark, fat and with a big nose, squeezed a long chord from his accordeon. The fiddler suddenly jerked into action, tapping his foot, sawing away with his bow, and shaking his head – and there was music. Real live music that everyone could listen to. But instead they kept munching away and appeared not to be listening. I seemed to be the only one listening, forgetting about my spoon and my

147

plate. But what amazed me was that the musicians also appeared not to be interested in anyone around. It seemed they were playing for their own amusement. And for mine for I, at least, was listening.

Masha looked at me and must have guessed my thoughts.

"They're local musicians. It's nice, isn't it?"

"I don't know," I said.

"It's an old waltz. I'll remember in a moment what their names are — yes, Mark Moishevich is the one with the fiddle and the other, with the accordeon, is Roman something. Eat up, will you, they'll be playing for a while yet."

This was something new: somebody asking me to eat up. I wolfed down what was on my plate but I refrained from licking it clean because I could see that neither Masha nor anyone else in the room licked theirs. Instead I wiped my finger round it and licked my finger. Then I stared at the musicians so as not to think about food. Mark Moyshevich was still tapping his thin foot and in the intervals between the pieces he called curtly to the sluggish and rather dim-looking Roman:

"Come on, ginger it up! We need more pep!"

I looked at the table and thought that we could at least sprinkle them a little pepper as a token gesture. Just so long as the waiter didn't get angry. Masha caught my glance at the table and immediately asked:

"Have you had enough to eat? Would you like something else?"

I heaved a sigh. How can you answer such a stupid question? How could I get it across to her that we, those from the special home, could eat an awful lot, as much as they would give us, and if they kept on giving us food we'd keep on gobbling it up. A hundred platefuls or more! Except that nobody was going to give us a hundred platefuls of food.

Masha drew her own conclusion from my sigh. She gestured with her hand and the waiter instantly appeared by her side. He bared his teeth under his moustache, looking at me as though he and not Masha were related to me.

148

Kukushkin Kids or the Cuckoos

Masha again reached into her bag for her coupons. I asked Masha about them. After all, the Cuckoos would want to know how to get hold of food in a restaurant, and I would have to tell them. Because they wouldn't have a dog's chance of finding out on their own, the whole thing was beyond their comprehension.

I knew I would never have another chance to get here once more. I had somehow managed to slip in, thanks to Masha, squeezed in through the narrow chink that was never intended for us jackals. Here I was seated like a lord, fed like a lord, yet no sooner would I leave this place than somebody else would leap in and take my table and my chair and my plate!

These were the funny agonies I was suffering as Masha was telling me about herself, and how she worked on a hospital train that ran to and from the front, treating the wounded soldiers along the way.

"Have you ever seen a hospital train?" she asked me, glancing at her watch.

I replied that these trains often passed through here – you could see the Red Crosses from a long way off – and sometimes the wounded men would look out and throw us a piece of bread or a rusk.

"Right. I have these special coupons for the railway which I can use to get meals at the stations."

"Have you got many of them?" I asked for some reason.

"Enough for you and me." She smiled.

A fine thing to say. She was really too dumb to understand. It might well be enough for her but there would never be enough for me. So I changed the subject and asked her about her hospital train. Where it was at the moment. Masha glanced at her watch again and explained that it was near Moscow and that once the wounded were transferred to the hospital it would set off again for the front. In the next day or two, their boss had told them.

The music played on and Mark Moyshevich, the fiddler, kept tapping with his thin foot, the public was focussed on their food as if impatient to get on with some urgent business. As far as I could see there were not a single kid among the restaurant

149

public most of which consisted of soldiers. I checked again but not even proper children were there let alone urchins from the special home like myself.

Masha was lost in thought, so I again started eating because the waiter had just put in front of me something that was much too wonderful for words. Suddenly Masha asked:

"Would you like to come away with me?"

"Where to?" I wondered with my mouth full.

"On the train. We'll pick up more wounded, then go to the rear, and then back to the front, and so on, together. Well?"

She looked at me, biting her lip. Her eyes expressed anguish as if she was torturing herself over something.

"What about the Cuckoos?"

I pictured all of us leaving the damned home with its prison-like routines to go travelling to and from the front. That would be great! And we'd get coupons that would let us eat off white plates at the stations. And we could drink the sweet red juice. What a life! Hey waiter, get us a hundred plates of goodies! No, not a hundred, a thousand, a hundred thousand! Quick!

But Masha said guiltily:

"No, they can't all come, Sergei. I can ask my boss on the train to let you come, as a favour. I've already mentioned you, I could speak to him again, as your aunt... I'm a good doctor, they value me. Do you see?"

I nodded. They valued her, but they did not value us, the Cuckoos. What would I do without them? It's all very well to have an aunt feeding you, but what about the Cuckoos? They had no food to give me but they were my own people. As for this aunt of mine, who knows where she fitted in. And then again, would they want to take me on board? Why should they? I'd heard a little story at the home, can't remember who told it. But anyway, there was this great big eagle flying around. One day he was joined by a little wee birdie. The whole of that day it followed the eagle, then the next day and another day, until eventually it grew too tired. As it fluttered its wings feebly it piped: "Excuse me, Mr Eagle, where are we flying to?" The

Kukushkin Kids or the Cuckoos

eagle thought for a bit and, without turning his head it gave an easy flap of its wings and replied lazily: "I'll be damned if I know!"

Why should we fuss about, racing after an eagle, or a hospital train for that matter, that like everyone else in the world could not care less about us? Just as they could not care less about Mark Moyshevich and Roman who tried so hard to make this heart-rending music.

They finished playing, packed away their instruments in silence and took a seat nearby. They were served some food on a plate, their payment, I reckoned.

And what if they were just like me? Down on their luck. They'd get their food and then be turned out onto the street. Nobody needed their music.

I finished off my food, there was still some brown gravy left on the plate but I didn't dare lick it up. The waiter stood quietly behind me, a knowing expression on his face, a smile playing about his moustache, keeping an eye on my movements. I guess he intended to take my plate away and lick it clean himself. I knew from his face.

Without looking at Masha I said:

"I can't go without the Cuckoos."

"Why not?"

Another stupid question.

"I just can't. They are my family."

"What sort of family is that? You are not related to them, don't you understand that?"

I understood well enough but obviously she didn't understand a thing. At the home we were all related to one another for the simple reason that we belonged to nobody. The same as a stray is related to every other stray. The Cuckoos were not simply a group of kids. We were all Kukushkins, that is one family.

"They're not Kukushkins, for heaven's sake! And you're not a Kukushkin."

"Who am I then?"

151

"You're Yegorov."

"And who are they?"

"Something else."

"But what?"

Masha looked round furtively. "Come on. The train is leaving soon."

We crossed through the hall again. I wanted to have another good look at the wall picture to memorize the forest and the bears, so I kept looking back almost twisting my neck. Masha walked quickly and I had to run after her not to be left behind. Mentally I was saying goodbye to this paradise where no one filched even the salt from the tables let alone the knives. The walls, too, depicted paradise. The last time I looked round I spotted the waiter smiling in a knowing way.

I offered up a silent prayer: "Oh Lord God, if you really exist, please fix it for me to come back here again, even if it's in a hundred years. Please, God! I'll be good, I'll put up with the home and the bosses and the rest of it. I'd even give up some of my rations if I knew I'd get to this paradise again!"

The train did not come straight away. Masha fidgeted and looked at her watch. She scarcely glanced at me.

"Perhaps I'd better be going," I said. "They'll be looking out for me."

"They'll manage," she answered curtly and took me firmly by the hand as though afraid I really would run off.

When the locomotive did appear Masha looked fearfully at me for some reason.

"Sergei, I want to tell you something..." She shouted but even so I could barely hear for the noise.

I nodded. Go ahead if you want to. I was used by now to her silly questions and didn't expect to hear anything very interesting. But if she was going to start on about her Anton Petrovich again then I'd be off, she was not strong enough to keep me.

"Listen, Sergei, I'll come again tomorrow. But only for half

Kukushkin Kids or the Cuckoos

an hour. There's a train that goes back right away. Be here tomorrow morning. Alright? Be here at eight."

"What about breakfast?"

I couldn't help asking because that was the way we were all made at our 'special' home. Give us a snack to be going on with, by all means, but don't forget our rations!

"I'll get you something to eat here."

I imagined that perhaps she would again take me to that forbidden paradise.

"But what about my rations?"

"How stupid you can be!" she shouted and ran to the train. She climbed the steps and the train started up.

She stuck her head out of the door and shouted for the whole station to hear:

"Sergei! Tomorrow! Eight o'clock! Be right here!"

I waved goodbye to her so she'd stop shouting like a moron. I would decide for myself how to get round the problem of the rations. I stood there for a little longer but then a copper appeared in the distance and stared at me. At once I headed off in the opposite direction to get home as soon as possible.

I had had a bad night. Not that I was upset about the way things had turned out with Masha. In wartime our nerves played us all up. In our village some people flung themselves under trains or drank vitriol or acid, even shot themselves. And Masha was plainly unhinged over that Anton Petrovich of hers.

Actually, in the village they spoke no better of us and the home. Some said we were just a gang of juvenile delinquents and the clink was where we belonged, and others believed us to be derainged and thought that's why they kept a close eye on us and did not let us go out unattended. When Hog had to get us out of the police station he would say we all had a screw loose: "This home is affiliated to the lunatic asylum. I take no responsibility for them," he would claim.

That was rubbish, of course. He just wanted to give them a scare and shirk his responsibilities. But come to think of it

153

often we really did behave like nutters. Take Sandra, for instance: on pay days she would beg at the gates of the sewing factory, and when she'd saved enough money she'd run to the station to catch a train to Moscow. Last time she even took Koreshok with her. They were caught when they had already taken seats in the train.

That day when Hog interrogated them in his office he asked: "What d'you want to go to Moscow for? Can you tell me that?"

Sandra was a mute so Koreshok answered for her:

"We were going to go to the Kremlin to see Comrade Stalin."

"What for? Had he perhaps invited you to visit?"

"We wanted to ask him who we were and where our parents are. He's the best friend of all Soviet children so he should know where they are."

"What parents are you talking about?" yelled Hog his face scarlet with rage. "You have no parents! And you have never had them."

"But what about the others?"

"What others?"

"I don't know..."

"If you don't know then just keep your mouth shut."

Just then a song was playing on the radio:

> All across our glorious country,
> Tough as nails through fight and toil
> Joyfully we lift our voices:
> Leader great and friend so loyal!
> Stalin is our battle glory;
> Stalin is our inspiration;
> Singing, fighting; fighting winning,
> Right behind him strides the nation.

Hog shot a savage look at the wireless, darted over to it and yanked out the plug. He had turned to the policeman who had brought Sandra back and shouted:

Kukushkin Kids or the Cuckoos

"You see, she's cracked. They're all cracked here. They all have to be institutionalized."

He dashed over to Sandra and scragged her by the neck. She ducked her head in fear, and we ducked, too. But he didn't hit her, just waved his fist in front of her nose.

"This is the third time you've stirred up the home. Now shut up. If you try that again you won't get away with it so easily. I'll get you behind bars. No, I'll send you to Kozel for a month of corrective labour."

What was the point of telling Sandra to shut up when she was speechless anyway. But the threat to send her to Kozel was something serious. Kozel was the station master, a wizened little old man with red lips and insolent expression. He supplied Hog with coal, sending it over and getting us to unload it. In return for this valuable commodity Hog sent girls to work for him. Once he sent Sandra but in an hour she ran away. She appeared all dishevelled, got into her bed and lay there howling. We never found out what happened but clearly she must never be let anywhere near Kozel. At the very mention of him she shuddered and turned white as a sheet. It probably suited them that Sandra could not speak, it would be even better if we were all mutes.

Next morning I raced to the station without a word to the Cuckoos who had been looking out for me since evening, dying to hear all about it.

I did not have great expectations of that morning but still I was half-hoping for something to happen. I deceived myself about Masha being not all there just to make it easier for myself to bear the disappointment if things didn't work out. But I really did not know what I was hoping for.

For the first time I walked to the station openly for I knew what I'd say if they picked me up: "My auntie's coming over on the train to see me. If you don't believe me just wait till the train gets in and you'll see for yourself." I had prepared that little speech and let them think what they would. By now I'd realized that having an aunt was not to be sneezed at. Nobody had bothered much with me when I did not have anybody, in fact I simply did not exist as far as they were concerned. But that morning they told me: "Go on, we'll leave you your rations." Previously I wouldn't have had a dog's chance if I weren't there.

When I got to the station I made sure to hover where there were lots of coppers. I wished they would ask me: "And where might you have come from? Not the special home by any chance? Perhaps the cooler's missing you?" And then I would tell them the whole thing. But nobody even looked my way. When my aunt would have departed for good then they would come. They always materialized when you were feeling low and had no one to stand up for you. That's one of life's stupid laws. Or maybe they could just smell misfortune the way animals smell blood, from a distance.

I loitered around the baggage depot, watching them load the stuff. But they didn't take too kindly to that. They were used to people always trying to pilfer something. Just then I did not need anything. My aunt was coming so I might even be going to the restaurant. I could not care less about their stinking baggage.

When I remembered the restaurant I decided to go and have a look at it from the outside. I'd been around there before but it was quite another matter now. From the outside you couldn't see in, though. It struck me that they were hiding what was inside from people lest they, and particularly all sorts of dirty rabble like us, might want to see it every day which was strictly forbidden for the kind of us. Only VIPs could go in, only they'd be let in. If there was a paradise at all then presumably entry there was restricted, by special pass only. If they let everybody in there wouldn't be enough forbidden fruit to go round.

It also occurred to me that neither Hog nor the others from the home had been inside but I had. I could even ask my aunt to go there again. I wished I could get them all lined up on the platform and I would saunter past them straight into the restaurant, and the twits would stare after me, green with envy,

Kukushkin Kids or the Cuckoos

their mouths watering... They might even beg to be let in too but the waiter would bark at them:

"Out with you, scum! Can't you see this is not for the likes of you. This is for special people. For those who have aunts. You don't have any, so get lost and shut up and into the cooler with you!"

What with all my day-dreaming I failed to notice that the train had chugged in and hissed to a halt. I stared at the carriages but couldn't see any sign of Masha. I started to get worried that she was not going to come and I'd been waiting like a fool. When I had worked myself up into a state there she was beside me. She ran over to me as if she'd lost and then found me and was afraid to lose me again. She took me by the hand and led me off.

We flew through the waiting room, ran out into the street and dived into one of the station's back doors. We went down into a chilly basement and suddenly emerged into a big kitchen. Right in the middle stood a great fat woman and the same waiter. They cottoned on at once and indicated: "In there..."

It was a very small room but it, too, had tables with white tablecloths and vases with flowers.

"We'll have a snack here," Masha said briskly, tossing her bag onto a chair. She explained that the restaurant up above was not open yet and she was hungry. She left Moscow at four in the morning and it would take her another four hours to get back.

White plates were set before us, I tried not to look at them but I could see what was on them anyway: bread, slivers of sausage, sugar and butter. Masha rummaged in her bag and brought out something wrapped in paper. I stared at the flower in the vase and suddenly noticed an ant. The poor thing had been plucked along with the flower and now it was fussing around, running up and down the stem, uncertain which way to go. You're in a mess, my boy, and no doubt your mummy and daddy are grieving over you somewhere in an ant hill, or if you don't have any parents then some orphan-ants...

157

"Eat up. Don't sit there dreaming," Masha said attacking her plate. "Eat and listen closely. Alright?"

I nodded. I was always ready to eat and my ears worked of their own accord. Many times I had to eat at the same time as keeping my ears and eyes open in case someone whipped the food from me or clouted me on the head. It was second nature, so to speak.

For some reason Masha looked about her. But there was nobody around, and even the slippery waiter had vanished into the kitchen.

"Listen, Sergei... As I've already told you, your dad was a famous engineer. He got a big prize for his aeroplanes back in the old days. But then the clouds started gathering, and he expected to be arrested any day. So, he did what I suggested and transferred all the money into a savings account in your name. He gave me the savings book for safe-keeping, and I gave it to a friend to hide. After I was set free I started searching for you, but of course I was searching for someone called Yegorov, while by then you were known as Kukushkin, so I couldn't find any trace of you. I made inquiries, telephoned and went to see people. And then, quite by chance, I came across a woman, also a doctor, she handled the children of enemies of the people..."

Generally speaking, I am able to swallow food without even chewing it, but at that moment a piece of food got stuck in my throat and I started choking. A morsel flew out of my mouth and landed on the table, but I picked it up again and ate it up. Only then was I able to ask Masha:

"The children... of who?"

Masha concentrated on drinking her tea and was slow to answer. Then she said, almost apologetically:

"That's what you're called... Sorry, were called. You must understand I wouldn't have mentioned any of this if I hadn't known that I might never see you again. Nobody else would tell you. The only thing is..." again she looked about her, although there was nobody in the room. "You mustn't tell anybody. You

Kukushkin Kids or the Cuckoos

see, it's a secret, a dangerous secret. For a long time I just couldn't make up my mind whether to tell you. But I decided that you're a big boy now and should know what people are hiding from you."

I looked at the ant: up and down the stem it was running. How much longer would it continue with its pointless search for a way out.

"Who's hiding it from us?" I asked not even looking at Masha.

"They all are."

"And do they all know what sort of kids we are? Do they?"

"Of course they know!" exclaimed Masha, and again she looked behind her.

"And does our director know?"

"Better than anybody!"

"Why don't we know?"

"Let's go! Let's get away from here!"

I got a little agitated: we'd eaten everything up, but the poor, unfortunate homeless ant remained − condemned to stay forever in this basement.

"Just a moment," I said, lending him a finger. He clambered onto my finger and together we climbed up and out into the street.

It was only when we reached the platform that Masha breathed freely. She was still clutching the packet. Once more she looked about her and, taking me to the far end of the station started telling me how she had searched for me and one day had found the strange woman who farmed out children, and who was herself a doctor. Her name was Kukushkin. Can you guess the rest?

"No," I replied. I bent down and blew the ant off my finger. Go back home you silly ant, and don't get caught out like that again. The people in the basement wouldn't let you out. It wouldn't even occur to them that you want to live, too.

"What are you fussing about with?" asked Masha. "Are you listening to what I'm telling you?"

Anatoly Pristavkin

"Yes," I replied. "Her name was Kukushkin. Just like ours. And mine..."

"That's the whole point! She gave you her own name. Don't you see?"

"Why?"

"She was giving you a new identity. To try and make things easier for you!"

"How easier?" I asked again.

"Oh dear," sighed Masha. "You were the children of people who had been arrested. You were better off without their names. That's the way she saw it. And so she gave you − lot's of you − her own name. She saved you! Do you understand?"

I didn't understand a thing. But I didn't say anything. Because I felt like that ant in the basement: there was no way out of the situation I'd been placed in when first I was picked along with the flower. Now Masha was trying to take me away on her finger. But where? She would go away, leaving me with the knowledge, that day, the next day and all my life, that I wasn't plain Sergei Kukushkin but an enemy, because my father had been an enemy. And that I had been hidden under a different name.

I should really have asked about the other members of the Kukushkin clan. But what was there to ask? Whose children those Kukushkins were? How should Masha know? They were just other children. Their names could not be traced.

I remembered the packet and asked:

"Can I have a look?"

"It's yours now," Masha replied.

I opened it up. Inside was a little grey book. On the first page was written: "Yegorov, Sergey Antonovich". There was a round stamp. Above this was printed: "USSR Labour Savings Banks. Account No. 4102", and beneath in small letters: "Manager of the Savings Bank" and a signature. I turned the page. It was empty. Or almost empty. In the top left-hand corner was a number. But I couldn't make it out. It was a strange number − all noughts.

160

Kukushkin Kids or the Cuckoos

Masha bent over and asked softly:

"Well, do you understand how much he left you?"

I shook my head. I understood nothing. But the word "left" gave me a funny feeling, and all of a sudden I wanted to cry.

"He was afraid you might not manage on your own, so he did all he could. He said: 'I won't be able to help him any more. It'll be difficult for him. But at least he'll have this, for a rainy day.'"

"How much is there here?" I asked, for I just could not make out this strange figure, even though I was pretty good at sums. I didn't understand all this "rainy day" business, either. It was forever raining!

Masha chuckled softly.

"You silly boy. Go on, read it. What's that? A hundred, isn't it? And those are noughts."

"So how much?"

"Think about it."

I thought about it, but couldn't come up with an answer.

"A hundred thousand." Masha said this in a strange voice, and again glanced behind her. "And now hide it. Hide it really well, Sergei."

She took the savings book from me and wrapped it back in the paper. And all the while thoughts were going round and round in my head. I was wondering what a hundred thousand looked like. The most I'd ever had was three roubles, and that had been a long time ago. I had only ever seen a hundred roubles in other people's hands. How many hundred roubles notes would I have? One, two, three... It was enough to send you round the bend! I could think of nothing else. Nothing but the stupid thought that I had no need of this book. What good was it to me? I'd have been happy to take ten roubles... maybe a hundred. No, on second thoughts, perhaps not – you could get your head split open here in the village for a hundred roubles.

As though in a dream I heard Masha's voice:

"I've put some other documents in with your savings book, so don't lose them. There's a birth certificate. Your birth certificate. And a signed statement from the Kukushkin woman to say that she states before the law that she gave you her own name, but that in fact you are a Yegorov. But for the time being nobody must know that. She'd already been roasted. She only got off by saying that none of you could remember your proper names, so that she had to give you her own."

"What if we really didn't remember?"

"Well, of course some of you didn't remember," replied Masha.

"Could I have forgotten something and then remembered it?"

"What have you remembered?"

"The camp," I said.

"What camp?" asked Masha, and it seemed to me that she gave a jump.

"The summer camp," I repeated. "There was a forest, a path and a song about a cuckoo."

"A cuckoo?" Masha asked stupidly.

"Yes, a cuckoo..."

"Ah, that's what you're on about," said Masha, as though emerging from a trance. She stuffed the package into my pocket. Take it and hide it. I would have brought you some other things − letters and photos − but they took everything away from me. That savings book's also a keepsake. You'll understand when you're a bit older. I would have hung on to it, but what with going to the front. Each time you know you might not return."

I listened, nodded, and all the while wondered how to give her the packet back. Eventually I decided not to bother. She seemed to want me to have it, so that was fine by me! It made no difference to me! I could stick it in the back of my history book. But I did have to find out about this memory I had.

Again I asked:

"So, did I go to a summer camp?"

"If you remember it, then yes," said Masha hurriedly, and looked away in the direction the train was expected. Sure enough, there it was, wheels clattering, steam billowing.

Kukushkin Kids or the Cuckoos

"But I don't know whether I remember it or not!" I shouted above the noise of the locomotive.

"You remember the song, though?"

"Yes, I remember."

"Then all the rest happened, too," shouted Masha, giving me a kiss on the cheek.

"They don't want you to remember anything! As if you'd never had any other life. But you did, you did!"

Anatoly Pristavkin is one of the more outstanding realist writers of the generation known as "the men of the 1960s" and currently heads the Presidential Committee on Clemency. His best known novel *A Golden Cloud There Rested* has been translated into many languages, including English by Michael Glenny.

The above is an excerpt from *Kukushkin Kids or the Cuckoos*, an autobiographical novel which won the author the prestigeous Pushkin Prize. It is set in the war years in a special orphanage for children of "enemies of the people" with its appalling atmosphere of administrative neglect and callousness. The children learn that their names are not their real names, but given to them to conceal their true identity. They try to find out about their parents and finally stage an uprising which is cruelly suppressed by the special police force, shooting many of the children as criminals. Despite this tragic setting the novel is not at all gloomy, Sergei Kukushkin and his clan of "Cuckoos" are lively, bright and resourceful in the face of extreme adversity.

Page 132: a detail from the drawing by Marina Petrova.

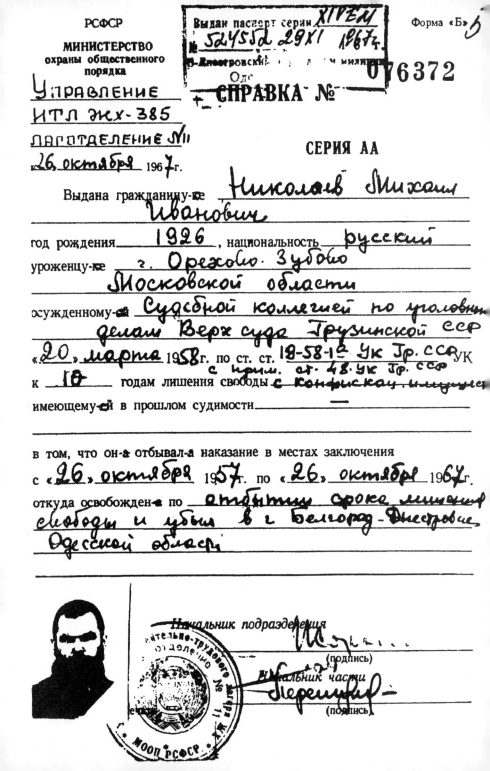

Misha
NIKOLAYEV

Orphanage

Translated by Robert Chandler

Last Day in the Camp

25 October 1967. My last day in the camp. I had years behind me. Tomorrow I would be free. Good bye, Mordovia! Goodbye? Or see you soon? Twice before I had believed I was leaving the camps for ever, but I was free for only 18 months the first time and six months the second time. Since 1950 I had been free for a little over two years. But in 1950 I had been a mere boy, while now there was grey in my beard; when my hair grew, it too would probably be half grey.

On this last evening I was walking about with Andrei Sinyavsky. He suggested I get myself a library job somewhere quiet and inconspicuous – after all, there was nothing in the world I loved more than books. Then I would be able to get my bearings and decide what to do next. I did not say anything. And not just because life had taught me to keep to myself. This time I had another reason for being silent. How could I say to Sinyavsky that I was afraid of the next day, afraid of being on the other side of the barbed wire and the watch-towers, afraid of this long-awaited freedom. Would he understand? He was always receiving letters and parcels, his wife came to visit him, even his friends came just to have a look at him through the barbed wire. They were all dying to see him. When his time was up his wife would come to fetch him. She would probably even bring him a suit – so he would not have to travel in his camp outfit. But there would be no one outside waiting for me and I was afraid of the next day. I was afraid, and there was nothing I could do about it. It's frightening to be forty, to be alone in the world, and to be beginning a new life, with no idea how and where, and with a certificate of release from prison instead of a passport. That was why I was silent: I was ashamed to tell the truth and I knew he would not understand.

I wound up my camp affairs. I gave away what in ten years had developed into quite a good library: four sacks of books, enough to infuriate the inspectors each time I was transferred

Orphanage

from camp to camp. I did the same with my album of newspaper cuttings on rockets and space research – somebody else in the camp would have to keep that up. I would be travelling light when I left tomorrow – with just a toothbrush, a towel, and a bar of soap. Empty-handed is easier.

I slept badly that night. I kept thinking about Belgorod on the Dniester: what would it be like, this town I'd been given a travel warrant to? Would I find a job there and a place to live? Where would I stay the night in Moscow? Would I be able to see Leonid R. who had been released earlier, in August, and who had left me his mother's Moscow address? What would it be like outside? Much would have changed in ten years. What kind of new life awaited me? No, I did not want a new life, I did not even want a nice quiet job as a librarian. I no longer wanted anything in this country. I'd just hang about Belgorod for a while – apparently it was not far from the border... I had to escape. I had had enough of this life, my new life as well as my old.

I had seen many people in my time in the camps, and had heard and read of many others, and I felt that day that I had been more unfortunate than any of them. I had heard people say with a sigh: "Stalin was the death of all Lenin's comrades!" Or: "Those poor Marshals – all shot without rhyme or reason!" Without reason? But didn't they all go along, until they too were destroyed, with everything that happened? Didn't they destroy one another, betraying their very closest friends, until their own turn came? This tendency to look on everyone who died under Stalin as a martyr has become quite widespread. In "Portrait of a Tyrant" Antonov-Ovseenko portrays his father as a pure and honourable Bolshevik who died innocent. He lays all the blame on Stalin and his surviving stooges. Yet his father was a high-ranking revolutionary himself, he had even been People's Commissar for Justice under Stalin. Had the son never thought about how much blood was on his hands? And how, after his wife was arrested in 1929, could the father have continued his career as a Soviet statesman? He did not throw his Party card

Misha Nikolayev

in the face of "the tyrant", he did not resign from all his posts, he just patiently waited for his own turn, or timidly hoped that "this cup would pass him by". I felt no sympathy for any of them: they had all received their just desserts. They had been willing participants, they had helped to make it all happen.

Whereas I had been thrown between the millstones when I was only a child, before I could understand anything at all. Why? Because of my parents?

My memory goes back, spinning like a spool of film. How had it all begun? Why had my life gone so askew? Who was to blame?

My Parents

Although I have an excellent, even excessively detailed memory, I have no clear recollection of life before the orphanage. I was probably just too small. But I do have what I call "pre-memories". They can hardly be put into words. They are neither thoughts nor feelings. They are my first sensations, which I remembered later, when I was nine or ten, and tried to interpret.

Here is the first picture. A dark night, it's raining, we're on horseback. There's a general sense of anxiety, something I'm acutely aware of, even though I can't yet speak. I still feel astonishment at how I could grasp all this without words. It is only later that I realized I must have been in my father's arms. I still have no idea who he was or what was happening, but I could sense the anxiety of the people riding beside us. I have no idea what the danger was, but it's as though we were escaping somewhere, running away from someone. When these memories (pre-memories, sensations, as you will) took shape and I began turning them round in my mind, I suddenly realized that we had been in the mountains. There was a mountain landscape imprinted in my memory: sheer cliffs on one side and gorges on the other. The only mountains like that are in the Crimea, the Caucasus, and Central Asia. That's all I remember about

168

Orphanage

my father. I have no idea how he was arrested, it may not have been in my presence.

I can remember my mother more clearly. The second of my most vivid memories is of walking along, holding onto the hand of a woman, my mother. We are in a large city: on a broad street with huge windows on the ground floors. It was only later I realized they were shop windows. Afterwards I somehow took it into my head that it must have been Leningrad. When I was there after the camps I kept hoping to recognize something. Needless to say, I did not. I think I must have been not more than three or four years old at the time.

Another picture I can see clearly is of a room in the evening. My mother and I are sitting together, she's cleaning her pistol on a table, beneath a hanging lamp. I couldn't help remembering the pistol. Since she had a weapon my mother must have been a party functionary. I can remember her talking to me. She had the same head of black hair as I was to have later. And she always smelt of fine perfume. Probably she was very young.

My mother's arrest has also slipped from my memory. A child must have some kind of defence mechanism against things like that. But strangely I do remember having a younger sister, I can remember playing with her. And then, before the orphanage, she died and was buried. I can remember a little coffin and the road to the cemetery, that's all. Somehow I'm quite certain that it was a little girl, my sister.

That's all I can say about my family. Why am I so sure my parents were arrested? Because there are always a few "kind folk" around who are only too eager to enlighten you. In my first orphanage – when I was five – I must have got into a fight or hurt one of the girls. Anyway, a nurse ran up to me and said with real malice:

"You little viper! Just like your parents – enemies of the people! You should be shot too, same as them!"

I was too small to understand, of course, but the words registered in my memory and surfaced again some time later. I should say that the word "kill" is common currency in the Russian language. As in: "I could have killed him!" or "Killing him would be letting him off lightly!" So what struck me may have been the word "shot". There's something else as well. In 1941, before I left the orphanage, I had a conversation with the director, Maria Nikolayevna. She told me that I mustn't be ashamed of my parents.

"Your parents did not abandon you, Misha. They were good people."

Frankly, I have been ashamed all my life of being from an orphanage, of having no family, of being almost a foundling. Even Maria Nikolayevna's kind words did not help; I still felt ashamed, I still tried to hide the fact that I was from an orphanage.

"You may not understand everything yet," she went on, "but when you grow up you'll realize that they were good people and they did nothing wrong."

She said that my father was no longer alive, but it was possible I might yet meet my mother. Years later I worked out that since I was taken to the orphanage in summer 1933, my parents must have been arrested before the murder of Kirov, in early 1933 or even in 1932. I have no idea at all when my father was shot or what became of my mother. I'm still astonished that Maria Nikolayevna was not afraid to say they were good people.

I never found my mother, nor did I ever learn anything about her, although I tried.

The Orphanage

How do I know what year I was sent to the orphanage? By chance. When Maria Nikolayevna invited me to her office to talk to me about my parents, we were sitting at her desk and she was suddenly called out for a moment. I was left alone with my "personal file" in front of me. A personal file exists for every Soviet citizen, accompanying them throughout their lives, but very few people ever get the chance to examine it. Of course I

Orphanage

was tempted... I opened it: attached to the first page was a small note with a stamp in one corner: "GPU Moscow Region". The note said: "Nikolayev, Misha, a four-year-old boy, is being sent to you..." And there was a signature: Executive Secretary of the GPU or OGPU. The stamp was dated 1933. I remember it well because it was my first document. From it I learned that I was born in 1929.

I often wonder at the number of people who must have collaborated in making orphans out of children like myself. I'm not just talking about the men who actually arrested millions of parents. There must have been someone who took me away; someone who decided which town and orphanage to send me to; some executive, probably a woman, a mother herself, who wrote out a document and signed her illegible signature. Doing this day after day, they must have wondered, they must have tried somehow or other to explain to themselves the appearance of so many orphans, to justify their own part in it all. But then no one finds it difficult to justify themselves.

It all happened on such a vast scale. Take Pokrov, where I was sent, and where I lived until the beginning of the war. This small town, a hundred kilometers from Moscow, had a population of five thousand. And no less than five orphanages. They were divided according to age, and I spent time in three of them: numbers one, three and four. The orphanages took children from the ages of three or four to the ages of fourteen or fifteen; orphanage children were only given seven years of schooling, from the age of seven. In my three orphanages there must have been a total of about four hundred children. There were also two other orphanages we never had any contact with. No one was ever transferred from them to us, or from us to them; their buildings were surrounded by high fences; the children never went to the town schools — did they have schools of their own? — and in fact were never let out at all. Who were those children? How many were there of them? All this makes six to seven hundred orphans in one small town. How many such towns were there in Russia?

171

Not a word was ever said to us about our parents, not one word. No one ever came to visit us, nor were anyone's parents ever found. We were all of us victims of the repressions; in the absence of plague or war there is no other way so many children could have been orphaned at once. Even close relatives were often forbidden to adopt children of enemies of the people; such children were hidden away by the authorities. The idea was that they should know no one and be known to no one, so they could forget about the past.

I used to know a woman named Nonna whose parents were arrested when she was five. Although she had relatives who wanted to take her in, she was packed off to an orphanage. She, of course, was too small to let anyone know where she was. Her uncle spent years searching in different orphanages; finally, because for some reason they had not changed her surname, he succeeded in locating her. They still would not let her go. After that he kept a careful eye on her, making countless petitions, until, after another four years, he got her back. It was quite a story – in the end he all but kidnapped her from the orphanage.

The usual practice, so they'd be less likely to remember anything, was to change a child's surname. The first name was usually left unaltered, since even small children are used to their names. I heard the same thing from Nadezhda Mandelstam – she worked for a whole month in an orphanage until the director finally dismissed her, realizing that she too was "undesirable".

Even now, near the end of my life, I still do not know my real name.

The authorities' purpose in taking orphans away from their relatives was that they should never think about their arrested parents. Lest they, God forbid, grow up into potential dissidents, potential avengers of their parents' death. It made very good sense to change a child's surname. I'm sure that the authorities achieved their purpose: the majority of the children, if not all, remembered nothing about their parents.

Before School

I remember my first orphanage in quite a rosy light. I was happy there. It was a fine, two-storey wooden building that had probably once belonged to a merchant or some local landlord. There was also a large orchard: apple-trees, gooseberry bushes, currants... The orchard was bordered by an alley of lime-trees. We used to play there both summer and winter – it was a good place to be. I gradually became used to the orphanage, and I felt no sense of loss at being there. No small child grieves for long over parents who have disappeared; at that age wounds inflicted by fate heal quickly. I soon adapted to the new conditions. The loss of my parents meant nothing to me then. I did not even remember them.

Strangely enough, I can remember, as though it happened yesterday, a winter holiday when they laid on some theatre for us: border-guards and saboteurs. Needless to say, it never entered our heads that the whole country was being carried away by this game – border-guards and saboteurs, upright Chekists and enemies of the people – and that it might have been in this very game that our parents had disappeared. That was more than we could take in. We were simply being imbued from our earliest years with the idea that the world was divided into "us" and "them", into Reds and Whites, border-guards and saboteurs. None of that meant much to us then. It was just a game we played: searches, reconnaissances, the pursuit and capture of the spy. Could we have imagined then that this game would continue for the rest of our lives?

The nannies were local women, good and kind. Pokrov was a small provincial town with its own traditional way of life. I can still remember the night watchmen, pacing up and down the streets with their wooden rattles as they guarded the sleep of the townspeople. If you woke during the night, you would always hear, close by or far away, the sound of a rattle. It felt very comforting. I can also remember the water-carrier. There was

Misha Nikolayev

no water main; right up until the war a man used to go round the houses distributing water from a huge barrel. Life in Pokrov was quiet and measured. Everyone knew everyone else and everything about them; it was a very closed little world indeed. Insofar as they affected the inhabitants of Pokrov, even the events of the external world were refracted through this traditional self-sufficiency. I would say that life in a small town like Pokrov – I had the same feeling in Tarusa and Borovsk – is a great deal more human than in the capital cities and industrial centres. Our orphanage was nothing like the Danilovsky orphanage in Moscow which, judging by the stories I've heard about it, must have been worse than a prison. The nannies looked on us simply as orphans - not as children of enemies of the people. They were sorry for us. One of them, Auntie Lisa took quite an interest in me. She used to stroke my head, I think she loved me. Sometimes when I was in bed, she would lie down beside me and snuggle up to me – I don't need to say how much the warmth of a maternal body means to a child. She had a daughter about my age who would sometimes come in with her – perhaps Aunt Lisa tried to feed her up a bit at the orphanage.

I really believe these women did all they could for us. The time one of them shouted at me that I ought to be shot, the same as my father, was very soon after the assassination of Kirov. What with the subsequent arrests and all that was written about Kirov in the newspapers the whole country was seething. Kirov's assassin was called Nikolayev – my own surname. The woman may have thought I was his son. But this was the only attack on me I can remember. On the whole, things weren't bad at all. I felt happy and had no inferiority complex at the time about my lack of parents.

Life went on like this for three years; it was much the same as an ordinary kindergarten except we never went home. In 1936 I was seven years old and it was time for me to go to school. I had to be transferred to the next orphanage, for school-children.

Orphanage

Alarm at Night

I was five or six years old, still in the first orphanage. In the middle of one night, when we were fast asleep, there was a sudden noise. I woke up to find the whole dormitory in commotion. As well as the teacher on duty, there were other members of the staff who usually slept at home. They seemed very agitated and were waking up everybody who was still asleep, saying: "It's all right, children, don't worry!"

Many years later I remembered that night and began to wonder why on earth they had woken us up. If they hadn't, we would have slept through the entire night and none of us would have worried about anything. At the time, of course, like the other boys, I took everything at face value. It was very odd, though: they'd woken us up to tell us not to worry. They said someone was outside in the garden. We were afraid, and infected one another with our fear and unease. I also remember feeling extremely curious: who was it down there? We began listening – yes, we could hear footsteps.

"He must be someone very wicked if he wakes children up at night," said the teacher on duty. We all knew, of course, that it was the teacher himself who had woken us up, and yet we believed him: that man out there in the garden had woken us up.

I was told to stand by the window and call out every few minutes, in as loud and grown-up a voice as possible: "Who's there?" I did this with great zeal. Outside in the darkness there was nothing to be seen. We were too small to go out into the garden at night, but the intruder had to be caught. And so the teachers put on a little show. (That is how I see it now – at the time I was impressed with their bravery.) One of them went downstairs, right out onto the porch, then came back and said:

"No, we'd better wait till morning. Who knows what this man might be up to. I don't want to leave you on your own with the children. Let's wait until morning. And you children go back to bed."

175

Misha Nikolayev

This went on for about an hour and a half. Everyone was awake and many of us were crying. Gradually we quietened down and went back to bed. I dozed off, full of the wildest notions.

In the morning, before breakfast, we older boys were taken outside.

"Come on, children. Let's try and find out who it was in the night."

To our horror and ecstasy we found footprints in the middle of the garden, scraps of bandage, lumps of cotton wool... Yes, he went this way, he stood here, he must have been bandaging himself. Now we knew for sure that a saboteur had broken into our garden, he had been wounded, he had been trying to hide. Our sleepless night had not been in vain. I felt very pleased with myself. I hadn't cried like some boys; instead I had stood by the window, calling out in a gruff voice: "Who's there?" It might even be me who had frightened the man away.

Simple little tricks like this (one member of the staff walking around the garden while the others work you up into a state of hysteria) make quite an impact on a child's imagination. This is how Soviet man was shaped: we were made to believe that we were surrounded by enemies. Then of course there were all the countless books on the Civil War, the underground fighters and the Socialist Revolution. And the films about border-guards and saboteurs.

Young Pioneer Camp

Every summer we had something to look forward to: Young Pioneer Camp. We went in separate groups rather than all together, and we stayed there for a whole month. What I particularly liked about the camp was that we were there together with children from other places, most of them from families.

Not far from Pokrov is a small town called Petushki; our camp was near there, in the village of Gribovo (Mushroom Place).

Orphanage

Now even the name sounds sweet to me. But at the time we were not very interested in mushrooms. The village lay deep in the forest, on the shore of a large, clean and beautiful lake. We swam several times a day, went for walks and hikes in the forest, and those who wanted to went fishing. I joined the fishermen's group for a while but soon got bored sitting there with a rod. I preferred reading.

There was, of course, a strict routine to the day: reveille and lights-out, roll-calls and morning exercises; all the same it was different from being in the orphanage and we felt freer and happier. To start with, we lived in the village huts, and this was almost like living at home. The office, the library, the various clubs, and the staff themselves were housed in the school building. Temporary shelters were erected for the kitchen and canteen. The children slept in the huts, eight in each one, while the hosts slept in the kitchen or a shed. We had camp beds and mattresses filled with straw. Some mornings the landlady would give us milk fresh from the cow. I have always thought of summer camp as the next best thing to living at home.

In the orphanage we were tormented by bedbugs. Especially in summer, when there was no getting away from them. On a summer's night we would be eaten alive, and could hardly sleep. What with bedbugs and the stifling heat, night-time was hellish. But children forget quickly and there was no one to complain to. And I had known nothing different. I imagined it was the same in every town. In Gribovo, however, there were no bedbugs and our beds smelled of straw; it was nice and cosy, and I decided you did not get bedbugs in villages. One has only one's own experience to go by. In short, Gribovo was a pleasant rest from our usual routine, from boring teachers – and from bedbugs.

As well as games and entertainments, there was work in the local kolkhoz, usually weeding vegetables. We would go once or twice a week, each unit in turn. On the way back we swam and played about in the lake; it wasn't really like work at all, it was more like another game.

The older boys would play war games: blues, reds and

Misha Nikolayev

greens. Each unit, naturally enough, wanted to be "red". Usually one unit would hide the flag, while another would try to find it. We would learn to be more observant and to get our bearings in the forest. We enjoyed pretending to be spies and soldiers, pretending we were bold and strong. But what I enjoyed most of all were our long hikes and the nights we spent by a bonfire with the stars overhead. This was probably when I first grew to love the night sky: if my life had followed a different course, I am sure I would have become an astronomer.

Once, in summer 1939, we had what seemed like a real alarm in the camp. During the morning parade the senior Pioneer leader announced that the programme for the day had been altered on account of an emergency. "We have been informed that some unknown persons have been spotted in the area, not far from the village itself. It is not impossible that they are German spies."

Somehow I can still remember that the spies were supposed to be German. These strangers, we were told, had to be found, and we were to assist the adults in this task. Each unit was to be entrusted with searching a particular area. You can imagine the excitement that gripped the camp, and the grief of the little ones who were left out.

The whole unit, thirty of us, set off in a direction known only to the leader. As we walked along the forest paths our leader kept finding signs and traces: here the grass had been trodden in a particular way, there someone had dropped a cigarette-end. Picking up the cigarette-end, the leader announced in a loud whisper – we all spoke in a whisper so as not to alarm the enemy – that it was a foreign cigarette-end, not one of our own. Inspired by the fact that we were helping in the struggle against the enemy, we searched in every direction, trying to make as little noise as possible. Being quiet, however, was not an easy matter – we were young boys and girls who did not know how to do anything quietly. Finally, with the help of the leader – although we were all convinced we'd done it ourselves – we stumbled across a little dugout covered over with grass

Orphanage

and branches. There it was, an enemy hide-out! Leading from it was an underground passage with a secret chimney so the smoke would escape sideways, underneath some tree or other. Who could have been responsible? An honest man would have had no reason to hide – it must have been a spy. We never actually found any spies, only the dugout. Nevertheless, we were extremely proud to have helped our border-guards in their search for spies and enemies.

All this was enacted with such absolute seriousness that there was no way it could have been taken for make-believe. It is only now that I understand the game the authorities were playing, the way they saw it as an essential part of our upbringing that we should be trained to mistrust strangers. At the time we were all ardent patriots, "eager for battle"; Germany had yet to become our "friend" and so anything that went wrong was blamed on the Germans. We listened to talks on Nazism and Nazi Germany, heroic anti-fascist Pioneers, etc. And none of us had minds of our own enough to wonder what Gribovo could possibly have to do with frontiers, guards and spies. Why on earth would a spy have been interested in that godforsaken village?

Misha Nikolayev (1929-1988) lost both parents to the purges and grew up in various orphanages before being sent to work at a munitions factory. By the age of fifteen he was fighting at the Front.
In 1950, Nikolayev was arrested for the first time. He had been standing outside a polling station, urging people not to vote in the fraudulent elections. In 1955, after three years in a labour camp, he was sentenced to a further two years for protesting outside Sverdlovsk jail against the execution of prisoners. After he attempted to cross the Soviet-Turkish frontier he was sentenced to death. The sentence was commuted to twenty-five years imprisonment, then to fifteen years, finally to ten.
On his release in 1967, Misha arrived in Moscow where he met and married Viktoria Schweitzer, a woman of great warmth, tolerance and understanding. In 1978, with his wife and daughter, Misha emigrated to the United States and settled in Amherst, Massachusetts, where both found work at the university. Those years were the happiest of his life.
The above is an excerpt from his book *Orphanage*.

Julia
NEMIROVSKAYA

The Garage
Insight

Translated by Marian Schwartz

The Garage

As a child I was constantly noticing how ephemeral reality is. Not that I didn't know how to live in the present. But the constant sensation of parting with it weighed on me. Staring at the burrs in the mown grass or the gentle slopes beyond the summer cottages, I would think: I'll be remembering all this before too long. Not that I had any grounds for supposing that we would ever go very far away for very long.

It was in the country, during a bad quarrel with my mother, that I learned about the malignant tumor they had removed from Papa's kidney. I'd never had the least suspicion when we were visiting Papa in the hospital, because he was always so cheerful and was always asking us about what we were doing, as if what was happening to him were trivial, like a pulled tooth.

Once when we were on our way home from the hospital, huge mongrels attacked a ragged little dog, evidently their recent companion. Mama's friend rushed at the pack and drove them off with her wool jacket. I felt relieved: I thought everything would turn out all right, although there was no direct connection between the dog fight and Papa's illness. When they removed the tumor, together with one kidney, the doctors had said that the risk of a new tumor appearing remained but you could say everything had turned out well for now.

The news of Papa's cancer closed off the air vent to my already panic-stricken mind. For a while I would sit for hours not moving, trying to get used to the idea. Hardest of all was the need to hide the truth from Papa. Maybe if he had known and we hadn't had to pretend life would have been easier.

I don't remember whether it was before or after his illness that Papa bought an orange car and an old widow sold him her garage. The garage was not far from our apartment house, but it was in a kind of neighborhood trains pass through on their way to the roundhouse: no buildings, upturned earth studded

The Garage

with pipes and broken fences. The only peopled place there was a filling station.

Driving up to our apartment in the evening after the theater or visiting, Papa would usually ask Mama:

"Natochka, shall we go park the car?"

Mama was fearful and didn't like to walk near the garages so she would think up excuses, and then I would chime in. Papa liked walks with Mama, but he would agree without a murmur.

So we drove to our garage amid the monotonous rows of other people's gates, and Papa opened it with an unbelievably huge iron key and switched on the light over the vacant cement space, which was ringed by shelves full of junk, spare parts, and canisters.

Then I held the steel door and Papa parked the car, and once the gate was closed we walked home. Behind us the smoke-stacks of the heating plant loomed over the horizon, to the left was a lonely TV tower, and ahead the white of our apartment building. We carried some sausage for the stray dogs that ran after us. Sometimes I told optimistic stories the whole way, with great enthusiasm, because to me any sadness was like a reminder of Papa's illness. Sometimes we talked softly through the wind, which roamed freely over the urban underbelly that surrounded us.

Papa had lived his whole life in Moscow and knew the length and breadth of it. He had been in the rumbles that were so common before the war between the inner city neighborhoods where he, Grandpa, and Grandma had been given a room in a communal apartment with seventeen other families. Their building on Luchnikov Lane has been razed, of course, but I remember the address: "4 Luch. Apt. 4." Papa ran away from nursery school for the first time when he was two and a half and the police took him home because he remembered his address like a rhyme. At ten he could get from his house to the Dynamo Stadium with his eyes closed; boys gathered on top of the wall and watched the soccer for free. He made his next escape to the war.

When Papa came back from the front he was eighteen. Of

Julia Nemirovskaya

all his many war stories, the one that amazed me the most was the story about the capture of Baron N.'s castle.

Papa's unit was stationed at the estate of a rich and distinguished German intellectual. The library there took up several floors, which were connected by a spiral staircase. The books, set out on semicircular shelves, were bound identically and stamped in gold on their spines.

The library was staggering: Papa picked up an art book of Duehrer, whom he didn't know at the time, went down to the ground floor, and started looking through the reproductions. All of a sudden a rhinoceros materialized on a thick creamy page.

I often tried to imagine WWII in both Russia and Germany, encirclement, battles on enemy territory, but in vain: the soldiers would turn out like stuffed dummies, and the dirt and fire smelled like the Borodino diorama. Only this rhinoceros, which I'd known so well since my childhood from Mama's scrapbooks, made everything real. A rhino-knight, as if composed of carved metal plates, the epitaph of German might, shakes off the book, grows, and rises in the whitened German sky above the exhausted soldiers, Europe, the whole cumbersome historic installation. Facts coalesce, dreams are explained, and scraps of someone else's past and future come to life in my memory.

In the castle, the looting proceeded full tilt. A comrade of Papa's from the regiment went down carrying a roll of canvases. He looked around, walked over to the far wall, where a barely distinguishable portrait was hanging in the darkness, got out his razor, and ran it around the picture inside the gilt frame. Then he deftly extracted the canvas from the frame, unfurled his fat roll, added his new trophy to it, rolled it back up, and walked over to Papa. A corner of the outside painting had bent back accidentally, and a grandee dead for centuries winked. Baron N. had had one of the finest collections of paintings in Europe.

A little later a round-faced soldier came to check out the ground floor and, scarcely able to move his tongue, explained that he had a gold cross in his mouth. Papa was too young to follow his two friends' example. He put the book back, thinking

The Garage

that it would be unhappy living without its companions, and made plans to return to the castle on the way home and examine the art books in more detail. Everyone was sure the war was about to end and they would be homeward bound any day now.

That night there was an order to pack up and move westward again. When they entered the forest they heard a crackling, as if someone had started breaking trees behind them. They looked around to see a column of fire where the castle had been.

There was an inspection on the morrow. When yesterday's soldier with the cross in his mouth walked past the commanding officers, smiling stupidly, he was called out, made to open his mouth, and sentenced to execution for looting. The generals shipped the confiscated cross, along with truckloads of other trophies, to their own families in Moscow.

No one suspected Papa's other comrade, and the roll of pictures remained there in his rucksack. "He must be a millionaire now, if he's not dead," Papa would add good-naturedly at the end of his story.

Papa's unit was still stationed in Germany when he was ordered to drive a lieutenant to Prague. It turned out that this lieutenant had one of what were at the time many dispatches telling of the victory and the war's end. Driving into the city, they stopped the car by the sidewalk and went to find a urinal. In a yard where all the windows were hung with white flags, there was a burst of machine-gun fire. The lieutenant died instantly; Papa only suffered a contusion. He lost his speech, but got it back in the hospital, stuttering at first, but then was back to normal. The convalescing soldiers would slip into town on the sly. Prague was honoring its liberators – no one then could have dreamed that twenty-some years later these same flower-strewn tanks would be covered with Czech blood. The women cried and kissed the silly beardless soldier boys. Papa decided it would be terribly smart to take a stroll through town in civvies. For his next sortie he traded a gold watch he had won at cards for a decent gray suit and a felt hat he thought captivating. When he saw himself in a reflecting window, he

185

decided that his crew-cut had grown out sufficiently to render him quite irresistible. The female residents of Prague, however, preferred a uniform, and only when all the servicemen had been taken, evidently, was it his turn.

Papa's Czech girlfriend was the youngest daughter of a university professor. I don't know her name – and Lord, there's no one left on earth now to ask. For both this was first-time true love. She took Papa to meet her parents. Despite his rich military experience, Papa felt awkward amid the paintings and bas-reliefs in the huge apartment. The only familiar object turned out to be a piano glimpsed in the parlor. Papa was taught to play the piano, but over the course of the war he forgot a lot of what he had learned and remembered only a few pieces by Chopin, Liszt, and Dvorak. Evidently, Papa's civilian suit and insolent look failed to create the necessary impression on the Prague professor's family. He felt the tension in them and even a certain desire to let him know that he was an outsider there. The professor sat down wearily at the piano and began playing some little piece, and his wife left the room. At this point Papa turned to his girlfriend and told her, as if by the way: "I don't like this Dvorak piece very much." The professor pricked up his ears. "Is that so?" he said.

"What do you like?" Crowding him over, Papa quickly bent over the keyboard and played another piece by Dvorak (as he later admitted, to flatter his hosts' national pride). That same evening the matter of Papa was decided positively. He became engaged.

A couple of weeks later a rumor went around that all foreigners returning to the Soviet Union with soldiers would be taken off the trains and sent to the camps.

Back in Moscow Papa looked forward to all kinds of wonders and successes. After plenty of boasting and losing his last remaining pocket watch, he came to his senses, finished the last three grades of high school by correspondence, and on the advice of his math teacher decided to study math at Moscow University.

The Garage

That was in 1948, and the anti-Semitic campaign was just getting under way, the Jewish Doctors' Plot and the rest. They didn't even let Papa take the entrance exams.

Apropos of this he always used to say: "So it was by sheer accident that I graduated from the Communications College, which may have been for the best." He was probably referring to his early professorship and other scholarly achievements. He was embellishing reality somewhat, however, because according to information I have from other sources, he walked out of the university vestibule and went wild, quickly turning to gambling. His other new enthusiasms were slick clothes and pretty women. On top of that, he was drinking, driving to resorts in his posh car, and creating scenes in restaurants. At the 1957 World Youth and Student Festival he was tossed into the Moscow River fully clothed.

Those were uncertain times, but however much you curse them, you end up making your peace with them simply because they happen to coincide with your life. At the age of thirty-three Papa married an eighteen-year-old beauty, a philology student at the university, thinking he could mold a wife to his own liking. His energy and bearish grace enchanted Mama. He invariably wore suits and narrow-brimmed hats, which were enough to drive you crazy. Soon enough, though, his cheerful boastfulness and simple ideas about life began to embarrass Mama. Her eighteen-year-old girlfriends were so sophisticated, smoking and discussing existentialism. Papa treated them loudly to fine wines and old jokes. My parents stayed together, alternating fits of mutual jealousy and extended quarrels with periods of married bliss.

I don't know whether or not Papa liked his work, but for the most part things went well for him. He didn't join the Party, but he showed his respect for the communications hierarchy. Papa studied the troposphere, which meant he got invited to international conferences, once an invitation was in the name of the Queen of England herself, of which he was especially proud. But ministry officials went instead, memorizing the papers they

187

had to deliver. From time to time Papa would get to hoping that they wouldn't dare not let him go. Then he would start studying the appropriate language and trying on his best suits, of which he usually had two, choosing which one to take. When he received another refusal, he pretended he wasn't upset. All in all, his life went unusually well, a fact he liked to reflect upon and talk about. Papa was one of the rare adults I knew for whom getting up in the morning, even a dark winter's morning, was a joy. Ever since I was a child, I've always felt exactly the opposite, so the optimistic tone in my dealings with Papa in the last years of his life was false.

Nonetheless, I loved to walk home from the garage with him. I loved going for the car on Saturday or Sunday mornings even more, especially in winter, when before you opened the garage you had to clear the area in front of the gates from the snow. All the years of my childhood the scrape of a janitor's shovel clearing away snow excited me. Simply producing this sound was happiness. Black trails of asphalt ran behind the moving shovel, and dirty mounds of cleared snow rose up by the opposite wall and dripped in the sun.

In the winter the car seemed haggard and unshaven, and it pulled out slowly, after warming up. When I inhaled the smell of gasoline amid the melting snowdrifts and industrial smokestacks, I was crushed by a sense of the world's ephemerality, so much so that for an instant I stopped breathing and seeing while Papa was transformed into a porcelain statue flying into a stone corner. I rushed toward him. Standing back, like on a staircase in a dream, I grabbed onto the running board of the orange car, crawled onto the seat – and there next to me was my soft, warm, lively Papa in his navy wool training suit.

He cleaned the garage and the car with zest, the way he did everything, secured the straps, and turning toward the sun growing right before our eyes, asked, "What's up, kid?" (he always called me kid).

And as usual I launched into a lie, as if the true reason for my fear would have come right through silence.

I talked about my successes and plans (assuming this would please him), invented minor problems that Papa tried to solve with his characteristic concern, and meanwhile Moscow whirled and twirled out my window, so that now after Papa's death I have a hard time looking at those surroundings.

Insight

I had my first political insight quite early on, although it was anything but independent. Mama informed me that Lenin was a cruel man who lusted for power and Stalin was a bloodthirsty maniac, but I shouldn't tell anyone that. I guess I was about nine. At the time this came as a shock to me.

What struck me wasn't that Lenin was bad but that the knowledge had to be kept secret. My closest friend, whom I clued in immediately, first making her swear several oaths as a precaution, said disappointedly that she had known all that for a long time. What do you mean — there had already been a search at her house, and her uncle was Sakharov's secretary. I knew about Academician Sakharov but not about the KGB, which my friend talked about with an air of importance.

In the evenings at the dacha Papa and Grandpa would lie in identical poses, their transistor radios propped up on their bellies, listening to the BBC and the Voice of America. The "Voice" wasn't jammed in the countryside, and the words "Sakharov" (a sweep of white wings) and "Solzhenitsyn" (the even buzz of a yellow bee) hung in the clear countryside air.

Like all happy children, I feared death to the point of neurosis, especially the death of my near and dear, and I was constantly thinking about what the world would be like without me. I was ten when my great-grandmother died. On the evening of the preceding day my great-grandmother had asked me whether Papa was at work because she would have to be buried. "I'm going to die tomorrow" — those were her last words. I pretended not to understand. On the way home Papa said that Mama's grandmother was very ill and I turned to stone, but I couldn't get out the words to Papa about her funeral. In the morning the telephone rang and Mama started to cry. I told her about what had happened the day before.

Later I made several attempts to form secret societies, but I was finally put off this idea by my classmate Petrov, who proposed bombing trains in the Metro in order to compromise the Communist regime. This was in the spring, and we had been gathering lilacs somewhere, so that I have always vaguely associated their smell with terrorism. My other friend and I swore to preserve Russian culture, especially the church, but neither she nor I yet knew how much of it had already been destroyed. Nor did we ever guess that very soon Pamyat (an extreme nationalist organization) would take up the protection of cultural monuments and our enthusiasm would wane.

For me, righteous political indignation was an emotion I'd been living with. In the fifth year of school I made friends with the daughters of the Ceylonese ambassador, who were less than a year apart in age. The principal called me in and asked me whether my parents were Communists and how dare I not inform the school administration about my ties with foreigners. I found this odd, since the ambassador's daughters were in my school and in my class and everyone knew that either I spent my evenings hanging around the embassy or else they spent theirs at my house. I complained to the two girls about the principal and totalitarianism, but when the ambassador asked me whether I saw any difference between the quality of Soviet and English films, I pretended not to understand the English word "quality."

Papa was a physicist and worked in a military plant. The KGB man assigned to watch over Papa was perfectly well informed about my relations with the embassy and had even given his assent when the ambassador and his wife got together with my parents. I remember Mama taking a long time to choose what to wear to a diplomatic reception and finally deciding on a long skirt. My parents were flustered by the ambassador's

Insight

receiving line and the hundreds of couples, most of them ambassadors from all over the world and their spouses. We could not visit them as private citizens, Papa's KGB man protested. To this day I can see my Mama and Grandma walking in wearing their fur coats, hats, and shawls, my three-year-old sister in her felt boots, and me, all covered in snow, and the ambassador and his wife are looking out through the snowy slit, looking for Papa, and the servants are hauling a trolley with whiskey, cognac, and other liquors.

This friendship so consumed us that I nearly became a Buddhist and the older Ceylonese girl decided to study Russian literature in college.

The departure of my friends was a great sorrow for all three of us: we said our goodbyes by candlelight, sobbing convulsively. For a long time I received no letters, and Papa reassured me that right after you get home there can be lots to do; then he added that it's not as hard on those who leave as those who stay behind. I still kept writing though. Six months later we had a phone call from the Sinhalese-born wife of the second secretary at the French embassy. She said she had letters from my friends. We met secretly outside Children's Department Store on Kutuzovsky Prospect, and no KGB agents snitched on us. The letter from the older girl was desperate. She told me there was an official invitation lying in the Soviet Foreign Ministry for me and one other classmate of ours to come to Sri Lanka, that she had sent me lots of letters by ordinary post and hadn't received a single one of mine. "Who is to blame in all this?" she asked, almost like the heroes of Russian classical literature.

Again I languished in impotent fury.

I did battle with the powers-that-be twice, the first time as a schoolgirl, the second while studying at Moscow University.

Once a friend and I were late to a movie house and they wouldn't let us in. At that moment a respectable-looking couple showed up and were immediately admitted by the same ticket taker who had turned us away. My companion lifted an iron urn and with a well-aimed blow broke down the movie house door.

Julia Nemirovskaya

We were taken to the police station. Recalling what someone had told me about how you had to bully policemen, I lied that my grandfather worked at the Moscow Committee of the Communist Party and if they didn't let us both go they'd be sorry. Strangely enough, they released us.

For many years there was an ongoing poetry seminar called Luch (ray of light) at Moscow University. The year I entered, its leader, Igor Volgin, was accused of abetting an anti-Soviet anthology being put out by some seminar participants. Volgin went to the University Party Committee, taking along several students with spotless reputations – me among them – to try to keep Luch from being shut down. The party secretary told Volgin: maybe you didn't know about the anthology, but the anti-Soviets came from your ranks. I shot back with a quick counter-argument: since the Communist Party came into being there had been thousands of scoundrels in its ranks, which meant they were criminals and the Communist Party should be shut down, too. It was the simple love of logic speaking in me, not fearlessness or hatred. I bore no passion for cheap heroism, and anyway the risk was slight: the worst the Moscow University Party Committee could do in 1980 was not let me finish my studies or go on to post-graduate school.

Two years later, though, Brezhnev died, and four years later perestroika began. My generation was lucky.

I don't remember there being any other more powerful political experiences than I'd known at nine. I was moved at the sight of my parents' joy over the perestroika Congresses of People's Deputies, but nothing seethed inside me. I was then interested in a certain nineteenth-century poet, Baron Delvig.

August 19, 1991, might have provoked a new upheaval in me. Especially since that is the birthday of my beloved, prematurely deceased Papa and also the Day of the Transfiguration. But I was already living in Boston, where the summer's heat is awful.

Winners of the Booker Russian Novel Prize

1996

Andrei SERGEEV
Stamp Album

Sergei GANDLEVSKY
Opening the Skull

Andrei SERGEEV

Stamp Album

A Collection of People, Things, Words and Relationships

I'm lying on mum's trestle-bed and through the planed-wood partition I can see the white flour-dusted figures in my room slicing up plump rolls of dough with kitchen knives. I have an inflamed gland in my neck. A portly, dignified-looking surgeon rides over from Malakhovka on a bicycle. I call him the Gastronome. He always brings chocolates and then one fine afternoon, on the table in the dining-room, my mum and gran hold me down under the lighted lamp and he operates.

"A job to suit a fine lady. No-one will ever notice those stitches."

I haven't needed the dummy for ages, but I'm sorry to part with it. Dad takes me down to the embankment, puts the dummy on the rail and gestures:

"The train'll be here in a moment."

I look towards Malakhovka. The train speeds past. Now we're back by the rail, but there's nothing on it. I'm relieved it's all over, and I don't feel sorry any more: just terrified there's nothing there at all.

Everything has to be washed. We wash the skinny carrots from the vegetable patch in the slops barrel. Doctor Nikolaievsky prescribes a thick salty-sweet nasty-smelling mixture as white

Stamp Album

as clotted milk for my dysentery. My belly aches for years and years.

Anna Alexandrovna, a nun, brings the news: some children – "the flowers of our life" – have thrown Doctor Nikolayevsky out of a train, at full speed.

CHILDREN ARE THE FLOWERS OF OUR LIFE is written on my favourite little fork. The iron knives and forks hold smells a long time. At lunch on the terrace mum or gran warn me just as I'm cutting:

"That's the fish knife!"

The spoons are nice though, especially the teaspoons. They're silver, and they have a stamp with St. George and the name SAZIKOV. That's a name no-one has.

Avdotya had a boy staying with her called Marxlen Angelov. His father was a Bulgarian revolutionary. Yurka Tikhonov got things confused straight off. He asked:

"Mark-Twain Angelov?"

Dad knows someone at work called Vagap Basyrovich.

Dad wanted to call me Victor; Mum named me in honour of Andrei Bolkonsky from *War and Peace*. The woman next to her in the maternity hospital was scornful.

"What kind of peasant name is that to give him?"

She had a baby too. She called hers Vilfor. Mum was sarcastic:

"What kind of churchy name is that to give him?"

The other woman was outraged: Vilfor was an abbreviation for "Vladimir Ilich Lenin Father of Revolutions". Mum's heart sank into her boots.

Mum and gran are always afraid.

"Don't pick it up – it's got germs!"

"Don't touch the cat – it might have rabies!"

"There's a dog – mind it doesn't bite you!"

"There's a man coming – mind he doesn't hit you!"

195

I look around and tense up, go wet under my armpits, feel tired and run to snuggle against my mum, my gran, to curl up and do something comforting – just to be alone and in peace.

It's amusing and calms me down to leaf through the coloured pages of my children's books:

Anna Vanna, our group wants
To see the little piglets...

The hippo fell into the swamp...

Now little girl, my dirty-face,
Where did you get so muddy?...

In the shop on the Arbat...

His teeth began to ache...

And without a wash or shave...

The man said to the Dnieper...

Never envy anybody
Even if he's wearing specs...

What an absent-minded man
From down on Bath-House Street...

Now my friend the crocodile...

Maybe we can fight again...

That means grandad needs his drops...

I get a cosy feeling copying drawings into my Pushkin Anniversary notebooks – the young Pushkin and Marshal Voroshilov. He's the best leader of the lot, only Stalin's better than him, the nicest, kindest, most reassuring – an esssential part of my childhood.

"OUR THANKS TO COMRADE STALIN FOR OUR HAPPY CHILDHOOD!" I imagined: winter, the sun is low, open space around four-storey houses with big windows – like new schools – people come out of them and cross the wide pavement

Stamp Album

without hurrying, children drag sledges along on strings. Everything sloping just a bit downhill.

Nobody taught me reading and writing, I did it all myself. Once in 1938 I pressed down hard on my red pencil as I traced out the indelible word SHIT on the front page of the new *Concise History of the Communist Party.* Dad didn't notice it at first, and he almost took it to his political studies group. Gran had to burn the book in the stove. I didn't get into any trouble, gran even said in a tender voice:

"Our own family saboteur."

The other boys say they've caught a spy in the next house. He was sitting in the bathroom at night, injecting military secrets into his arms above the elbows.

The grown-ups say the poems by Pushkin on the covers of my Pushkin Anniversary notebooks are counterrevolutionary. If you turn Kalinin upside-down in the calendar, then you get Radek. Radek makes up all the jokes but they haven't shot him, because then who would write the editorials?

In the beautiful blue history book for fifth grade I discover a clear Nazi symbol on the button of Lenin's grammar school uniform.

Agniya Barto prompts me:

Our neighbour Ivan Petrovich
Is always getting it wrong.

The woman activist from the Red Corner Club explains:

"Gofman's been arrested because they found a photograph of Trotsky at his place."

Gofman, a partisan from the Far East, kept two Alsatian dogs behind a fence. All our mums hated him: he was always jumping the queue, waving his Red Pass about.

The grown-ups always pronounce the words "R e d   P a s s" slowly and cautiously. But they openly call our house the Big

House – it's the biggest in the street, five floors and a basement. The little old houses on both sides have subsided, but our lovely house was put up in 1914, right on the river Kaplya. When a tram drives down Kaplya Street the window-panes shake in their frames.

On the corner of First Meschanskaya Street there used to be a small church, the Trinity of the Little Drop. It was built by a tavern-owner who agreed with his customers to short-serve them all by just a little drop. There's nothing on the site but puddles with bright-red shards of brick, the same as in gran's yard, and beside the empty plot is the tall, grey house with post office number 110. On the First Meschanskaya side there is a colonnade and dad leads me up on to the dais between fluted columns. Dad is delighted with the new m o d e r n First Meschanskaya, except the windows in the houses are too low. And in the middle of the street, there used to be marvellous trees – they cut them all down.

In the winter street a man with no coat and a swollen face wearing glasses asks mum for twenty kopecks. She takes out a rouble: "Poor man."

When I'm in t o w n with her, she buys me a sliced bun with a hot Mikoyan meat ball in it, and she waits.

I think the Mikoyan meat ball tastes better than a home-made one, but I can't say so – she'd be offended. And I don't like chewing on it there in the bakery where everyone can see me – as though someone's hurrying me.

Old ladies ask across the counter:

"Are your French buns fresh?"

There are adverts on the walls of the houses:

HE DESERVES JAM AND PRESERVES

EVERYONE SHOULD BE AWARE
JUST HOW TASTY FRESH CRABS ARE!

Stamp Album

In the evenings they show films on the blank end-wall: three piglets with sweet wheedling voices sing:

"Eat more ham!"

On pay-days dad brings home two hundred grammes of fine sausage, already cut into thin flakes in the shop.

Mum gives away the Brockhaus-Efron encyclopedia to the book-pedlar, it took up all the shelves on the side of the marble windowsill right up to the top. When he gets home from work, dad almost pulls his hair out: all that's left is the Small Soviet Encyclopedia with some of the volumes missing.

Dad doesn't cut articles out of the Encyclopedia or paste over the portraits in it when somebody is arrested as an enemy of the people.

In summer in Udelnaya our half-crazy lodger Varvara Mikhailovna showed mum a book with pictures of Timiryazev and Stalin:

"Look at Timiryazev's noble face. And the other one hasn't got any forehead at all!"

Dad tells us about things in the Timiryazev Agricultural Academy: his colleague Professor Dyman turns up at church on Sundays trying to spot people he knows. A Party assignment.

"A nasty assignment," says mum, emphasizing the rhythm.

The Dymans come calling on us several times each winter.

Great Ekaterininskaya Street. We are sitting on a bench in front of the stove. As soon as it starts warming up, we have to close its door fast: a waste of firewood. It's fun to watch the flames, but we can't. Today we can, though.

Gran goes through a velvet family album with gold clasps and cuts the heads out of soldier's greatcoats with epaulettes:

"Just as long as the faces are all there!"

Sometimes she talks to the wall:

"Sadist!" Or the window: "Syphilitic!"

Andrei Sergeev

I heard her confessing to mum in a half-whisper:

"In the toilet I come across portraits in the newspaper*: I crumple them up as much as I can but then I turn them over anyway, after all it is someone's face..."

Gran is so much a part of everything that once when boasting to a boy my own age in the yard, I shouted conceitedly:

"Only your mum had you, but my mum and gran had me!"

No-one tries to tell me what I should do and what I shouldn't, but I only once told another crazy lie in the same yard, when I said my father was a tsarist general. I didn't get into trouble that time either.

Another time I tried boasting it worked better. Klara Ivanovna – Kayanna – leaned over me.

"Say that again, Andrei, go on, what did you just say?"

"My dad's a soldier, my mum's a soldier woman, and my gran's an old soldier-woman."

Uniforms and badges of rank are bewitching – pips, chevrons, four diamonds and a star, red cuffs, stripes sewn on sleeves. Most splendid of all are the stripes down the Cossaks' trousers, and most thrilling of all are Budyonny's moustaches.

The long point of the Budyonny cap is a cunning military tactic. If the pointed tip shows over the top of the trench, the enemy will shoot straight through it.

In a colourful book Budyonny visits a nursery school and lets them touch his sabre and his moustaches. The book is called "The Budyonnikins".

Mum has brought me to the new hairdresser's in the Central Army Club. I can't take my eyes off the woman in the flying uniform who looks like a man. Raskova? Grizodubova? Osipenko? Mum doesn't turn a hair at asking. Vera Lomako. Another one getting ready to fly all the way from Moscow to the Far East.

_____

*Old newspapers were used as toilet paper until quite recently

Stamp Album

Names of my childhood:
The aeroplane Maxim Gorky – the ice-breaker Chelyuskin
Otto Yulievich Schmidt – Captain Voronin
Molokov – Kamanin – Lyapidevsky – Levanevsky etc.
Chkalov – Baidukov – Belyakov
Gromov – Yumashev – Danilin
Raskova – Grizodubova – Osipenko
Dadanin – Krenkel – Shirshov – Fedorov

The most important is Valery Chkalov. Lots of boys younger than me were called Valery. Suddenly one day all the mums are talking to each other and crying. They say Chkalov has crashed into a tip. I imagine the back entry, the janitor's lodge, the big wooden bin for peelings – with a little aeroplane sticking up out of it.
Maybe the Tartars are gawping at him from the janitor's lodge.

The Tartar rag-and-bone men yell underneath our windows:
"Any ol' rag-bone, ol' rag-bone!"
They bring them in to the kitchen through the back entryway. The nannies frighten the children with their sacks.

There are nannies everywhere. I once had one called Matyonna – Maria Antonovna Venediktova, a friend of gran's. She used to take me round the churches, she could have baptized me in secret. Mum and gran didn't have me baptized quite d e l i b e r a t e l y , they said when I grew up I could get baptized myself if I wanted.

In the quieter streets g r o u p s of children are walking along the pavements, five or six boys and girls in a row. The old woman in charge is talking some foreign language...
"I've put mine in the German group."
"Mine's going to the French group."
"Why'd you put yours in the English group?"

Andrei Sergeev

I didn't go to any group. Or to the nursery school behind the fence.

In Udelnaya the glaziers walk down the street with wooden boxes on their shoulders:

"Windersglaze! Windersglaze!"

Or the odd-job men:

"Fixin'n'solderin', fix your buckets here!"

Once in summer the sanitation man Ivan Ivanovich turns up from Vyalki. He scoops out the shit from under the house with a long-handed shovel and carts it off to the pit by the gates in an iron hand-cart.

At Udelnaya and in Moscow scrawny one-legged organ grinders come wandering around – toora-loora-loora-loo. They're all one-legged because of their one-legged barrel-organs.

In the yards they sell "Chinese nuts". They're not nice, they taste of soil and castor oil, but if you take one out of its shell and split it open, at the top of one half there's a little Chinaman's head with a beard.

Women are hawking scarlet lollypops on sticks in the shape of a rooster – horror for the mums!

"Just crawling with germs!"

On public holidays there are lots of them on First Meschanskaya Street.

They tried changing First Meschanskaya (Middle-Class) Street to First Grazhdanskaya (Civic Duty) Street, then they made it First Meschanskaya Street again.

There are people walking along First Meschanskaya. Not many of them are very tall. When one does go by people yell at him – "Uncle Sparrow Grabber".

On ordinary days on First Meschanskaya Street there are carts, sleighs, vans, horses. As many horses as motor-cars. The horses aren't interesting, but there are different types of cars. The ordinary ones are grey and worn-out. Ever so occasionally an impressive black one will come rushing through the middle, all shiny, with a squeaky treble voice shouting something like:

Stamp Album

"Ovid!"

On the corner of Third Meschanskaya Street by the co-operative shop, by S o k o l o v ' s , a woman stands with her tray, selling fudge, toffees, wafer shells with white or pink filling, chocolate bombs − inside they're empty. They say they used to have wonderful little trinkets inside them. It's all very e x p e n s i v e .

Most tempting of all − because they're forbidden − are the home-made toys sold by the pedlars.

A paper ball filled with sawdust on an elastic string − smack it against the forehead of the person standing next to you.

A nightingale − a bright-red wooden thing with a lead core. Press on it and it spins round and trills and warbles.

A bumblebee − a small clay cylinder on a string on a stick. Whirl it round and it hums.

A "whirr-whirr" − a small pipe with a blockage in it. Blow into it and it sings − more horrors for the mums.

"One mouth into another, spreading germs everywhere."

To defeat the hawkers, in a small toyshop on First Meschan-skaya Street they bought me a box just like a match-box, only bigger, with ten painted soldiers and a painted officer, all packed in cotton wool.

New soldiers appear in ones and twos. On Great Ekateri-ninskaya Street I show my granpa:

"A standard-bearer, a bugler, a machine-gunner, an infantry-man, a cavalryman."

Granpa points at a soldier charging into the attack in a gas-mask.

"An attackerman."

On Kaplya Lane while mum is cooking in the kitchen I'm playing soldiers on the oak parquet floor. There's only one table − our writing-desk and/or dining table. The radio is broadcasting

Andrei Sergeev

a discussion on the theme: Did the Garden of Gethsemane really exist?

Every morning at ten o'clock I listen to a children's programme:

> *Forty sparrows*
> *Lived in a flat,*
> *Forty sparrows*
> *Happy and fat.*
> *Nasty black bugs*
> *Lived in the flat.*
> *They starved them*
> *And froze them*
> *And scalded*
> *And dosed them.*

Also fairy-tales and stories, I always get absorbed, except when: "The text was read by Nikolai Litvinov." He speaks as though he's sucking up to someone, that i n g r a t i a t i n g voice, as though he's always lying about something.

After the children's programme comes the programme for housewives: socially active wives winning bicycles, the Khetagurova-girls. A song: The Girls are off to the Far East. A song about a heroic railway pointsman.

> *It may cost him his life,*
> *But he will never, never*
> *Let the foe destroy the line.*

Mum only turns the speaker off when she puts me to bed, or when they start talking about Pavlik Morozov who squealed on his father.

At eight o'clock dad listens to the n e w s   b u l l e t i n.

Sometimes the Comintern station broadcasts *No pasaran* from Madrid. The programmes are all full of hiss and crackle, and the most crackly of all are the ones from Madrid, and what's r e c o r d e d   o n   t a p e.

Stamp Album

Dad takes me for a ride on the metro. I catch my breath when the train crosses the Moscow river and I can see the Kremlin through the window, with its rabid-red stars. Everyone knows that Kiev station is the most beautiful.

For the Revolution Day dad took me to see the lights and he showed me the new locomotives at the railway station, the JOSEPH STALIN and the FELIX DZERZHINSKY, all done up in ribbons like horses in a book.

I vote like the grown-ups do. Dad lifts me up, and I drop it in the box – for Bulganin.

In the yard at home I'm like everyone else, I want to be like everyone else. I'm afraid of Arkasha from the small house, I bully Rickets – that's Rafik from the janitor's lodge. I ride my sled, riding downhill standing up is too scary. I'm clumsy, so I avoid skipping across the asphalt on my way to class. I play at war, at hide-and-seek, once I played family.

As soon as I get involved in a game, mum sticks her hand down the back of my neck:

"Wringing wet, like a mouse out in the rain."

Things are difficult enough without her – this constant feeling of being annoyed (I'm not fast or deft enough) and offended (although no-one has offended me). I get tense and nervous, I get tired for no reason, I get so furious I black out. A girl from the fourth floor began arguing with me, so I hit her on the head with the edge of my iron spade, and made it bleed. Mum went running off to apologize and said I should be ashamed. I wasn't ashamed, I was scared: what had I done, what would happen now?

(I don't know whether or not to believe what mum remembered later: "You always wanted to be the janitor. You said: I'll get up early, take my shovel, and then when the people appear I'll throw the snow under their feet – whoosh! whoosh!")

The scrawny, hungry milkmaid comes into the kitchen with her milk-can. She fills a cup with milk from the full can, then

205

afterwards pours it back. She shakes the can, slopping the milk about. I bring her something disgusting – a salted cucumber with jam. Ekaterina Dmitrievna sees it and says in Ukraine they eat cucumbers with honey. Mum doesn't say anything. Dad is drily delighted with me:

"Oh, that's delightfully disgusting!"

But I heard Nyusha whispering to mum that her sons the flyers have come to stay with her and she's a f r a i d of them.

Gran loves treating people who are ill, and mum's always getting treatment.

The words of my childhood: cupping glasses, mustard-plasters, blue lamp, calcium tablets, aspirin, etc.

Translated by Andrew Bromfield

Andrei Sergeev, born in 1933, won the 1996 Booker Russian Novel Prize for Stamp Album about growing up in Stalin's two-faced pre-war Moscow. A pastiche of fragmented memories, letters, family documents, newspaper clippings, slogans and even a shopping list, *Stamp Album* recreates the very texture of that terrible time.
The above is the first chapter from his prize-winning novel.
A translator of English and American literature by profession, Sergeev appears in English translation for the first time.

Sergei GANDLEVSKY

Opening the Skull

It was a holiday morning, Victory Day, May the 9th 1984. I was in the kitchen mixing kasha for my nine-month-old daughter, Lena was changing her diapers in our room. My brother was in his room, and my parents in theirs, when suddenly my father rushed into the kitchen, shouting, "Quick, your mother's died!" I followed him. My mother's mouth was wide open, yawning terribly. My brother, who was a doctor, took the scarf from her head and adjusted it so that it held her mouth shut.

"In her heart your mother was a deeply religious person," my father said in a croaking voice, finally managing to light the spiral red candle in its decorative candlestick.

Smelling burning milk, I rushed back into the kitchen.

Then they came to take my mother away.

"Wait a minute," I said as I kissed her forehead. So it really is true: the dead cool down just as quickly as a hot kettle.

Two men placed her naked body in a plastic container, closed and locked the lid, and carried her away.

"I think I'll have a glass of cognac," my father said, pointedly not inviting me to join him.

"By all means," I reassured him, "I'm going to church."

The agony had begun the day before. My mother was unconscious, crying out our names, and kept on asking for her bag.

"The one with your make-up?" I asked, not understanding her.

My mother didn't answer. "Give me my bag!" she insisted.

Ten days before her death my mother had thought that she wouldn't survive the night. "Don't go anywhere today, please," she had asked me.

She asked my father to gather those whom she was closest to — Myuda, Yura, Katya, Gorya, Yana, Nina; no one told my mother that Gorya himself had died just days earlier. Her family and friends duly arrived only to find my mother sleeping off the after-effects of her medicine. Myuda, herself ill with the cancer from which she would die six years later, was sitting at the bedside of her sleeping friend and was thinking of leaving when my mother opened her eyes and exclaimed: "So that's our farewell."

"Still a little longer yet," my mother pronounced with a guilty smile after they had left.

The following morning we all watched the May Day celebrations on television.

"Interesting," I wondered, "do the old men on top of the mausoleum know that people only come along for the extra day off?"

"Maybe that's why they're standing there themselves," said my mother.

That year spring had come very early and the courtyard of the Novodevichy Monastery was swamped with lilac blooms. I bought a candle and placed it in front of an icon. When one of the old women who looked after the church came up and carefully rearranged the candles, I felt upset that I could no longer distinguish mine from the rest. Going back out into the light for a smoke, however, I felt just how right the old church biddy had been. If that was a collective spirit, I had nothing against it.

I have ended up doing many stupid things in life — insulting and horrible things. But more than anything else, there is one small mistake, an oversight which sticks in my heart. I was visiting my mother in the Oncological Hospital — her second-to-

Opening the Skull

last port of call in her illness – to tell her that I had been in touch with Lena and asked her to forgive me and come back home.

"Of course, you mustn't offend her," my mother said happily.

Depressed by the sight of her, which left no doubt as to the outcome of her illness, I kissed her and hurried away, practically fleeing her presence. Only when I reached the metro did it hit me – she would have been standing at the ward's second-floor window waving after me. As long as she still could walk, she would stand there and wave – as she had a hundred times before, when she let me out as a child to play in the yard, or saw me off to my exams or on some journey... May you go on waving at me for ever! Weak as I am, self-centred, carried away with tenderness, I still beg you: wherever in the heavens you may be now, and whatever effort it might cost you, don't for a moment let your arm fall. Until I finally turn round, shaking from tears at the impossibility of our meeting.

After my mother's death our family fell apart quickly, and it became obvious who had really held it together – and who had just blustered with a pretence of power. All her life, like some eternal guide, my mother had carried my father along, suffering as he did from a weak heart – in both the literal and the metaphorical sense. I know, I hope, who I resemble. Lena, young as she was, lived by her principles and felt nothing for my father or brother – well, no one survives long on principles alone. The mutual frustrations I had felt over fifteen years with my father flared up again, and the usual Soviet flat-swapping strife, coupled with my brother's predictable selfishness, only added fuel to the fire. The strength of the hatred in that Yugo-Zapadnaya flat became so suffocating that I was ready to do anything to escape it.

My father was an intelligent and decent man who loved his wife deeply and took pride in her beauty. However, his happy marriage was the only piece of luck that fortune threw his way: either fate proved stingy when it came to the follow-up, or

Sergei Gandlevsky

eventually it just gave up, not anticipating the demands that would be placed on it. A man made for the arts, with an erudite mind and a touch of the Voltairean, for thirty-five years he had been tied to his engineering, and he had always excelled faithfully in his work. In spite of a personal shyness that he concealed in front of others, for thirty years he had assumed positions of authority at work. A despot at home, he had later been faced with the drunken disobedience of his children. In spite of my exaggerated aspirations to culture he went on pronouncing words with their accents in the wrong places, and, forgetting his son's uncompromising corrections, would say something outrageous like, "Even the brilliant Lunacharsky..."

The best memories I have of my father are from childhood, of course. If he was coming home with good news, his step showed it straight away: he approached with a determined, swinging gait, his hands gesticulating animatedly. That would mean that I had only to look around carefully and I would find some well-hidden present, or that my father had found a motorboat that would take the five of us, including our collie dog, from Uglich upriver to Baskachy. For the last fifteen years of his life he moved around in a different way, his hands drooping mournfully – and that was largely my doing.

After my mother's death my father made it very clear to me who he thought had been the ruin of her, and who had wrecked his own life into the bargain. Once, when we were working together on the dacha allotment we had just been given, frenziedly and in silence, he dropped the hint that my motivation was strictly material. I threw him the dacha keys, and the four of us – by then Grishka had appeared on the scene – left home and went off to live with Lena's mother. Besides Tatiana Arkadievna herself, Lena's brother was already living there with his wife and nine-month-old son, and we were left with the passage room. The three children wailed and fell ill one after another, catching infections from each other. The television was on full blast all day long. During our rare, anxiety-ridden couplings Lena's brother, dressed in his underpants, would invariably cross

210

Opening the Skull

the passage to the other room. And each of my clumsy movements brought another of my mother-in-law's innumerable knick-knacks crashing down and smashing to smithereens.

My father died in 1990 from his fourth heart attack, and today my brother, my step-mother and I are still waiting for his dollars earned in Iraq to reach us from the Central Bank. My father was Jewish, never belonged to the Party, and sympathized with the state of Israel – and it turned out that he had corrupted himself all his life at the behest of the stinking Soviet regime and its bunch of criminal sub-scoundrels – Castro, Qaddafi, Hussein and the rest of them – and with the diligence typical of his race he spent his career perfecting rockets that would in their time be targeted on Tel-Aviv.

I remember him standing in the kitchen at night, in his black underpants which stretched down to his knees, medicine glasses and bottles shaking in his hands. "Sixteen, seventeen, eighteen..." he would count his heart-drops falling into a glass. My father was small in build, balding, with a face aged by his heart disease. His eyes seemed small and far-away behind his minus-seven lenses; his stomach was fat, and his sagging, flabby chest and back, overgrown with grey hair, were those of an old man. When I came in he turned around, looking at me over his shoulder with the expression of a hunted animal, ready for rebuff or attack.

At the gathering of friends which we held after my mother's funeral I stood at the window with Myuda and launched into a tirade about my father.

"I know," she answered, "we were here on the day she died and he was putting out plates and glasses on the table, singing Soviet songs – as if it was some sort of pathetic challenge. I begged him to stop, but he went on all the same."

"Damned, bloody family," I said, exaggerating the drama of the phrase in my drunkenness.

"All families are that way," Myuda corrected me.

And now my family is no more, and the circle of friends which went with it is long gone too. Out of habit I still go to

211

the cemetery every year on my birthday, December 21, taking the number 39 trolleybus there.

When I was born, my father's colleagues congratulated him on the birth of a little Joseph, but he would duly disappoint them. I can imagine my mother, recovering from the birth, as she went up to the window of the Grauerman Maternity Hospital and looked out on to the snow-covered roofs of the Old Arbat – they would soon be knocked down – and I can picture how young she was, how beautiful, how happy. But today, on my birthday in this year, 1993, it's difficult for me to behave in the right way for a son – the whole weight of my soul hangs on the results of a diagnosis. As the trolleybus goes along, my indifferent eyes rove around the Danilovsky Monastery, the market and the church on Khavsky.

Then the International Friendship University, and, next, my stop. I enter through the crematorium gates, walk along its snow-covered path. I walk on, leaving the main building to my right, pass a mess of cemetery rubbish, and find the right path. My head is aching as usual and an insistent dry march resounds in my ears – no music to it, only the bare bones of rhythm. A strange couple approach me: a man of my own age, well dressed, leading an older lady by the hand; she is dressed in a fox-fur coat and crimson shawl, like a gypsy, with heavy make-up which has altered the natural lines of a face that was once beautiful.

"A cold, gloomy morning," she wheezes up to her taller companion.

My parents are in the outermost niche, three layers up –hello, there! – two oval containers made of porcelain which stand on a metal shelf meant for flowers which my father had made for him at work. The wall itself is not even solid – a concrete parallelogram, almost a cube. The formality of its appearance is usually disguised by lilac, but today, in December, all is bare. First breaking their stalks, I lay my flowers down flat on the snow-covered shelf.

Suddenly my mind goes back to ten o'clock one Moscow summer morning – birds twittering, the horn of Gorya's Moskvich

Opening the Skull

sounding at the two windows of our first-floor flat at number 28 Studenchesky. Out we came with our baskets and our bags full of provisions: my mother resplendent in her mature beauty, my father with his early baldness and his eternal irony pursed in the corners of his tight mouth. My brother carried our badminton rackets, while I, a pimpled fifteen-year-old, had a volume of Pasternak, complete with the preface by Sinyavsky. My literature teacher, Vera Romanovna, had lent it to me for the three days of the holiday, telling me to look after it as if it were a treasure. We had a reservation at some holiday hotel outside Moscow, and all the way my father, his face stony, railed about some overweight woman with a bulging shopping bag in one hand and a potted plant in the other, ridiculed the red-banner slogans we kept passing and harrassed Gorya about his driving, sending my brother and me into fits of hysterical laughter.

I light a cigarette, and out of habit go on with my walk along the ranks of cemetery urns, passing the names and faces which I have known for a decade – the Mytlins, the Derzhavins and Ilya Tsypkin (1953-1975). We were at school together, and once, in the sixth grade, during lunch break, he had nicked a set of used Rio-Muni stamps off me – I was collecting flora and fauna in those days. It seems, my friend Tsypkin, that we may soon have the chance to return to this long-ago property dispute. There were four of them, you remember, four unforgettable colonial beauties – a rhinoceros, giraffe, hippopotamus and elephant.

This summer, I was getting on the Gagarin-Moscow train at Tuchkovo – a whole crowd invaded the compartment, but amazingly I managed to squeeze my way past the bags on peoples' knees, past the baskets and the rucksacks into the middle of the carriage; I threw my bag up on to a shelf and then looked around me. I was hanging, suspended by the sheer pressure of the crowd, directly over my friend Tsypkin's mother. It was remarkable – in thirty years she had not changed at all: still stout, well-built and beautiful, a proper officer's wife. My

213

Sergei Gandlevsky

migraine and the rhythm of the train seemed to beat in unison, but I could make out what they were talking about – the usual stuff about what to do about these suburban trains, and how to best preserve vegetables. Amazing, I thought to myself, here is the mother of a boy who had killed himself discussing with the woman next to her how to pickle tomatoes. But what would you prefer – that they swapped advice about how best to do away with yourself? Tsypkin's telephone was G9-16-49. Sometimes I almost want to rid myself of my so wickedly perfect memory.

A sense of dismal thrift comes over me – I see that there is still room in the cemetery niche for a third urn. I should slip the idea to Lena, pretending it's my black humour again, otherwise they'll send me to a graveyard in some faraway industrial dump, where no one will ever come and visit – and quite right not to.

I reach the end of my cigarette, wrap the butt up in an old tram ticket and put it away in my pocket. Casting a last glance at the two porcelain oval forms, I walk towards the tram. On the journey I stare, without focusing, through the window, and think about preparations for my own funeral party. There's always the risk that Lena will turn sour and forget to ask someone – though thank God I have collected enough friends along the way. Then I think of a solution: Natasha Molchanskaya only has to ask Slovesny for permission to have the party in the conference-hall at work – and then my closest friends can come on home afterwards and go on drinking there.

Getting out at Vishnyakovsky Lane, I turn down on to Ostrovsky Street and buy a chocolate cake in the shop, fresh as could be. It's still early to go to work, but there's no reason to go home either, so I head for work. I say hello to the door-woman, and collect the key with its green plastic label; going up to the second floor, I unlock the door, put the cake down on the little tea table, and sit down at my desk without taking off my coat. I hold my face in my hands, suffering from the aching inside my head, from my fear of death and from the events of Friday.

Opening the Skull

Back on Friday the 17th, as I came out of the Burdenko Hospital, I thought how lucky I was that Semyon Faibisovich was having a preview for his exhibition today; I could say farewell to people who were dear to me, and enjoy a drink as well, if that was how it was to be. But I wouldn't say anything to Lena before Monday, no reason to get her nerves working before I had to. I had felt good.

At home I had taken a shower, first hot, then cold, and thought about my disfigured brains as they went first hot, then cold. Grisha Dashevsky called to ask how I was.

"Do you want me to spoil your day?" I asked.

"Just tell me the truth," he asked.

Next I rang Natasha Molchanskaya, my friend and boss.

"You won't die, probably, but you could well end up an idiot," she responded with characteristic straightforwardness.

How do you like that! I started getting dressed up, I'm an expert on that – red goes with grey, black with almost any colour. Lena arrived, she had taken the children off to their grandmother. I told her that the results would be ready on Monday, at the clinic, and to take some extra trouble with her appearance. The preview was an important event, after all.

"If you go on at me like that," she answered, "I'll turn up bare-footed."

Our wardrobes at home are full to bursting with all kinds of excellent second-hand clothing, bought from some Montreal jumble sale or handed-out for free at some Jerusalem outlet, and my wife goes around in the first thing she happens to grab – she has a boyish style, cheap trousers and cowboy shirts. Before he introduced us at his birthday party Soprovsky had warned me:

"A friend of mine from the expedition will be there. You'd better go easy with her – if she doesn't like something, she won't hesitate to thwack you one. In Sebastopol once I even saw her refused entry to the women's toilet, they were convinced she was a boy."

Instead, she turned out to be a wide-eyed slender beauty,

215

Sergei Gandlevsky

and I thought again that Soprovsky didn't understand anything about women. My drunken delight was such that I woke up in the lavatory — our first meeting! All she wanted to do was create some antediluvian idol out of clay, or draw some primitive mystery on bleached butcher's boards.

I like her realistic manner best, her pen-and-ink drawings such as dacha fences, telegraph poles, old Moscow gates. But I'm afraid that, sullen as she is with her mixture of shyness and pride, she won't sell anything at the Izmailovo or Krymsky Val street markets.

"How's your head?" Lena asked, distracting herself from her make-up.

"Oh, same as ever."

My poor head — better not to think about it.

"Put on your fur coat tonight," I ask her.

"But it's slushy outside!"

"Please."

As always we are a bit late, but not terribly so. When we get to Turgenevskaya Station we almost quarrel deciding how to go on from there, and Lena turns out to be right. We go up Myasnitskaya Street in the direction of the Garden Ring. I can see almost nothing from my right eye, while my left has double vision.

Darkness has fallen, and it's sleeting. It seems a funny thought that here I am, hardly able to see a thing, on my way to an art exhibition. Again we lose our bearings, but then spot, directly across the road, a huge glimmering, faintly blue window in front of which Misha Zaitsev, Timur Kibirov and Lev Rubinstein are standing smoking. Judging by their cries and gesticulations, they are already well away: we appear to have arrived late for the champagne. Picking up the hems of our coats, we make our way across the damp and falling snow of crowded Myasnitskaya — I balancing on my heels, Lena on her tip-toes and go into the gallery. Then we lose touch of each other and wander around on our own, smiling, saying hello to people, dropping passing politenesses.

Opening the Skull

I have always felt out of my element at openings and presentations, and today I was even more oppressed by the extra challenge of not giving anything away about my incapacity.

Once, in Sukhumi, I witnessed a pack of street dogs crossing a road. One driver couldn't slow down quick enough and drove straight over one of them, flattening the animal's pelvis bone and back legs. I watched how, despite this, the injured dog hurried after the rest of the pack, yapping loudly, supporting itself only on its front legs, dragging a bloody mush behind it, trying desperately, in the way it moved and by its bark, to convince them that everything was all right.

That was just how I felt yapping out the usual dutiful phrases as I wandered along past Semyon's canvases, screwing up my useless right eye so as to see better. I like some of his paintings, and I respect Semyon himself for the fact that he is no charlatan, that he doesn't aim to shock his audience.

At another exhibition like this I had once wandered around, bored, past one empty, cold work after another with titles like "Installation No. 1", "Installation No. 2" and the like, until I ended up in front of what seemed a final "Installation No. X", an ordinary writing desk with plastic cups standing on it. One of them had been knocked over, and a little puddle of wine or juice had spread over the polished table top. Then Lena and Varya came up to me, seeming less impressed by its effect, and gigglingly corrected my error — there was nothing specially artistic about the table or the glasses, they were just the left-overs from the previous day's binge.

Peering and blinking at the huge pictures, I realized what pleasure I derived from looking at monochrome canvases; I suspected the painter himself was colour-blind, a typical deficiency in the Gandlevsky family.

"Sergei, tell me, what do you think of that picture?" a female acquaintance asked me.

"These slanting waves make my head spin," I answered, trying for words which wouldn't give away the fact that I had suddenly forgotten her name.

217

Sergei Gandlevsky

It was the truth. My head hurt, aching with such an intensity that I couldn't distinguish the rumble which was going on inside it from the reverberations of the tall, crowded room or the noise of the television cameras.

Then the tipsy Alexander Genis appeared, along with his wife, who was she? Nina – no, not Nina, maybe Tanya, no Vera – or do I mean Olga – yes, Olga! With Olga Trofimova, or was it Tikhonova, or Timofeeva, that was it, Olga Timofeeva. Alexander Genis? Yes, that was his name. Go up and say hello to him, but don't try and speak too fast or you'll get your words mixed up.

"I was at your office today, they said you were having some tests done. Everything's okay, isn't it?" Genis answered my greeting, before being distracted by the rush of someone embracing him from behind.

I was wary of a longer conversation with Genis, and was glad that he had detached himself so lightly. Two years ago, thanks to the all-powerful Lena Yakovich, he and Peter Weil had gone in for a debate with Kibirov and me, for the Literary Gazette. It was about this and that, nothing in particular, with a free glass of vodka thrown in an the end. Later Krava told me that the two critics had praised my conversational reaction. I like to be appreciated, and did not want Genis to see that in only two years I had declined from an elegant speaker to a slow-witted idiot. I was spared. Earnestly I started shaking my head, looking around busily. Deprived of the gift of speech, half-blind, with a full aching migraine and trembling hands, I looked out for my wife and for the vodka which had somewhere been put aside for me. Why was it that everyone around me was already drunk, while I, who needed it more than anyone, was as sober as a stone? Misha Zaitsev, standing at the window, was furtively unscrewing the yellow stopper which stuck out of his bag, and I made my way through the seething crowd, apologizing, towards the brightness of its metallic glint.

I downed my hundred and fifty grams in one gulp, and felt a rush of relief. Who was here? Valya, the beauty of Kalmykia,

Opening the Skull

Koval's wife; Alena, the Jewish beauty, Aisenberg's wife, and Anya, the Russian beauty, wife of Zaitsev. For full harmony of colour we were missing only a black beauty. I settled in their company, tired of wandering unthinkingly through the hall.

The chirping of the women's speech calmed me down, made me feel as if I was lying in a meadow out at Tuchkovo, with a little bird flying over me in the hot sky, singing. And next to me was my dog Charlie, his exotic nostrils flaring, the first notes of a bark reverberating in his throat.

They brought around champagne a second time, and I captured two glasses, one for myself, one for Lena, and put them behind me on the windowsill in reserve. Lena, Kibirov and Rubinstein, always a bundle of energy, approached me. They were going out to smoke in the cold street, to drink and crack jokes. Faibisovich's wife whispered to me as she passed by:

"Soon it will end here, and then we'll go on at our place."

The preview duly wound itself up and those who had been invited stretched their way in the directon of the Garden Ring, in groups of three to five, heading for Faibisovich's place.

I ended up with Zaitsev and Kibirov. On the way we discussed an unlucky publisher, who had paid us in full, but hadn't published our books. Kibirov did most of the talking.

"Lev may swear that it's all the same to him whether anyone reads his work or not. But I want people to read me, I want to be published, I make no secret of it, and I don't see anything disgraceful in that," he said.

Zaitsev followed him up − all the contract deadlines had expired, he said, and somewhere he had a disk with the ready versions of our books, that the work was already ninety percent, if not a hundred percent finished, and that all we needed to do was find a more dynamic publisher.

So, I asked myself, with your new concerns, do these problems irritate you? No, I answered myself honestly − they do not. Or would you want your friends to be going through the same thing you are, if only so as not to be so lonely? No, I

219

Sergei Gandlevsky

answered again in all honesty – I wouldn't want it that way. Or do you, caught up in your lofty terrors, despise their egotistical gossip. No, enough of all that. I felt good once again.

Excerpt translated by Tom Birchenough

* * *

In the poet's vegetative life
There's a period to regret, when
He shuns the heavenly light
And is afraid of human judgment.
From the well between tall buildings,
Scattering grains to town pigeons,
He swears a terrible oath to get even
When he gets the chance, but

Thank God, at the dacha's porch,
Where jasmin reaches out to touch
Your hand, we learned to fly
From Vivaldi's fit of violins – and so
The emptiness climbs in height.
And from the empty height the soul
Falls to the ground, and lays still,
But the flowers brush the elbows...

We don't know a damned thing,
We play the coward, get trashed,
From agitation snap our matches
And out of weakness break dishes.
We promise to speak without flattery
The blunt-truth, point-blank, like it is...
Yet poems are not weapons of revenge,
But a springwell of silver honor.

Poems

* * *

The self-judgement of my sudden maturity
Is a spectacle you will hardly enjoy,
It lacks the general pleasure
Of walking the shore of a quiet river,
Reflecting in rhyme. A silence
Has long watched over my words.
Barkhudarov, Kriuchkov et. al.
Must be a gift from grammarian gods.

There is a custom in Russian poetry
Of breaking mirrors with disgust
Or concealing kitchen knives
In the drawers of writing desks.
A fogey in a hat spattered by a pigeon
Reflected in my mirror, a trophy of war.
Don't starve me with a creative hunger –
That comes quite on its own power.

It was like a ship, a yawl,
Sparrows in an empty hammock.
Is it a cloud? No, it's an apple,
An alphabet in a woman's hand.
The alphabet of tender habits,
Scrape of oarlocks on dacha ponds.
He licks a scab, asks to be held –
I won't give you up to anyone.

Slavery, jealousy, and torture now,
The motifs spilling drop by drop.
Choking on words I moo and mew,
Embracing my head in open palms.
Why must I have as my inheritance
Someone's mask with ambiguous mouth,
The tragedy of a one-act life,
A philosopher's dialogue with a fool?

Sergei Gandlevsky

Why, my unfaithful muse,
Explain to me when I die
Why you sat with an evil smile
In one unending feast
And fooled the dreamy child,
Picking at the festive tablecloth?
Is it an apple? No, a cloud.
I'm not expecting mercy from you.

* * *

I was a little beast on a thin umbilicus.
Watched the pattern in frosted glass.
How secluded I breathed in the middle
Of infancy, that remote forsaken place.
Sun streamed down in a dusty band.
Blood circled its way through me.
Thus little by little the Babylonian din
Of times and fates tided in from outside
As a pendulum toiling in silence.

We – the inarticulate horde of children
Ran along the sandbars naked –
Until in the sweat of high fever
I learned by rote your image forever.
I was a body, lived by bread alone,
When from silence, syllable on syllable,
I evoked Catullus' beautiful Lesbia,
Diluting stunned flesh with heavens –
And an angel carried my shadow along snow.

Infancy, wait a few more moments.
I'm ten years old. My soul's living.
I'm the bitter fusion of lymphocytes
And God, already deity prevailing.

Poems

A snow-laden road trampled down.
A school bench, its paint peeling.
A fishing bob, the heart trembles, and drowns.
Chalk is crumbling. Biting hangnails,
I write out the letters "I'm no longer I."
And my giddy dependable friends –
Honor students, athletes, castoffs –
Are saddened. I trudge down the hall,
Open the very pupils of my eyes,
Wipe my face with a hand, seeing a light,
And past bulletin boards, pennants, trapezes
I go out onto the porch of the school.
Five wild senses merge into a sixth.
January air is like a penetrating knife.
I hold myself so I don't drop in snow
The empty mirror of my future life.

* * *

In the beginning of December, when nature dreams
Of autumn ice-drifts, of winter's cabinet of curiosities,
I decided I might as well undergo a little treatment
At Mental Hospital #3, the one next to the jail.
Patients of all sorts – ninety of us in all –
Troubled with the can-can of prophetic dreams
Rambled in pairs in our ill-fitting pajamas
Around the oval yard of Sailor's Silence.

All day long the floor jostled like a market.
Reveille, saunter, sleep, clean floors, retreat.
I remember a quiet hall, an aquarium without fish –
One can't sweep away with a broom the litter of memory.
A hospital veteran taught me, an ignoramus,
To open a lock from the inside with a piece of iron.
After that I made my getaway, procuring street clothes,
But returned to sleep in Hospital #3.

Sergei Gandlevsky

Here's occasion for a poem with a misty hidden motive
About life locked up, grinding a perfect key
To one's own jail. Or about a lonely life
Outside one's own jail. Teacher, don't teach.
To hell with this profundity, my spectral reader!
I wouldn't ever bring my secret grief and life
Under the playful common denominator
Of commonplaces for nothing. On the run I jumped

For the trolley. A wet snow fell. Fellow citizens argued
About passengers' rights. Above, in every key
An invisible ballroom pianist at a grand piano
Scored out the film of hope and dire need.
And so what is this musical scale I hardly hear,
The traditional delirium of poets and cripples
Or a carnival attraction (the tamed mice running
In a toy car) with a gray snow heavily falling?

This December was sad. No matter where I knocked
To share my premonitions, I was barely believed.
Will there ever be an end? – the blood grumbled.
My poor carnival's over. Time for the madhouse.
When I would fall asleep, the hospital chamber
Let in snowfall, the torpid frozen forest,
A train station deep in the country, the clock face –
It's getting dark. I have to wait, but time is running out.

Translated by Philip Metres

Sergei Gandlevsky, 44, won two major prizes in 1996: the Little
Booker Prize for his first novel, *Opening the Skull,* and the Anti-Booker
prize for his poetry. His novel is a deeply personal and poetical
reminiscence of the 1960s and 70s, a period which the writer wanted to
preserve for posterity. Gandlevsky was then part of literary underground
circles where his poems were avidly read in samizdat. His friends of
those dissident years, now well-known writers and artists, are featured
under their real names in his autobiographical novel *Opening the Skull*
in which the hero suddenly has to face the reality of dying from a brain
tumour.